D1073314

Spilled Milk

Veronica Christopher

Christopher Kastrinos Printing
Lincoln, Nebraska

ISBN: 978-0-9600339-1-1

First Published- December, 2018

Printed & bound by Christopher Kastrinos
Cover design by Veronica Christopher

VeronicaChristopher.WordPress.com

Published by

"She believed she could so she did."
-R.S. Grey

This book is for Cypress, my Heartstrings, for always believing in my dream of becoming an author, and for reminding me that the storms were a test of my foundation. Thank you for your faith.

I love you.

PROLOGUE

The prickle of the rope furiously itched my neck but I refused to loosen it. I deserved its wrath. The covered bridge I sat in was old and rarely traveled on. Its red paint chipped in several places and the wooden planks held unknown strength. No one had torn it down due to its historical prowess and nobody ever would. It'd been built in the 1700s and connected two mountains that sat close together. The bridge was impassable from late December through early February—our snowy season.

The ground a good 100 feet below was littered with boulders and shards of rock, countless that had been crushed by elements over time to form a blanket of rough landscape. A brook squirmed through the stone valley as it spilled down from Mt. Cranmore.

Mt. Cranmore and Mt. Jolly sat on either side of the bridge. The covered section was only about 50 feet in the center; the rest of the passage was uncovered and paved road. The bridge was dubbed the Jolly Pass by early settlers and the name stuck. To those of us who lived on this mountain range, it was simply the Red Pass.

The mountains were adorned with quaint towns and villages far and few between. Here, the people exploded with telltales proven true and dramatic revelations better left unspoken. We weren't uncivilized, just isolated. Isolated, but not desolate. We still had neighbors we saw once in a while at the town shops, most we'd grown up with. We had internet access, we didn't willingly fuck our dads, twiddle wood on our rickety cabin porches, or daydream of sheep's ass holes.

Up here, where the sun forgot for half the year and calls of coyotes and other animals echoed in the valleys, the people suffered in different ways and addictions of all sorts ran rampant. Our pickings of friends and lovers were scarce that we had to settle for what we'd been offered. Karma, if she truly did exist, fed off our weaknesses and continuously cursed our souls. She mocked our fingertips as they foolishly reached for floating dreams.

I gazed down at my hands that had been guilty of so much and had strained to grab a hold of a dream or two along the way. I began to weep again. The palms were cut and stung from the splinters that burrowed deep and poked mercilessly. The claw marks were puffy and light pink, and swelling even more. They traveled up both arms and some streaked my face, but those had already turned numb.

It had rained relentlessly the entire day and only yesterday it was 50 degrees. The snow melted at an alarming rate which sent people into town to gather supplies to prepare for flood season. Townspeople stocked up on food and water, batteries, canvas covers to protect their roofs, and sandbags to save the houses, shacks, and cabins that dotted the land.

Our basement flooded every March and April. Our yard developed small ponds and streams and our driveway became an annoying pond, never mind puddle, that seemed to rise with every drop. Mom and I had to park our cars at the top of the driveway and walk the 80 or so feet to the house. It

SPILLED MILK

was a pain in the ass, especially since when we'd reach our doorway, our pants would be soaked from unskillfully trying to dodge unforgivable puddles.

My little sister, Sephora, loved when it rained. She'd change into her Little Mermaid bathing suit and splash about outdoors. Rorie, Sephora's preferred nickname, would take out her purple raft and cruise around rain-formed ponds for hours on end until I beckoned her inside so she wouldn't catch a cold. Rorie hadn't done those things for a while now- a couple years almost. Not since Dad left her and Rose left me. I always ached at the thought of Rorie and cursed Mom for never aching at all.

Mother's children all had our own justified reasons for resenting and fearing her. She'd damaged each of us so irreparably that no shrink could help us had any ever bothered to try. A high school guidance counselor had once attempted to reach out but had failed miserably before finally giving up. We were a lost cause- the St. Germaines. The whole lot of us; every generation- destined to travel the road less traveled, a dirt path decorated with tears and blood and endless failures, failures that would curse the generation after us and the one after that.

Mom had the responsibility of leading us to that other trail, the one with the plush green grass and tall oak and white birch trees lining the way. Yet she didn't and I hated how I still needed her, loved her, and how that love was never reciprocated.

Despite how Dad used to hold me after Mom would beat me, and how he would run his fingers through my long hair and tell me it'd be all right, I didn't feel a bond with him. I

3

missed him, I loved him, but something within me distanced myself from any kind of attachment to him. So when my older sister Rose killed him, I didn't cry. The tears just never came even when the heavy sadness and weight did. I didn't even cry when someone planted a sign in our yard after his funeral that said "Never rest in peace".

He was a man was how I condoned my lack of sensitivity. Men and boys were weak, poorly-constructed puppets made of rotting flesh and hollow bone. Easily discarded, more easily forgotten. Our family had seen the demise of many a boy or man. It seemed only I was incapable of forgetting them.

Dad was aloof and our blood but that didn't mean we saw him a lot before he passed. He didn't even live with us though him and Mom never divorced. He was just some guy who lived on the other end of town who we were required to see every once in a while by some law of nature. The betrayal he borne consumed him eventually and cursed his soul, and had cost him his life. After all he'd put us all through when we were younger, he deserved to lie in the cheap wooden box he was put to rot in. Yet the vague memories of him still hurt.

The spirits of my younger brothers, Henri and Clyde, deserved better than to eternally rest beside our fathers. They had still been pure and the rest of us were always miles from spotless. Losing them was hard on me and especially hard on Rose who cared for them as a mother. Rorie seemed to have forgotten as she was young. I still had Rorie though and worrying about her kept me going after Henri and Clyde were gone. Kept me going- until now.

SPILLED MILK

I wondered if Henri knew what was happening as he fell to his death, or if he died after an episode of blurs and weird sensations he wasn't quite old enough to distinguish. Falling to death must've been some kind of family inheritance along with bullets piercing flesh. Only Henri didn't hang himself when he was four years old- he fell out a second story window.

In the fifth grade, my best friend hung herself too. Her brother was watching her one weekend while their parents were in Concord, the capital, visiting a relative who had gone into labor that morning. Kristy's brother decided to drive 20 miles to his girlfriend's house- not exactly just around the corner- and left Kristy home alone. It was a normal occurrence as she was 11 and old enough to stay home alone for short spans of time.

Her brother had returned home by morning to find his little sister's body, wearing a white cotton nightgown dotted with faded blue flowers, dangling from the banister in their front entryway. I always felt she was crying for help, even as she hung herself, as she'd done it in such a public area of her house.

Of course, when I learned the news of my best friend, such thoughts didn't enter my brain. The older I got and the more I thought of her, I wondered how her family could miss the signs and not see what she was suffering through. By not stepping in to see what was causing her pain, they contributed to her death and that prevented me from calling them years later to make sure they were getting by okay.

To hang yourself meant that you had a big sack of balls, right? It had to take fearlessness to get the rope, fasten it to

5

you, and then muster up enough courage to take the leap. Did you feel your neck break and then die of asphyxiation? Or did you have a split second where you felt the most incredible pain before fading away to unconscious oblivion? Right before 'the end' greeted, did you think of the kitten that used to purr by your head at night? Your boyfriend? Your Mom? A premonition of what would have, could have been? If you did have a premonition, would you realize what it was or see it as a random vision that destiny used to tease you with, reminding you of what you never had?

But now, being that person, I knew it wasn't fierce bravery that led me here doing what I'd previously felt was a sin, the un-do-able. I was full of regrets and guilt and scared like I'd never been scared before, and all my life I'd feared much. The intensity of life and of last night weighed heavily. What had led up to last night weighed even more. It wasn't a pressure my shoulders or my soul recognized. This was different.

Before, I'd clung to precarious wishes although I'd been silly to believe. I'd never had proof that dreams and wishes were something worth fighting for. I was never destined for greatness. The world let me know that. So did Mom when she reminded me near-daily.

I stood up slowly and faced the eastern gray sky. The sun was due to rise shortly and I'd make sure I wouldn't be around to witness it. I didn't want to see any promises of redemption or be graced with beauty. My mind was set. I prepared my heart and brain of what was to come. I willed my innards and my conscious strength as soon the blood would stop flowing, veins would collapse, and everything I'd ever known would no longer exist. I would be without memories. All I'd see ever again would be nothingness. Heaven did not exist.

I cried harshly, shaking violently with sobs. "No!" I howled to a world that was never any good at responding, and "fuck!" to the moon that was so beautiful it still stole my breath away. Even now I laughed at myself for thinking that maybe I still had a chance if beauty could still affect me.

Freezing cold sprinkles landed softly on my welcoming skin. The rain had ceased but Mother Nature, like most women, still had some shit to get off her chest.

I again checked the rope to make sure it was tightly tied to the wooden rail of the Red Pass. I wanted to dangle freely once all life left my body instead of resting on a valley of sharp rocks where my body would surely be discovered by some conservationist passing through. The bridge wouldn't only know the history of our hills as soon I would become a part of its story too. I climbed out the small carved-out square that served as a window and leaned over the wood rail as the tears fell and blended in with the rain drops.

The dawn was so still but for a stubborn sporadic wind. The brook below broke the silence as it babbled steadily. Even the wildlife was hushed. Was I a fool for thinking they were silent in honor of me? I had no purpose. I didn't deserve love or respect or even the shitty existence forced upon me.

I'd be trapped here. Heaven, if I'd been wrong and it did exist, was too good for me and my kind. Hell would be too overcrowded and Lucifer would have to implement a waiting list. I didn't know how such a list would work as there was no other place to go beyond Hell, was there?

My eyes stung from yesterday's mascara and eyeliner and remembrances. My cuts ached and my bruises were sore. The guilt and shame unfairly crushed me with every breath even as I stood here in an attempt to solve the problem. I still wanted to be someone's daughter, someone's baby, anyone's best friend, and my arms still wanted him in their embrace. Shamefully, I still wanted him...

As Mother Nature's aftermath slapped against my raw face and body, I heard the child-like melody of Rorie's voice. But she was off hiding somewhere, alone. I chanted her name and shouted apologies at failing her, just like Mom and Dad and everyone else in her life had, and for failing myself too. Rorie's voice blended in with the pulsating in my head- a steady *thump, thump* calling my name.

The constriction around my throat agitated and consumed me with purpose. Nothing else mattered. I'd done all the living there was for me. I'd never known unconditional love but I'd come close enough. I found a small moment of profound bravery. I gulped in one final breath and muttered my goodbyes...

SPILLED MILK

CHAPTER 1

"Have a good sleepover," I told Rorie as she climbed out of the car's backseat. I got out to help with her overnight bag.

I unlocked the trunk and pulled out a pink backpack with soda stains on it and a zipper that always snagged. I handed over her pillow with a unicorn on it and she hugged it close to her. That pillow case had been passed down for generations-not because it was some priceless piece of fabric, because we believed in the 'waste not, want not' philosophy.

"Are you coming to get me tomorrow?" she asked as I shut the trunk.

"Around supper time," I answered and noticed her disappointment. "Do you want me to come earlier?"

"Why can't I stay with Sara?" she asked, a blank expression on her face, gazing at little Sara's front door.

I started toward the house- a large garrison colored white with blue shutters and a front porch that held the quintessential porch swing with a cushioned seat. The yard was dotted with children's toys, a snowed-in sandbox, and a large wooden playground set fully equipped with a slide, two swings, and a jungle gym. Anyone could understand why Rorie wanted to stay. She'd stay forever if I let her.

Rorie had been friends with Sara Huntington since birth. Sara's mother had reached out to our family once she learned Mom had a new baby girl. Sara and Rorie immediately took to one another and would probably be friends for life, even if Sara did often rub it in Rorie's face how poor she was in comparison. Our lives were cursed the very moment Mom and Dad fell in love with each other.

"You can't stay," I told my 10-year old little sis. "What would I do without you?" I looked down at her once we reached the porch steps. She smiled up at me slightly.

Sara heard us on the porch and flung open the door, a huge smile on her pale face. She had a sticker of a pink star on her left cheek.

"Rorie!" she cried and the girls hugged, the unicorn pillow between them. "Hi Amber," she turned to greet me.

I rubbed her hair, messing up her baby-soft blonde mop. "How goes it, Sara? How's your mom and dad?"

"Mommy's inside. Wanna come in?" she asked and grabbed a hold of my hand to pull me inside. I resisted and let go of her sweaty little palm. "Hungry?" her offers continued.

I peered past her to see a pristine house filled with nice furniture and pricey décor, and I smelled beef stew coming from the kitchen. My stomach clenched with the insatiable urge to eat the entire pot.

"No," I answered. I placed Rorie's overnight bag on the floor inside by the doorway. "Tell your Mom I said it smells great but I really should get going."

I leaned down to plant a kiss on Rorie's cheek. "See you tomorrow around dinner time. Be good." The affection was not returned, as it never was in the company of others-especially Sara.

"Feed Bart," Rorie reminded before going inside with her

friend and shutting the door. The barricade didn't shut out the smell of stew that still lingered. I heard giggles and four small feet race across the house on spotless shiny wooden floors.

Bart was the fish Uncle Jeremy had given to her for Valentine's Day. It was red and blue and sat in a tiny fishbowl that sat beside her bed. A Chinese Fighting Fish named Bart. Rorie loved that fish like she would any cat or dog.

As I stepped off the porch and head to the car, I heard Mrs. Huntington behind me.

"Amber," she called gently and I decided against pretending I hadn't heard her. I reached my car and looked her way.

"Hi," I greeted.

I watched her walk towards me. She crossed her arms over her chest and smiled sincerely, her long blonde hair tossing in the breeze. She wasn't wearing a coat, just a small navy blue tee that brought out her eyes. There was still quite a chill in the air.

"Why didn't you come in, Amber?"

"I noticed you were cooking and didn't want to disturb you." An honest answer.

I don't know why she chuckled but she did, and added, "It's Dennis' favorite. I even threw in a little venison for added flavor. If you're hungry, it'll be ready any moment now." We both looked at her house as if the house was a huge pot of beef and venison stew.

I was famished. There were no groceries at my house. I shook my head. I'd rather starve than accept. She insisted I wait a bit and at least take a tupperware home. "No, really. I have plans," I said, "but, honestly, thanks."

I noticed the goosebumps on her arms and contemplated offering to let her sit in my car but I wasn't any good at socializing and didn't want to give her an excuse to prod me with a hundred questions.

"So," she continued after a small moment of awkward silence, "how are things?" That was one question. I expected 99 more…

"Things?"

"Things," she simply said. Her smile never disappeared even when the worried wrinkle on her forehead appeared. "You know…at home?"

I reached for a cigarette in the console of my car and lit it while admiring the mountain peaks behind her house. She saw where my gaze fixed and silence met us again. She knew I didn't like talking about how things were. After all, she was at Dad's funeral over year and a half ago. She couldn't bear to go to Clyde's funeral as she'd known my brother well, but she did make it to the wake and cried the entire time on her husband's shoulder while he stroked her hair. It was the first time I'd witnessed a loving touch granted to a woman by a man.

Mrs. Huntington reached out and touched my forearm kindly. I pulled away instantly. It was a reflex. I should have apologized but I said nothing.

She studied me, my facial expressions, and asked, "Are you okay, Honey?"

"Of course I'm okay," I cracked a smile and shrugged. "Why wouldn't I be okay?"

She smiled slowly, "Of course you're okay. But if you ever need anything I'm just a phone call away. If you ever need a hot meal or a place to rest or someone to talk to, vent to, I hope you know my home is always open to you and to Rorie."

I nodded as I did know this. I sat in my vehicle and started the engine. "I know and thank you"- I didn't know how I should greet her- Heidi? Mrs. Huntington? Sara's mom?- "but I really should be getting home." I closed the door and rolled the driver-side window fully down.

"Okay, Honey," Mrs. Huntington smiled down with her pity, "take care of yourself."

"Mom's making supper," I lied, not knowing why I did and backed down her driveway. She didn't turn to leave until I honked at the end and pulled away.

On my ride home from Prescott Notch, where the Huntingtons lived among the region's elite, I contemplated stopping at The Express, the town strip joint, to apply for a job. I needed more money than I earned at my present job. I shouldn't have to send Rorie off to Sara's house for a nutritious meal or a place to relax with no hypothetical eggshells littering the floor. And she needed a new overnight bag too.

I even went as far as to drive into the club's parking lot. I sat for a while staring at the small white building stained with dirt and sin, and at the men that went in and out sporadically. It filled me with distaste but my desperation lurked and weighed heavily. What would I tell Rorie? Where would I tell her I was going every night and during the same hours Mom was away?

Mom stripped at Glitter, in Temple, about 40 minutes east in our nearest excuse of a city. Mom would kill me for working at The Express. She called it a hole in the wall. She said ugly girls who couldn't dance at Glitter worked there.

Mom had two jobs. During the day, she was shut up in her bedroom performing for her fans online through her webcam. Sometimes she performed solo but mostly she had extras- men, women, a group. Then at nights, she'd head off to Glitter to spin around a pole and tempt strange men until one in the morning.

Tonight she was off from the club and was hosting a party at home. Her and her friends would drink and drug out for a few hours until their brains were decorated with blur, fuzz, and oblivion, before retiring to the bedroom to a camera ready to capture scenes of pleasure, mocking, shame.

Carmen would be coming over to join in on the festivities. Her much-older boyfriend was away on business for a few days. He was mid-40s, balding, and owned a trucking company. He also drove and delivered and was on such a run in Florida and Georgia.

For some strange reason, Carmen really liked my mother, even after all I'd told her about how Mom used to kick the shit out me while growing up and how Mom tried to get me to sniff lines a bunch of times to loosen up. She liked how Mom was sexy and pretty and how men wanted her, how women were intimidated by her. She liked how Mom still acted like she was our age, how she dressed. All my guy friends in high school had a hard-on for Mom and she loved the attention.

Men came at me too. I looked like her. Same big light brown eyes, same long black eyelashes, same full lips, identical dark brown hair with caramel streaks. I didn't like the attention the way she did. She knew she was good-looking. I knew I was pretty, too, but I wanted to be recognized for something greater.

A tap on my car hood interrupted my thoughts. I looked up to see a tall, skinny man dressed in a dark blue and gray flannel shirt and dark blue denim pants smoking a cigarette. He leaned against my car as if he belonged there. It rubbed me the wrong way.

I honked my horn and then rolled down my window with my left hand while grabbing for my pepper spray with my right.

"Hey, ass wipe!" I shouted, "You scared the fuck out of me."

He approached and leaned down to peer in at me. He had a wrinkly face though he couldn't be more than 45, and yellow teeth. His top canines were missing and his gums puffed dark pink at the edges, revealing evidence of gingivitis.

"Well, hey Miss," he said as if we were lifelong buddies. I prepped my finger on the red button of my pepper spray ready to douse the bloodshot eyes out of his wrinkly head.

The man continued, "You were spacing out. I was watching you."

"Why were you watching me?" I asked and muttered "creepy" under my breath. My tone was harsh with him. He inhaled a deep drag of his cigarette, no filter, and blew it in my window unintentionally, rather subconsciously, but quite rudely.

"Why are you crying anyway, Miss?"

"I'm not-," I started defensively. Instinctively I reached up to my face to feel for dampness and I felt it. I hadn't realized I'd been crying. I shrunk in weakness and started the engine. The guy backed away.

15

"You take it easy," he spoke between drags, now leaning against a rusty yellow pickup truck I assumed to be his.

"You too, Mister!" I shouted and peeled off. A couple of dancers who had been smoking by the side door looked in my direction. I didn't belong here but Mom did.

On my ride home, as my bubblegum pop music blared on the only mainstream radio station up here, I was angry at myself for the tears I'd shed. I was especially upset I'd been caught, even by a stranger. Why should I give a shit if he saw? But I did. How long had he been watching me? More importantly, how long had I zoned off?

I hadn't cried in a while. Not since Rorie started acting herself again and that was only a few months ago. She hadn't been the same since Rose killed Dad. She was only eight when it happened.

I swung into the local McDonalds and ordered two burgers from the dollar menu. I paid for my meal with dimes and a couple of quarters lying around the car. The drive-thru lady offered me ketchup even though I didn't order fries and two pennies for change. I declined both and drove off. The burger wrapper was off by the time I exited the lot and cruised along the lower half of Kancamagus Highway. The second wrapper was shed by the time I reached my road.

I lived on Sandman Road, a two-mile strip that started near downtown and ended in neighboring North Connolly. Our nearest neighbor was half a mile away and they lived in a dark brown shack the color of rust that was falling apart. Most of the people in our town, Little Bethlehem, had grown up here.

Our high school had seven attending towns and still the

graduating class was less than 50 kids. Everyone literally knew everyone else and newcomers were easily spotted. Some blended in eventually, others left within just a few years. It took a special kind of person to make it in our mountains. My family had lasted for generations. That had to mean something about our stock.

Once I neared the bend before my house, I could see lights on inside and a dozen cars dotted our driveway. I had to park on the side of our street as not to get blocked in once the party got rolling and more guests showed up. I locked my shitty Hyundai and turned on my key chain light to help navigate the long drive. We had no lamps to illuminate the driveway to the house. It was about 7:30 and getting dark even though we just turned our clocks ahead a couple weeks ago for daylight savings.

A couple of my mother's friends were sitting on our front porch banister smoking cigarettes. One man eagerly tossed back a Rolling Rock. A younger man I recognized from one of Mom other parties whistled at me as I neared. He didn't rise once I stepped onto the porch, only grinned and blew out a big cloud of smoke.

"Damn," he said in appreciation. The other two men just looked at me and nodded their approval. One had a joint half gone and offered it to me while saying, "Damn, you still looking good, Amber."

I muttered a "Gee, thanks," and sucked off the joint, not really wanting to go inside but wanting to all the same. I wanted the alcohol and treats but I didn't want Mom. I could hear her giggling even as the bass on the stereo thumped inside.

I passed the joint to the rotting-teeth guy whose name I'd forgotten and whose name I didn't bother caring to know. He still stared at me, a squint in his eyes, a sleazy grin on his dry cracked lips.

"Come on, girl," he said. "Come find a seat. Tell me what you and your hot lil' friend are up to."

I didn't bother to sit. And I didn't want to talk about my 'hot lil friend' either. He was the prick who always referenced for a threesome, with either me and Carmen or me and Mom. Both Mom and Carmen would be here tonight so I knew this jerk might be a problem later.

One of his buddies, with a gray hoodie sweatshirt and beige cargo pants that didn't match, spoke up, "You can find a seat right here," and patted his lap. The third guy, with a plain black baseball cap, a green and black flannel shirt, and fading thin jeans on, only laughed then chugged at his beer slowly as if he and the bottle were having a love affair. The rotting-teeth guy chuckled and didn't cover up the fact that he'd been goggling at the side view of my ass.

"Ugh," I snorted and opened the front door.

Their laughter blended into the blaring music and noisy chatters of the dazed and drunk occupants that polluted my house. I shot the guys a dagger of death before slamming the door.

Once inside the front door, a staircase was directly ahead against the right wall which led straight to Mom's bedroom on the second floor. To the left of the stairwell was a small hallway which led to the dining area that we set up as the family living room. Just as you entered the front door and looked left, Mom's spare room greeted through a white doorway.

It used to be the boys' bedroom when all the St. Germaine children were together, alive, and under the same roof. It was only unoccupied a week after Clyde died before Mom moved her shit into it. She claimed she needed her privacy most and needed her own living room away from the family's living space. Knowing Mom and her lifestyle I couldn't dispute her on that.

I could hear my mother in her downstairs room but I couldn't see her in the small crowd of people. I could see and hear others partying in the family living room. A small crowd gathered in the kitchen which was past the living room through a tiny storage room.

There was a side door off the kitchen so a few people were in the side yard although the temperature had dropped drastically from earlier. They were probably smoking or hanging out on the trampoline Dad had gotten Rorie about a month before he died. Rorie hadn't used it since he left her.

I entered Mom's room and finally saw her in the far corner, her head bent down as she prepared to sniff a line of her white sanity. One of her dancer friends sat beside her on an overturned milk crate, her rolled-up dollar bill ready by a nostril. She and Mother giggled like schoolgirls.

"Go!" Mom shouted and they raced to see who could inhale their line the quickest. Mom prevailed.

"Hey, Am," I heard somebody greet behind me. I turned away from my mother and her show to see a girl I'd gone to high school with.

"Hey," I said, giving her a small hug, "what's up? How are

you?"

She smiled, a wine cooler in her hand. We had gym class together during sophomore year. She was quiet mostly and only socialized when her best friend was around, but then her best friend moved to Concord junior year and stayed away for good. Her friend was smart and did the right thing by leaving.

"I haven't seen you in forever," she said.

"I know." It had been a long time. Her name was Rachel. "Did mom invite you?" As far as I knew, we didn't have any friends in common and I wasn't aware of any friendship she had with Mother.

"Your Mom's awesome," Rachel said happily. She looked over my shoulder to Mom and drunkenly hollered "What's up, Momma?" then swigged at her raspberry iced tea wine cooler.

Mom's eyes met mine briefly. "Baby!" she called back to Rachel and never bothered to greet me.

I nodded and smiled, trying desperately to fight back the jealousy that overcame me as I watched my mom banter with a bunch of young girls my age, but could never banter with me. Mom waved Rachel over. As if I'd vanished, so had our conversation.

I made my way past scantily clad and heavily made-up girls and women, drunk leering and groping men, and clouds of smoke from more than once source to the kitchen. I grabbed three Smirnoff Ice's from the fridge and small-talked with a guy around my age who had been over to have drinks with Mom on more than one occasion.

"Have you seen Carmen yet?" I interrupted talk of his girlfriend's D&C at the Emergency Room last weekend.

He shook his head and I apologetically excused myself

from a conversation I hadn't paid too much attention to. I didn't believe in spewing forth your problems to an almost-stranger in an attempt for sympathy and found that men did this more often than women.

I made my way up the stairs that fed off the storage room by the kitchen, to my bedroom, which was to the right at the top of the flight of steps. Rorie's bedroom was to the left. To access Mom's bedroom, one would have to cut through mine or use the front stairwell. It surprised me that no one had snuck up to use my room yet since it didn't have a lock. I heard sounds coming from Mom's room which was only separated by a thin wooden door. You didn't have to be a genius to know what the moaning and groaning sounds were that crept through.

I sat on the edge of my bed and stared at myself in the mirror that was screwed to the dresser. The mirror was outlined with brown. Pieces of the cheap paint on my dresser were cracked and fallen off which revealed the pea green color it formerly knew. The white was discolored anyway and the drawer knobs were missing so I couldn't fully shut the drawers, or end up annoyed with having to pry them open later.

I chugged down a few gulps of Smirnoff and remembered the joint I'd tucked away yesterday. Mom bitched about how she had four joints already rolled and one went missing, as if it sprouted legs and frolicked off. I found it on the microwave later in the day, just lying there. Mom must've warmed something up and rested it.

So I took it, allowing her to think it truly did wander away. I didn't know why she hadn't accused me of stealing it when she actively accused her friends..

The bass on the stereo downstairs vibrated the flimsy door of my room and the sole window shook gently with the beat. The loud voices downstairs collided with laughter and conversations- some distinct, others a murmur of words. Mom's laughter was heard every now and then and each bout made me cringe. I pictured her downstairs cracking jokes and piping crystal meth or cocaine down the noses of her friends. The more fucked up they were, the more fun they had.

I occupied myself with my Smirnoff's, my joint, and thoughts of Rose. I hadn't heard from my older sister, Rose, in almost a year. I went to visit her after I hadn't received a phone call or a letter from her in a bit, and was sent away. The guard had let me know that Rose didn't want any visitors and that she'd send word when she was ready to see people again. When I asked the guard if 'people' included her sister, he said that 'people' specifically included her sister. I hadn't heard from Rose since, until a couple of days ago.

I had picked Rorie up from school on Tuesday and found a letter from Rose in the mailbox, a big heart on the back of the envelope colored in with blue ink. There was a smiley face after my name on the letter's address line. It was as if we had communicated all along with no break in between. I never told Rorie that our big sister had written.

I tried my best not to mention Rose, Dad, Clyde, or Henri in her presence, because now Rorie's fine. She was outwardly over it. I didn't know what ran through her internally. I could only imagine how a 10-year old little girl felt being one of two kids left, when we started with six.

Rose's letter was short. Usually her letters were a few

pages long, detailed with jail life. She'd often write of her cellmate, Kara, and the stuff they knew about each other's past. Kara's life was just as messed up as ours, except she never killed anybody. She'd sent tales of the friends she'd made and lost, fights in the yard between two pissed off prisoners, her job on the inside in the kitchen, the college courses she was taking and loving.

At least being sentenced, she now had the opportunity of a college degree she'd probably never get to use but tax dollars paid for anyway. Rose was serving life- her degree would mean shit once she walked out of prison in 40 years.

Rose would be 63 when she'd be a free woman again. I'd be 61. We always joked that when she finally got out, we'd have wheelchair races and cane fights. Rorie would be 50 and could soon join in with her own wheelchair that she'd probably paint purple.

This letter was different. She asked me to send her 50 bucks and visit her the first Tuesday of next month, which was quickly approaching. Her words on thin, recycled, yellow-lined paper reeked of defeat. The sentences no longer read of acceptance but rather of a loss of who Rose used to be.

It was only a paragraph long and lacked details of the prison life she'd grown to accept as her fate. But I hadn't lost all hope- the smiley face and colored-in heart let me know she was still managing. If anyone would be all right, it was Rose.

The cell phone on my nightstand vibrated, indicating an incoming message. Cell service was blotchy up here, especially where we lived. The one tower was in nearby North Connolly and the townspeople had put up quite a fight to not have one built but came to realize we had to move with the times or be forever left behind. Radio stations had a hard enough time with clarity and uninterrupted service.

I read the text from Carmen that she was on her way. She lived with her boyfriend in Eastman Valley, a town much like where the Huntingtons lived in Prescott Notch- upper class, sprawling acres of land, expensive cars dotting driveways and garages, swimming pools in backyards, kids toys outside that weren't purchased at the Dollar Tree.

Carmen liked her new life in Eastman Valley. She liked having dollar bills in her purse when before she'd only had loose change in her wallet and some guy's number in her back pocket.

I lit a cigarette and took out my flat iron to straighten my hair. While it warmed, I attempted to text a reply but the cell service disappeared. The best service was in the center of North Connolly or on the outskirts of Lil Beth.

As I stroked the flat iron through my long hair, someone knocked on my bedroom door. It was too soon for it to be Carmen.

"Yo?" I hollered, not inviting my guest inside.

"Am?" It was Mom. She sounded drunk when she spoke next, "Hon, open the door."

I let her in and went back to the mirror. Hearing her call me 'hon' sent shivers down my spine. Rarely, and I mean rarely, was she ever nice to me.

She came in and I noticed her bloodshot eyes. Her black tank top was low-cut and two C-cups threatened to spill loose. Her stomach was revealed atop her tight black leggings. The silver butterfly belly ring glistened.

SPILLED MILK

She took a cigarette out of the pack on my nightstand and lit it. She sat on the edge of my bed to watch me. It made me uncomfortable so I switched the flat iron off and looked at her reflection in the mirror. Even wrecked, she was pretty. Even calmly stoned, I wanted to hit her still.

"Yes?" I asked, suddenly wanting to throw up from the bass downstairs. I was still hungry even after my two burgers. The pot had given me the munchies already.

"Nothing," she said, smiling while she fluffed her hair with her fingers. "Just seeing how my girl is."

"Your girl?" I asked, obvious sarcasm in my words. I sat beside her and laughed, "Since when am I 'your girl'?"

I took the cigarette out of her hand and helped myself to a couple drags.

"You're always my girl," she answered without confidence. "So, listen," she smacked my leg, "I need a few bucks."

I burst into laughter and returned the cigarette. "So," I said, "the truth comes out. What for?" I stood up, clicked on my straightener, and carried on with my hair.

"I just need a few bucks, Amber," her voice lost some of its previous fluff, insulted I didn't just fork it over like I normally did. She couldn't slap me around with her guests over. "I'll pay you back with my tips tomorrow."

"What do you need money for? I have another pack of butts if you need cigarettes," I offered.

"A 30-rack," she blurted. "And a bag."

I scoffed, hair finished, and started to freshen up my makeup. "A 30-pack of beer alone is more than a few bucks," I stated the obvious, "and a bag of what?"

"What the hell does it matter?" my mother asked,

standing up to get closer to me. "I get crazy tips on Saturday nights, you know that."

"Well," I gave off the impression I was contemplating, and finished with, "…no."

"No?" Mom asked in a how-dare-you manner.

"No," I confirmed, " I'm broke. Ask one of your friends."

"You have at least a 20 hanging around." I didn't. I hadn't cashed my paycheck yet. It was stated so matter-of-factly that it angered me. What angered me more was that she was in here asking me for money when she was the one working two jobs, and I only worked 30 hours a week for minimum wage at the movie theater in Connolly.

She began to open my dresser drawers, fumbling through socks, underwear, and sweaters looking for money that didn't exist. After finding nothing but clothes, she moved to my nightstand to look through note paper and old letters from Rose. I assumed I wasn't her 'hon' anymore.

"Mom," I said louder, "I have maybe a dollar in my car. You can't get a bag with a dollar. I can't believe your friends don't have any."

"All those fuckers brought was weed," she exasperated and crossed her arms over her breasts. Her eyes still surveyed my room for some mysterious hiding spot where some unknown stash of money or drugs lay hidden.

"Fuck," she muttered, uneasily shifting her weight from one leg to the other. She wasn't at the point of withdrawal as she'd just plowed down a line or two, or three, but she was uneasy knowing she may run out tonight and wouldn't have the funds for more. Her dancer friends were like her- fiends

26

who blew their tips then scrapped around for more loot to re-up.

"Amber," my mother spoke more seriously, resting against my dresser to talk to me, "if you spot me a 20, I'll pay you back with interest."

"I don't have any money," I insisted, pushing the eyeliner back and forth under my lower lashes to draw a bold black line.

"I'm your goddamn mother," she spat, then ripped the eyeliner stick from my grasp and tossed it across the room. It hit the wall and landed behind the large heavy bookshelf that held my written works from throughout the years. I didn't write anymore.

Just then, Carmen knocked and entered without an invitation. "Hey," she shrieked in her giddy, girly way then rushed over to hug me. Mom still eyed me until Carmen threw her arms around her neck and squealed, "I missed you."

"At least someone around here gives a shit about me," Mom said, throwing me a glance. She twiddled with Carmen's hair.

"What do you mean?" Carmen asked and Mom engulfed her into a mini conversation about how family was supposed to look after each other and I couldn't even lend her 20. Of course, if I let Carmen in on the real reason Mom wanted the money to begin with, I'd have to suffer the repercussions afterwards. I couldn't throw my own mother under the bus like that.

While I finished with my mascara and brushed through my hair one last time, I saw Carmen hand Mom some money out of the corner of my eye. Mom hugged her in gratitude. Always unable to hide my true thoughts, I subconsciously let out a chortle that went unheard.

Soon, the three of us were downstairs. The party was in full force. Music exploded and people were so inebriated that love was everywhere. Mom had given the 20 from Carmen to a friend of hers who disappeared for an hour or so. By the time he returned, I was so drunk that I didn't say a word when Mom jumped up to greet him and stroked his groin right there in front of everyone. No one reacted.

Mom and her drug-runner scuttled off somewhere while Carmen and I sat around the round kitchen table and played Truth or Dare with a couple of our high school friends who'd stopped by. After every answer or stupid dare performed, we took a shot. There were no rules.

We were just having fun like the good old days, when fun was just that- fun, and there was no guilt involved. I even humored myself when Mom came back, who was happier than when she'd taken off, and took a shot of Jagermeister with her. She joined in on our Truth or Dare game and chose 'truth'.

"Best oral?" my high school friend, Erin, asked. Being girls, we all giggled and the small crowd that gathered, mainly men, joined in on the *ha ha ha* chorus. The rotting-teeth guy from outside loved the question.

Mom pondered a second. I watched her think, probably comparing her long list of playthings in her head. My vision was blurry by now but I swear I saw penises float above her. I hoped she didn't say Dad.

"JJ," she answered and playfully shoved at Rachel, who'd

Carmen, in my mother's bed agitated me most of all. It made me sick. All day, I had plotted different ways in which to ruin Carmen's bubble that she'd always live in.

I could fuck her balding boyfriend and plan it so she walked in while I rode his short dick like a stallion. Then I could live in his fancy house in Eastman Valley. I could blindfold her while she slept and torture her in silence so she'd never know it was me- torture her in ways she deserved.

I'd pluck out her pubes one by one, slowly, then I'd punch her pretty face around until the red trickled out of both nostrils. After a few nicks and some cuts and bruises, I'd convince some STD-infested guy to fuck her senseless in every orifice his dick could fit into. I'd take off her blindfold and send her back into the world, permanently scarred- both her skin and her spirit.

I didn't know why I didn't plot revenge on Mom like I did Carmen. I'd grown used to Mom. Maybe it was because I subconsciously preferred her the way she was now rather than how she used to be. She used to hit me a lot. I'd spill paint, she'd hit me. I spoke out of turn, she'd hit me. I'd lose a Barbie shoe, she'd hit me.

She used to beat Rose too. She'd tie up our wrists to a doorknob and put a rag around our mouths so we couldn't scream. But when Dad moved out when I was 11, Mom started partying with friends again and smacks were replaced with insults or nothing at all.

Rose and her letter also nagged at me. I couldn't clearly define what exactly about her letter caused me dread. It could have been the abruptness of it, the boxed shape of her letters when usually she wrote in cursive or bubbly large font, the fact she'd asked for money when that was never Rose's way, or it could have been that I only now realized that blue-ink heart on the back of the envelope and that penciled-in smiley face next to my name was a cover-up. They were placed there for my benefit, so that I wouldn't see that possibly she wasn't okay like she let on.

My big brother, Bret, also nagged my mind. I'd been dreaming of him again lately. The dreams came and went and I wondered if they were there all along and it was only at times that I couldn't remember them. Not the kind of dreams where you woke up and recalled bits and pieces. All I ever recollected was the stubble of his facial hair. Bret was 25 years old and the black sheep of our family. He was a ghost now like Rose. A long lost memory that no one spoke of. The road to his cabin would be open and I could visit him.

I'd smoked three cigarettes before I pulled into the parking lot of the pathetic movie theater. My shift started at four and it was 4:28. I was working with Frank tonight and, besides his rusty old truck, there were two other cars in the entire lot. Small as it was, it looked depressingly naked. Not exactly the theater's busy time, so I didn't rush.

I took out my cell phone and wandered around to find a good signal. Almost immediately, a voice mail and a couple of text messages came through and my phone chirped. An envelope icon flashed on the phone's screen. The voicemail was Frank telling me to hurry my ass up and the text messages were from Mom advising that she couldn't pick Rorie up, like the note I'd put beside her car keys before I left for work told her to. I'd forgotten I had to work when I'd promised Rorie to get her around supper time and I felt guilty about it.

I scrolled through my contact list to find the Huntingtons number and called it. Mrs. Huntington told me, her voice dripping with honey, that it wasn't a problem if Rorie spent another night over and she'd be glad to drop her off tomorrow anytime. They were having such a great time.

Rorie then hopped on the line and breathed deep as if she'd ran to the phone. "Oh my God, Amber," she giggled, "thank you so much. Me and Sara are playing dress up and Heidi has this really cool scarf that I used as a belt for that white dress that Sara has. Remember the one I told you I liked? You know, the one you wouldn't let me get at the mall last summer? The one with the yellow flowers on the bottom of the skirt."

My little sister took in a breath so she could blab some more. "Well, the scarf looked so good and then Heidi wrapped it around her head and pretended to be a hippy. Then Dennis found an old hat from the basement. It was like a cowboy hat and a farmer hat, and he put a carrot in his mouth. We even put a hat on the dog," she giggled and I couldn't get a word in," but he didn't really like that very much. It was so funny.

"So, thanks for letting me sleep over again. Heidi's warming up leftover beef stew for dinner. You should've stayed for supper last night- it was so good. The carrots were perfect. When you make the carrots they're too mushy. Heidi's are just right. And the beef chunks were so tasty. You missed the boat," Rorie snickered again.

"Have fun," I said when she was done telling me her entire day in probably four breaths. "Tell Heidi and Dennis I said 'hello'." 'Heidi' and 'Dennis' were emphasized. I couldn't even refer to Mrs. Huntington as anything, never mind her name, and here Rorie was referring to Sara's family as if she'd taken them as her own. In a way, she had. She was there so often. Little Sara never came over to our house. She'd never been invited although I wouldn't have minded. I just didn't want to corrupt the poor girl.

Once I finally walked into the two glass doors that led into a small lobby carpeted in red, Frank laughed, "You're hungover, aren't you?"

I hip-checked him once I walked behind the candy counter to the registers. "Do I look like shit or something?" I fiddled with my hair and clocked in. I did feel a little woozy still. I hadn't eaten yet and I'm sure two cups of coffee and two sodas didn't help much. It sucked being broke. We ate like crap.

"You never look like shit. I just assumed, being a weekend...," as if I got drunk every weekend. He looked at his watch then added, "And you're so late."

I rolled my eyes, "I love how you throw the word 'so' in there. My car ran out of gas," I lied, "my mom had to come and bring me gas. It took forever." I rarely talked about home life or Mom with Frank so he had no reason to disbelieve that Mom would go out of her way to bring me a jug of gas. I looked around the lonely building, "Besides, who the heck cares? There's no one here. You should've thought to clock me in at four."

He laughed and handed me a large plastic cup. We prepared for a routine work night. Just a few customers here and there and plenty of time to munch on popcorn and

SPILLED MILK

Swedish Fish, and toss back free soda and lemonade. Frank and I usually worked together and ended up with the 4-10 night shift.

Every once in a while, I got stuck with some flaky girl named Heather who was a junior at Three Rivers High. It was the same high school I'd gone to so it didn't surprise me when she made the comment, on a few occasions, that she'd rather work at the movie theater than get a real job because at a real job you actually had to work.

Three Rivers, as a whole, stunk but its politics reeked even more. If you were a girl who wasn't halfway decent, people knocked you by calling you "ugly" or "skank" or " fat ass ho" even if you weren't fat. If you didn't smoke pot or drink beers, the other guys didn't like you and tormented you in the halls and at lunch. If you were really disliked, your mailbox was smashed regularly and your house saw many bags of manure and vomit tossed there by asshole kids with nothing better to do.

Carmen and I weren't one of those people. We were pretty and fun and partied like there was no tomorrow. Our home lives weren't so thrilling but, at school, able to get away and be ourselves, we flourished, and we ruled. Everyone knew who we were. Even my coworker Heather had heard of us and we graduated when she was a freshman. I imagined Heather, cute and flaky, fit in at Three Rivers just fine.

About three hours into my shift, still snacking away on candy and chips and talking about random subjects with Frank, my uncle strolled in. His hands were jammed into the pockets of his khaki pants. The sight of Uncle Jeremy always sent my mind racing.

Tonight, the sight of him made me want to laugh. Maybe it was my mood. I started off anxious, then had to paste on a fake smile for Frank's sake, and now I wasn't feeling so bad. Frank's talk of his Mom and her garden and helping set up the pool at his brother's house in Connolly, another neighboring town in our region, helped to brighten my mood. He loved his family. I could appreciate that, even if I couldn't appreciate mine.

"What's with the hunting jacket?" I asked Uncle Jeremy. One of his hands left a pocket and took off his baseball cap colored brown. The hunting jacket he wore clashed in the worst way with the tan khaki pants and his dirty, old, steel-toed work boots. The baseball cap didn't help matters either.

"What's with the glitter eye shadow?" he returned.

"Going to the can," Frank said to avoid the feeling of being third wheel, and head off towards the men's room.

Uncle Jeremy shifted his weight and I could tell he didn't like being alone with me. His eyes lingered on the cotton candy rack, then a honey bun.

"Munchies?" I offered while handing him a large cup to help himself to a drink.

He set the cup down on the hard plastic counter that was constructed to look like real glass. "So, how have you guys been?" His voice was deep and his Adam's apple bobbed when he spoke.

Uncle Jeremy wasn't a bad looking man. He was about 5'10 with a medium build. His light brown hair complimented his eyes- the same color as Dads, a caramel brown with a black ring around the iris. The same eyes I had. I could tell he hadn't shaved in a week or so.

"We've been okay. You?" I sat down on the stool and gnawed on some strawberry twists.

"All right," his eyes fidgeted more. "All right," he said again. "I was in town picking up some things for the house and thought I'd swing on by."

Uncle Jeremy rarely stopped into my work. As a matter of fact, this would be the first time. He usually swung by the house a couple times a month to check on things. He'd bring Rorie a present, like a DVD, a new shag rug for her bedroom, some funky and colorful T-shirt, or a fish like Bart. He never brought anything for me. I never wanted anything.

"What's new?" I asked.

He shrugged. "Fixing up the house and getting the bike ready. Spring's coming. Got to have The Bitch ready for summer." He referred to his motorcycle as 'the bitch'. He loved his bike. There was no crazier sight than a man wearing work boots and a hunting jacket riding a bike down the Kancamagus Highway.

"The bitch," I chuckled. I looked at my uncle and felt a sudden pity for him. He had no one. No wife. No bastard children. His parents were long gone. All he had was Dad and Rose stole that from him. "Are you okay in that house all alone?" I asked then added "You should find a lady friend" to make the conversation light.

"The last thing I need is a lady friend," he finally cracked a smile without answering the part about him being okay or not.

"I disagree," another quip to fill the time. "So," I urged, "what's up? I have to get back to work soon."

He scanned the empty movie theater. He knew as well as I

did that everyone drove to Temple to the 3D theater there. They had 3D glasses and everything. They had a fancy, recognized corporate name while Connolly's venue was called "Movie Magic" and listed three or four movies at any given time. Plus, we closed at 10, last showing at eight depending on the features' length, and the one in Temple shut down at midnight on Friday and Saturday nights.

"Business is on fire, I see," said my uncle.

"Yeah," I tittered, "I call it 'job security'."

Uncle Jeremy boomed. It felt good to see him laugh.

Once the seconds passed and the wise crack became a has-been, he let me know that he'd found a sleeping bag in his basement last weekend while he was lining it with sandbags. That reminded me that I'd have to find something for our basement. Flood season was coming.

The sleeping bag was of black exterior and lined on the inside with purple material. He figured it was Rories, as anyone would have. Rorie and purple would have been best friends if purple were a person. I told him that I didn't remember her ever having a purple sleeping bag, never mind one at all. She didn't like camping because that meant possibly getting 'nippy' or overheated. Camping also entailed creepy crawly bugs and bears finding her snacks then eating the entire family after it devoured her Cool Ranch Doritos and Twinkies.

Frank had returned from the bathroom and saw that I was still busy with my guest and started to mop. We didn't usually tidy up until closing time. I called to Frank in our friendly joking way, "Holy shit, Frank is cleaning. It is Saturday," I then pretended to check an imaginary watch on my wrist, and finished, "7:44 pm, and Frank is at work actually working," pretending to be making some kind of national announcement.

"Ha ha," his mop moved from side to side on the small tiled section where a table sat for movie-goers to sit and have some nachos or shoot the breeze. No one ever sat there but good old Frank cleaned that floor anyway. "Good one, Amber."

"I'm going to head out," Uncle Jeremy replaced the cap back onto his head, "and let you get back to work. It was nice seeing you, Amber, real nice. Let Rorie know I asked about her." His hands reunited with the pits of his pockets.

I nodded.

"I'll come see you next weekend," as if he worked a 9-5 during the weekday instead of collected social security checks and couldn't find the spare time. "Check with Rorie about the sleeping bag, will you?"

"I will,"

He turned away, and his back said, "See you girls next weekend."

I turned to Frank and so began a lengthy discussion about how the process of camouflage in the chameleon worked. The thought absolutely blew our minds and I made a mental note to do some research on it later. It'd make a nifty documentary. My buddy, good old Frank, even if he did fart a lot and they always reeked of eggs. No one else I knew liked to talk about actual topics with substance. With everyone else, it was *them, them, them* and some *blah, blah, blah* on top of that. Frank- not your typical guy, definitely not.

I ended up leaving the theater a little after 10. My entire

shift saw maybe a dozen customers. We only made $17 at the snack counter. Most people knew to wear a large purse or puffy coat to smuggle in snacks and drinks. The irony of job security hit me. I always wondered how Movie Magic could afford to pay me let alone the four other people it employed. I humored myself with thoughts of my short fat boss, Elvis, with his yellow shirts and his loose-fitting pants attached with suspenders, dealing crack out of the back door of the theater.

Maybe he was a grave robber at dusk and hocked the valuables taken from the coffins for extra cash then sold the body parts on the Black Market. Or he could be a pimp and took commission from a ring of hookers that were at his beck and call. Good old Elvis. I supposed the only thing that mattered was that I was still employed and got some kind of a paycheck once a week, and care less about where that check came from.

Frank stayed behind to make sure the entry door and all the counters were free of fingerprints and germs. Nancy, a crabby middle-aged lady from Red Center, south of Lil Beth and one of our areas poorest towns, would be opening up tomorrow and Frank didn't want her bitching about how lazy we were. Nancy liked to complain. It somehow made her feel superior. She desperately needed this measly job- she had four children and a disabled husband to care for. Frank needed this job too, he always said- he had three cats to feed.

Once by my car, parked directly by Franks, I dug deep into my purse and retrieved a condom in a transparent green wrapper. I placed it gingerly under Frank's windshield wiper blade- a gift from one friend to another. A couple of days ago, I left him a banana peel with a half-dollar-sized ladybug sticker on the white side under that same wiper blade.

I immediately reached for the joint that waited for me in the ashtray. I lit it and turned the engine. One of my favorite songs was midway through and I cranked the knob up. My shitty stock speakers complained and I had to adjust the dial just right so the speakers would stop crackling and ruining the song. They desperately needed replacing.

In fact, I needed a whole new vehicle. My Hyundai wasn't cutting it anymore. She was a gas pig, the engine struggled at 35 when it was cold outside, and the passenger door window got stuck at random times like during a rainstorm when I had to rush out to the liquor store for Mom. Carmen had come with me and had cracked it a little too far down to smoke her cigarette. The window was stuck for two days until I hit it out of frustration and it suddenly worked again. I didn't foresee buying a new car, or even a used car, anytime in the near future. I couldn't even get new socks.

Movie Magic sat in its own parking lot alongside Route 4, which was also known as King Valley Road, a mini highway. It didn't resemble a real highway with two or more lanes in each direction, separated by a median, and lines on the road to give instruction. There were no toll booths waiting at the end or grid marks on the edge to startle sleepy drivers back to wake. It was an ordinary road, like any towns' Main Street. All the so-called major businesses sat on or just off of Route 4. The only thing that made it a 'highway' was its speed limit.

Route 4 wound north and connected to the Kancamagus Highway, nicknamed 'The Kanc' by locals. The lower part of Kancamagus, another road pretending to be highway, was always open, during all seasons. Once you started to climb Mt.

Jolly it was closed off with a chain from two posts and a large wooden log. A bright orange sign on both posts read "Closed. Trespassers will be prosecuted." The road was dangerous when it rained heavily and snowed. It could only be traveled upon during designated times and months.

Barely anyone lived high on the mountain, just some loner or misfit or outcast, although state law prohibited residency during off-season. Bret lived up there. He'd been sent to some Boys Home when he was in the fourth grade and when he moved back he didn't stay long. He left again when he turned 18 and lived with his girlfriend at the time. They broke up and he was forced back home to crash in the basement on a fold-away, raggedy, old cot. He moved out around the time Dad moved to Uncle Jeremys.

But instead of bunking with someone else, my brother decided to build his own cabin. It was tiny and the logs weren't painted, but he loved it because it had been constructed with his own hands. He didn't mind being shut up year round in his cabin. It sat secluded on a long, skinny dirt road that fed off of the Kancamagus. Bret was the outcast in this scenario. Maybe a bit of loner, but not a misfit.

The blockade on the Kanc had been removed recently and I could see him again. It was rough on me sometimes not seeing him for a couple months. I'd spend all spring and summer with him then, when the road got blocked up by the State Park officials and I couldn't see him for a while, I was miserable. Eventually, of course, I livened up and carried on with life and its' responsibilities. I just didn't like the immense pressure I felt within my chest walls when I thought of him or woke up after dreaming of his facial hair.

SPILLED MILK

I hadn't stopped by his cabin when the log and chain were finally removed from their posts. A nor'easter hit a couple days after- the day before I'd planned to go- and it wasn't an easy climb up the mountain. The officials had to temporarily block it up again. That didn't bother me- my car couldn't handle it anyway in the snow.

When finally they did unblock it, I was too busy with Rorie because the Huntingtons went on a mini vacation to the Cape. I found that silly of them as I'd pictured Cape Cod to be a summer getaway. What a difference it made when Rorie wasn't away a few days out of the week. My wallet felt the impact when it came to the bill for groceries and paper products.

As expected, nobody else was on the highway. The setting sun was hidden behind Mt. Washington. The dirt road to Bret's place was a compacted layer of mud. Melting snow fed off of mountaintops and onto the roads. I had to drop my speed considerably. Soon, the melt would find its way down into our valley at the bottom of the mountains and cause a mini ruckus in our towns, and create a mini play yard for Rorie.

Bret's driveway was just as bad as the road. His black minivan sat close to the cabin. It wasn't an old person minivan nor a family minivan. It was a simple black van with a red line around its body towards the bottom. He had the thing since he was 18 when his girlfriend kicked him out for catching her cheating and calling her out on it. Uncle Jeremy and Dad helped him fix it up to mint condition. The three of them worked on it for a month solid and drank beers the entire time. They worked better drunk.

I parked and honked my horn three times to let him know I was here in case he was naked, taking a dump, or masturbating and not prepared for company. He came to the door and leaned against the door frame, a smile on his face when he recognized my car. He looked handsome in his jean pants, a loose-fitting black tee, black sneakers, and that smile that made many girls' hearts skip a beat.

I nearly flew out of my car and jogged to him. His arms welcomed me and I stayed within his embrace as long as I could without it being awkward. I pulled loose and looked up into his eyes, brown like mine but without the black ring around the iris. His brown eyes were speckled with black ovals and it was beautiful. His arched eyebrows were full and his nose was just right. He sported a mustache and a short beard.

I reached up and rubbed his chin. "What's with the mop?" referring to the beard I wasn't sure I liked. I preferred when he looked like he hadn't shaved in a couple of days. He looked better rugged. The extra facial hair made him look like the typical mountain man in these parts. Bret wasn't that guy. But maybe, like the rest of us, he was hiding from something and ,instead of hiding behind phony smiles, he hid behind a beard.

He led me into his cabin and I breathed in the familiar scent of it. It always smelled of pine. We sat side-by-side on his fluffy blue sofa. He gazed at me. I resented Mom for forcing him to the Boys Home when we were younger. I missed him and I could've used a guy around the house to help out with things I wasn't destined to be good at. I also needed his wisdom- a man's wisdom.

"You don't like it?" he tugged at his beard.

I squinted, "I'm not sure. I'm soaking it in."

It was so still in his cabin. He only had a television in his bedroom but no cable nor did he own a landline telephone. He did own a stereo but it was off. There were no pets around to break the silent air. It was perfectly still but for the two of us.

After about an hour of catching up and filling him in on Rories' happenings, and chit chatting it up about what we'd been up to and how life was going, I mentioned Rose's letter.

"How is she?" he asked. He and Rose weren't very close. Rose was closer to Dad, and to Rorie. I became Rorie's favorite when Rose got locked up. Bret and I had always stayed in touch and remained good friends besides being family. I trusted him and I think he trusted me.

"I don't know," I answered honestly. "She wants me to go see her."

"Are you going?"

My eyes widened. "Of course!"

He shook his head and rose. He looked down at me where I sat, looked as if he was going to say something, then stopped and went into the kitchen. His cabin was a one floor, open-concept style so I could see his every agitated move. Rose wasn't a good topic with Bret, or anyone else in my family. The day she shot Dad was the day Rose was as good as gone forever. No one even liked Dad all that much, except Rorie. Rorie always liked visiting Dad and Uncle Jeremy. It got her out of the house and away from Mom and the nonsense.

He started washing dishes and said, "How the hell can you keep on defending a murderer? She fucking murdered

47

your father, for Christ's sake."

"He was your father too," I reminded him, then said harshly, "she's my sister," feeling the need to defend Rose. Every killer had to have their reasons. I got up and walked over to the kitchen and plopped down on one of the bar stools besides the counter. "She's *your* sister too," I pointed and watched his strong hands clean a pan. I had to remind him of where his roots lay and where he came from.

"And?" he asked.

"And?! How can you just cast her off because she made a mistake? You fuck up all the time. The one time Rose screws up everyone turns a cheek and pretends she never existed. She's our sister. She's cleaned our scrapes and cuts. She fed us. She took care of us." I supposed shooting someone in the head, especially the man who created your existence, was more than just a mistake.

He said nothing, only scrubbed.

"Why is that?" I asked. "That no one can repay her for what she's done for our family?"

He said nothing.

"Well, I'm visiting her."

"Nobody said you couldn't. Do what you feel you have to do. But what if Dad had killed Rose- would you still be involved with him?" I thought a moment, and thought even harder when he added, "That'd be like spitting in Rose's face. Don't you think?" How could I disagree? Rose would be pissed. It would definitely be a betrayal.

I searched his rugged face and looked for any sign of emotion left for our big sister. Bret was hard to read but I knew him better than anyone. My brother was hard-headed and knew exactly what he liked and didn't like. He stood his ground. He fought the good fight.

I, on the other hand, spoke through my eyes. I didn't hide my feelings well. I'd had lots of people throughout my life tell me my eyes looked older than my chronological age. A boy I'd dated in high school told me one day that my eyes looked like they'd seen a lot. I never knew if he was serious or if he said it because he thought it sounded deep, like he had substance. Turned out the only substance he had was in his pants.

"You don't miss her, do you Bret?"

He stopped scrubbing, turned off the sink, and dried his hands on a nearby rag. His Adam's apple bobbed, "What the hell do you want me to say, Amber? What do you want me to do- go to that jail, throw my arms around her, and tell her what a good job she did wasting Pops?"

I stood up and went to him at the sink. I put my arms around his waist and rest my head on his chest. His arms felt good around me. His big hands were soothing as they pressed against the small of my back.

"She loved you, Bret. You were her 'booga'," a special nickname Rose came up with just for him when he was about six. They were only three years apart and used to run around in our yard together often before Mom sent him off to the Boys Home.

Young boys who needed discipline and a more structured environment were sent there to live and receive their education. Frankly, it was just a place to dump your kid when you couldn't handle them anymore. Mom had run to her mother by the seacoast and gave her some bullshit story about how Bret needed special attention in order to thrive, and her mother, having favored boys over girls, gave in and forked over a check to see Bret through until he turned legal age.

"I know," he said into my hair and he breathed in deep. Did he inhale the scent of my strawberry kiwi shampoo or did he fret over Rose? He never said though that he loved her, and he'd never admit if he was, indeed, in pain over losing her.

We smoked cigarettes and I watched him drink a couple of beers. I offered him a hit off of my pipe and he declined at first, until he saw me smoke it. It only took a couple of puffs for Bret to feel high. After all, he was stuck up on this mountain all alone in forced sobriety. He had to stock up on food and supplies in the fall to see him through until February. He made pretty good money logging. He lived stingily and saved most of what he earned, so it lasted him during the winter.

Bret and I were still on his comfy sofa. He leaned back in the corner of the couch by the right arm and my head rested on his lap. We spoke every now and again but the silence didn't kill us. It didn't matter I hadn't seen him in over two months- we were comfortable in each others presence. Even when he was gone all those years when we were kids and he came back there was no awkwardness like there always was with Dad.

I glanced at my cell phone that sat on his dark oak coffee table and saw the time. It was late. I hadn't realized how much time had slipped by. I sat up and startled Bret who had drifted off. He wasn't a big smoker. He was too active to sit around and smoke pot for long periods of time. If he sat around, he drank beer. Hard liquor wasn't his friend- he turned rude, mean, obnoxious, boisterous, and he wasn't any of those things. Not to me anyways.

"I should get going," I stood up and stretched. He sank lower on the couch and yawned. I felt kind of bad for getting him so stoned, but it was also a good thing. He'd sleep like a baby for once as he rarely slept a full night. Bret always had too many thoughts.

Our eyes met and a part of me wanted him to ask me to stay. It'd been a while since I had good company. Rorie was okay most of the time but when she acted up she was out of control and I usually had to leave the house when that happened and go for a ride. Not exactly the most responsible choice but I did it anyway, knowing full well that I always should have stayed and worked it out with her.

I lingered by my brother's cabin doorway.

He didn't ask.

I didn't stay.

CHAPTER 3

Nobody knew what I was up to as I snuck around the house like some robber. I didn't want anyone to question where I was or why I had gotten home so late. The drive down the Kanc was hard at night with no street lights and only headlights or the moon for guidance. I missed Bret already and I'd just left his company.

I was sure I'd get an earful from Rorie when she woke up. She hardly ever let me sleep in. No way in hell Mom would get up at 7:30 to help Rorie get ready for school. She was in the fourth grade and old enough to care for herself in some ways but not old enough in most ways.

Even if I didn't set an alarm and snoozed away, she barged in my bedroom and woke me herself. I fed her. I put the clothes on her back. I put bandages on her scrapes, and kisses on her scars. I went to her parent-teacher conferences. If all that defined being a mother then I was it. If blood defined being a mother then Rorie was blighted with Nicole.

My head spun and although my mind was filled with thoughts and memories, nostalgia and disquietude, I felt the heaviness of sleep. I marched up the creaky back stairs taking the steps two at a time and popped my head into Rorie's bedroom. She always slept with her door ajar. Her room was so small she felt claustrophobic with the door closed. Her dark brown hair poked out of a faded purple comforter. She snored gently and hopefully dreamed sweetly. She was at peace. That made me smile.

I closed my bedroom door; I valued privacy. I'd grown up in a house full of people. Before, there had been a Mom, a Dad, a big brother, a big sister, two little brothers, and a little sister. Once, there had been eight total. Now we were down to three but still lacking solitude.

I didn't bother to set an alarm. I knew Rorie wouldn't wake me up until about 10. It was a Sunday. She probably stayed up late watching Cartoon Network as soon as Mom left for Glitter, and she probably waited for me. The thought of my little sister in her white pajamas sitting on the living room sofa, watching the door for my entrance, gave me a pang of guilt.

I wanted to go into her room and lay beside her but she was too old for that now. She let me know everyday that she was no longer a little girl. She was in the double digits now. How dare I treat her like a kid? 20 wasn't exactly a big person either, she debated. I altercated that I'd soon be 21 and that, my friend, was an adult.

I quickly changed into my gray sweat pants and black short-sleeved tee, eager for the comfort of my bed and squishy blue corduroy blanket. As soon as I rested my head on two pillows and smooshed a long body pillow between my legs, I shut my eyes and sleep found me. So did dreams of my childhood with Bret. Never did I dream of him the way he was now; we were always kids.

At almost nine in the morning my door knob turned and in came Rorie, still sleepy-eyed. She'd just woken up and wanted cereal. I told her to get it herself; I was too tired. She muttered something about my being lazy then left to pour her own Frosted Flakes.

She didn't shut the door so I heard the cupboard smash, a bowl smack onto the counter, a drawer being pulled open then slammed shut, a spoon clank into the bowl, then a loud crinkle, and finally flakes hitting the ceramic. A fridge door was then yanked open and, after she poured the milk, it was pushed shut with small force. Condiments encased in glass jiggled on the shelves inside.

"Shhhhh!"

"Shhh yourself," came Rorie's voice.

"Close the door," I said loudly and covered my head with a pillow.

She picked up her bowl and it landed on the kitchen table with a clank. She pulled the chair out from the table and it squeaked against the cheap linoleum floor. She even crunched her breakfast loudly.

In between a bite, she said louder than I, "No! You're lazy and you're closer."

That would have been a good point had I not been annoyed with her and at being woken up. I had to work at four and planned to get some shut-eye until at least noon, then I wanted to take a long drive and get lost on a deserted road to kill some time.

Mom would be at work so Rorie would be home alone as usual. Of course, I'd call the house and ask how her day was then I'd remind her to brush her teeth and take a shower. She'd shower but she wouldn't brush her teeth- she'd only say she did then chew on a piece of mint gum for a minute in case I smelled her breath for proof. I knew her tricks. Unfortunately, she knew some of mine too.

I pulled the blanket off of me, got up, stomped to my door, then slammed it shut. Mom shouted from her room, "Shut the fuck up!" I climbed back into bed, fell against my pillow, and waited for my heart to stop racing. Mom's voice above a certain pitch gave me anxiety. She used to be funny when her mood was just right. Now, she had nothing. Not even dignity- if she'd ever had any at all.

When I finally did wake up for good a little after noontime the house was creepily quiet. I welcomed it. I was surprised Rorie allowed me to sleep in this late. She must've been outside playing by herself. There wasn't a neighbor her age for miles. She used to ride her bike two miles down the road to play with a little girl who had an above-ground pool. Rorie stopped playing with that little girl once she turned 10 in December. Again, she was in the double digits now. The little girl was only six.

Usually I wasn't hungry when I first woke up but I was famished. I looked inside the refrigerator for a bite. All I saw was expired milk, a ketchup bottle nearly empty, butter, a plastic jug of blue juice that held no nutritional value as it cost me 99 cents, and a few mustard packets I'd brought home from the convenience store in town where they sold hot dogs.

I chugged down a bunch of the blue juice, enough to fill my stomach and ease some of the hunger pains, and rushed back to my bedroom. I grabbed my thick cotton bathrobe and a clean towel so I could jump in the shower.

The bathroom was off the family living room. It wasn't a very private location being in the main area of the small house. When people were over, urine landing in the toilet bowl echoed. For that reason alone, no one ever took a shit at our house. Our bathroom was narrow too which made it an uncomfortable place to be with the door closed. At the end was the toilet and tucked away in a left cranny was the sink.

The tub sat right against the wall and doorway so baths and showers weren't private either. Nobody liked taking showers at our house. I didn't like it when they did either because I was the one stuck with removing hair globs from the drain.

I peeked between the blinds that hung from the small window that looked into the side yard. Rorie wasn't anywhere to be seen. It was sunny outside and I wanted to get out there and enjoy it before work. I jumped in the shower and rushed to get dressed, curious as to my little sister's whereabouts.

Just as I scrambled to find my car keys for the fifteenth time this week, I heard soft R&B music playing and muffled moans from Mom's room downstairs. She was filming another show on her webcam. A part of me wanted to sneak in her room one day while she was at the club and go through her personal site to see what kind of people viewed it.

I wanted to see if people asked her to stick abnormally gargantuan dildos in her ass hole or screw a dog or something equally sick. A small piece of me wanted to know what her world was like and why she stayed in it for so long.

I surveyed the land beyond our dark blue New Englander-styled home for Rorie. I called her name a few times and received no reply. I got into my car and started the engine but I couldn't leave. My eyes scanned the surroundings for the shape of her body. All I could think was that she had gone exploring, fell down a ravine, and broke her neck- still alive and longing for help.

I went back into the house and looked around the living room and kitchen for a note from her. I didn't find one. I didn't find one in my bedroom either. Knocking on Mom's door to ask if she'd seen her youngest daughter would be useless. Mom hardly paid heed to Rorie. If I interrupted her anyway, she'd be pissed, pause her webcam, and rush out to slap or yell at me for screwing up her cash.

Instead, I went into Rorie's bedroom and looked through her desk drawer for a piece of paper and a writing utensil. I found a green colored pencil and tore off a corner of a homework assignment to jot down a note for her: *Where did you go without telling me? I will be at work at 4 so call me there right when you read this! XO, Amber.*

Frank laughed as soon as I waltzed through the door of Movie Magic. I knew what he was thinking and laughed too. I was late again. I got lost on my ride. I saw parts of our county I hadn't been before. I found a very skinny road hidden between trees and took it. Another narrow road fed off of that one. I kept taking small roads, some that led nowhere, some that led to tourist viewing spots, others that led to other roads.

Eventually, I didn't know what roads I'd driven and what direction I'd taken them on. Finally, I reached an area where signs pointed toward the interstate. Once I got to the highway, I found my way, and here I was 40 minutes late.

"I should start charging you to punch you in on time," he said.

I put my purse down and picked up the telephone to dial home.

"Why?" I asked as the phone rang and rang with no answer, "Did you punch me in?"

"Hell no," he roared with laughter. Frank was so jolly. Nothing brought him down. "You didn't pay me."

"Next time, just bill me," I joked.

He chuckled and ritualistically handed me a large plastic fountain drink cup. We were ready to start our long shift of ass-sitting.

"Did Rorie call?" I hung the phone up after I'd counted 14 rings. Elvis would have been pissed had he walked in just then to see me with a phone in one hand, a drink I hadn't paid for in the other, instead of a broom and cleaning spray.

"No," he answered, "was she supposed to?"

"Yes," and left it at that. I waited until he took a bathroom break to dial the Huntington's phone number. Sara answered on the second ring. It was as if she waited by the phone for it to ring, but I could also picture her flying across her spacious living room once it sounded. Her and Rorie could talk for hours about everything and about nothing. Even little girls at their age blabbed on and on just like girls my age did.

Sara didn't know where Rorie was and hadn't heard from her but, as soon as she did, she'd let me know. I told her to take down the number to my work and she giggled as if I should've known better, "Caller ID! "

Right then, her mother asked "Is that Amber?" in the background. A television sitcom could be heard too. Loud studio laughter boomed. It was Three's Company. Jack Tripper made some sort of wisecrack. I could picture their little family unit- Sara, Heidi, Dennis, and their dog- on their black leather sofa laughing along with the studio, eight eyes on a large flat screen posted to the wall.

"Mom wants to talk to you," she chimed. I hadn't heard her Mom ask to speak with me exactly.

Sara handed the telephone to her Mom, who jumped on the line with me. "Amber," came that honey-smooth voice, "how's it going? Is Rorie missing?"

"No," I scoffed, "she's not 'missing'. I just don't really know where she is at this moment-"

"That means 'missing', Amber," she stated in a friendly manner.

"Did you try the house?" I wanted to slap her through the phone. Of course I'd tried the house.

"No answer. I'll keep trying, thanks." I hung up the phone after she had started to say something that started with "how". I couldn't handle her questions right now. I couldn't handle lying to her and telling her that everything was all right. It wasn't. It'd never be. We all just pretended that it was. Only a fool would admit their misery.

I kept to my word and kept calling the house. I even called Mom's cell phone which went straight to voicemail. Good thing for Frank and his mood that could always lift mine. His presence helped, and so did his jokes and spouts of wisdom, but Rorie still crossed my mind.

Frank and I grew bored, and sugary snacks and fatty munchies filled our stomachs so we couldn't eat anymore. I had given up on trying to reach Rorie. Cleaning helped occupy my mind. The theater was spotless by the time Frank and I got through with it. Nancy would have no reason to snitch to the boss tomorrow when she opened, about somebody's fingerprint still smeared on the popcorn counter or a square of toilet paper left on the men's room floor.

Uncle Jeremy's truck was beside my car at the far end of the lot. In the passenger seat was Rorie. I smiled when I saw she was safe but, as soon as she returned the smile, I got angry and let her know it.

"Where have you been?" I cried when I pulled open the passenger door. Uncle Jeremy watched us and tipped his hat in greeting.

"With Uncle Jeremy, duh," was her smart ass remark.

"How?" I asked, looking at him particularly. If she'd been with him all day long he damn well should have notified me before now. It was past 10 and too late for most children to be awake still. Rorie wasn't like most children though.

"I stopped by the house," he answered. "You were sleeping and Rorie didn't want to be alone so we went into town. We took a drive out to Woodstock to see if the bears were out yet." He was referring to a popular attraction which boasted bears and an old-fashioned train. Some guy dressed up in furs, and who wore a patch over one of his eyes, called 'The Wolfman', chased the train in a little motor car. The kids loved it. I'm sure that guy thought he had the best job in the world.

"I thought you were stopping by next weekend," I pointed out and he explained that the plans he'd had for working on the house didn't pan out too well. He wanted to see us girls and stopped in. I wondered if Mom and Uncle Jeremy exchanged pleasantries when he came, or if she stayed shut up in her room all day and ignored the world.

"I still will. Hungry?" he asked and Rorie scooted over to sit in the middle of the truck bench. She was all grins. She must have had a nice time hanging out with Uncle Jeremy.

I didn't have cash and I rarely let someone else pay my tab. I tried to hold onto my checks until mid-week when necessities started to overflow and Rorie needed this or that, or I had to buy food and items for the house or Mom. Mom hit me up for a loan every week- a loan she never repaid and I never pestered her for. I didn't know what she did with all the money she earned and I couldn't say I didn't care, because I did care. Maybe caring was my downfall.

"Not really."

He snickered and so did Rorie without knowing what he was going to say. "Filled up on cotton candy and popcorn? Can't fit in any real food?"

"Maybe next time," I let him know, "but you guys head out. I'll pick Rorie up at your place in about an hour."

Rorie scooched back over to the window seat, ready for her take-out with Uncle Jeremy. I'd visit with Bret again or find something to do if he was busy or sleeping.

Uncle Jeremy asked if I was sure and I confirmed that I was. I watched his truck drive away and Rorie's small head in the passenger seat disappeared. The worry was over- I knew where she was. I'd have a good talking-to with her on our drive home later tonight. It may have been okay for her to pull that shit with Mom but she could not pull it with me.

I took the journey to Brets and stopped in the lot of The Express again on the way. One day, I'd grow enough balls to walk in the place and ask to speak with the manager. My measly paychecks weren't cutting it and Rorie was growing at an alarming rate and needed more. In fact, her entire spring and summer wardrobe needed to be replaced.

We'd pulled out her box of warmer-weather clothes and she tried them all on, piece by piece. Only a few old shirts still fit. All of her bottoms were too tight. Last year, she was a skinny little thing but meat was finding place on her bones the older she got. It stressed me out since we pulled out that box that I wouldn't have enough funds to clothe her for the season. She needed new shoes too.

Bret's minivan wasn't parked in his driveway and I immediately panicked again. That made two siblings that took off without telling me in one day. My panic subsided when I remembered that Bret didn't have to tell me where he was going- but Rorie did. He probably ventured into town or into Temple to grab a few drinks at a bar. I parked my car anyway and tried the door to his cabin to see if it was unlocked.

It was common practice up here to not lock doors. You could leave your door unlocked for an entire weekend and come home to find that no intruders had bothered and that all of your belongings were still in their rightful place. It was locked. I tried the windows but they didn't budge either. I waited by his cabin for a half hour before I hesitantly left.

I had to get Rorie at Uncle Jeremys on the other side of town. I ended up having to wait around for Uncle Jeremy and Rorie to show up. I waited on the front porch steps and smoked a joint. His truck pulled in, at last, and Rorie hopped out, a fast food bag in her hand. She rushed over to me and shoved the bag at me, that big smile still on her pink lips. I didn't look inside.

"It's an apple pie," she said happily.

"Thanks," I told her. "Ready?"

"Yup," she said and hugged Uncle Jeremy. He turned to me, "Your mother said you're going to see Rose."

I looked into Rorie's face when the name 'Rose' was mentioned, and she hadn't flinched. That bothered me. What bothered me more was that Mom knew. How did she know? Did she find the letter I hid in my nightstand drawer?

"How did she know that?" I prodded. I then told Rorie to go sit in my car. When she started to complain, I handed her the keys and told her to put on some music and sit in the driver's seat to pretend to drive.

We sat on his porch on a couple of white lawn chairs. He was wearing the same clothes he'd been wearing when he stopped in the theater to see me. The hat was different; this one was navy blue.

"Your Mom," he said, "she seemed…," he tried to find the right words and couldn't. "Did she get drunk again last night?"

I shrugged. "I don't keep tabs on my mother."

"Right," he said. "You nervous to see your sister?"

"Why would I be nervous? I've visited her in prison before." On many occasions. "How does Mom know I'm seeing Rose?"

"Who knows," he answered, "and I didn't ask how she knew either. All I know is that she knows." He studied my face and couldn't determine the expression I tried to hide. "Is it some state secret? Is that why you didn't mention it to her?"

"It's just none of her business. Whenever I do mention Rose, Mom either ignores the topic or she goes off on tangents about how Rose is a loser or a bitch or a filthy murderer. Maybe I just don't feel the need to have to defend my own sister all the time."

Of course I'd always defend Rose. Some saw me as a traitor by seeking the enemy but Rose was no traitor, nor an enemy, nor a murderer- even if she did shoot another human being in the head.

"Until everyone forgets what happened you're going to have to defend her. I don't foresee people forgetting anytime soon." Uncle Jeremy was wise.

"Why not?" I looked at my dad's brother, seeing Father every time I looked at him. It wasn't only in appearance; it was everything else- the way my uncle talked, his motions and movements, the remarks and quips he came up with, how he walked, his love for things like hunting, fishing, fixing cars, and riding motorcycles.

"Everyone seems to have already forgotten her," I carried on, butterflies in my gut. Conversations like this caused me discomfort. I should've stayed hidden inside my house like I had been for a greater portion of the last year and a half. Ever since I ventured back into the outside world, people were coming at me left and right with questions and comments regarding my family's dark history. "Bret has, that's for sure."

Uncle Jeremy looked at me and lit another cigarette. "You saw your brother recently?"

Last Halloween, while he and I took Rorie trick-or-treating in North Connolly center, the subject of Bret came up. Uncle Jeremy had told me I shouldn't spend so much time with Bret. I asked why and he never answered. I never knew why the two of them stopped being buddies just before Dad's murder. Bret and Uncle Jeremy used to do all kinds of guy stuff together.

I nodded, "Yeah, I went to his cabin."

He looked at me deeper and I squinted, hoping he'd fill me in on why the friction in our family was so heavy even before Rose killed Dad, and why so many St. Germaines parted ways. "You sure it's a good idea?"

I didn't know what he meant. Rorie honked the car horn and her hand waved madly motioning for me to hurry. "Why wouldn't it be a good idea?" Another honk and I put up a finger gesturing for her to hang on.

Uncle Jeremy looked straight ahead and took a long drag off of his Pall Mall. "How's he holding up?"

"He's okay," I said to my uncle, then yelled to Rorie who had honked a couple of more times, "Two more minutes!" Back to Uncle Jeremy, "You should stop by his place and say hello. It'd be nice if he knew someone still gave a shit about him."

"That's not fair," he flicked the filter of his cigarette onto the dirt walkway, then looked at me defensively, "Bret's my boy. You know I care about him."

"Oh really?" I got a little defensive myself. Tonight was a drag. First, I had to stick up for Rose, now Bret. "Is that why you haven't talked to him since Dad died? Even before Dad died?" I lit another cigarette myself. I was getting more stressed. Anxiety would prevent me from sleeping tonight.

"Amber," his tone was lower this time. "What am I supposed to do? Go out of my way to make sure everyone's okay? Your father is dead," he stated, "and his children are alone. I get that. But I can't keep reaching out to your brother and getting nothing in return. It's not me why we don't talk. It's his choice and he chose it."

"You make sure me and Rorie are fine," I pointed. Rorie quit honking and cranked the stereo. "What makes us so special?"

He looked at my car. "She's a good girl," he said and I nodded. Rorie had her moments and she made me proud a lot of the time. "She's a young kid. Your father would've wanted me to look after her."

"I can look after her just fine," I said.

He took off his baseball cap and placed it on the porch beside his boot. The wind blew harder. I pulled my jacket around myself tighter and started to count the number of hairs on his chin- *one, two, three...* It was all that prevented me from fleeing.

"That's the thing," Uncle Jeremy said. I could feel his eyes on me.

Twenty-two, twenty-three, twenty-four...

"You're not even 21," he reminded me, although I felt well beyond my years, "You shouldn't have to take care of your little sister. You should be out having fun, going to college-"

"College?" I laughed and stood. "Nice thoughts, Uncle Jeremy, but unrealistic. I've got to head home. Rorie has to get to bed."

"Am," he stood too and jammed his hands into his pockets, "have you tried talking to your mother about Rorie?"

"What about Rorie?"

"About Rorie not being your responsibility."

I turned to leave. "Please," I scoffed, "we both know who

my mother is. Therefore," I said over my shoulder as I paced to my car, "we both know that Rorie is my responsibility."

"See you two next weekend!" he called and I waved.

I got in and Rorie was still having her own mini dance party. Her little hands moved about the air and her body moved side to side with the beat of the song. She sang the parts she knew out loud and slurred the parts she didn't. I turned the dial down and we drove off into the night, the moon low and ahead of us.

CHAPTER 4

Talking with Uncle Jeremy got me thinking about Dad and death. Thinking about death brought Henri and Clyde to mind. I was 'Ammer' to Henri and 'Sissy' to Clyde who loved me best.

Henri came first. He was born when I was eight. Clyde was born soon after. They were only 11 months apart. Rorie would be born after Clyde- they, also, were 11 months apart.

Henri passed when Rorie was only a couple of months old. After he died, so did everything else associated with him. We rarely spoke his name. I kept a picture of him in our living room- until Mom destroyed all family momentums when Rose and Dad left.

I kept my own photo album until she found it and destroyed that as well. I was only left with one family picture and Mom looked gorgeous as always in it as she held Clyde in her arms. Everyone looked happy- but we weren't. That was the point of pictures.

I was young when Henri came. Once Mom let me know she was pregnant, I burst with excitement. I couldn't wait to have a little sibling I could play with and keep me company. Mom was pretty happy too. I overheard her talking with Dad the night she told me of the new arrival. She mentioned to Dad that the baby within her was her fresh chance to do it right. She'd already messed up with the rest of us.

SPILLED MILK

When Henri was born, Mom's family came up from New Bay to celebrate. It was the third time I'd met my maternal grandmother. It was the first time Henri met her- and the last. Mom and her family weren't close. She was the black sheep. Although her family lived in the same state, they didn't make any effort to come see us. Then again, we made no effort to see them either.

Henri brought Mom back to life. She radiated and even laid off of hitting me and Rose so much. Prior to those days, she hit us all the time- morning, noon, night. Rose took the beatings better than I did. I didn't learn to take the hits until I realized they would always come no matter what I did. Had Henri been grown enough to contemplate the world around him, he would have thought Mom to be some great women or something. She *was* great when he came- even Dad saw it.

I liked to watch him crawl, smile, and play. I never enjoyed changing his diapers, even though Mom made me often, but I did enjoy how he stared at me as I did. He smiled and kicked his chubby legs when I plugged my nose and made gagging sounds. I felt he needed me and, at age eight, I hadn't really felt needed or wanted before. Henri made me feel good about who I was when, before him, all I'd felt was bad.

Only Mom, Dad, and Rorie were home when Henri wandered to the second floor window when he was two years old. Rose and I were in elementary school. Bret was at the Boys Home. Rorie had been sleeping in her playpen. Nobody had been watching Henri and he must've pushed the screen in the window too hard so it fell out, and he fell out right after. Mom was the one to discover him. She had noticed the screen

69

missing and a curtain swaying in the wind. When she looked out and down to the ground, her little boy lay there mangled.

I remember when I got home from school the day Henri died. Rose and I had seen the flashing lights of the police cars, ambulance, and fire trucks down the road. The other children on the bus stood up and madly chattered about the commotion. Once everyone learned it was at our house, they hushed. Even without knowing the details of what had taken place, everyone knew it was serious because there were so many emergency personnel.

Rose and I had looked at each other and I remembered the fright in her eyes. Maybe she'd already recognized the enormity of the troubles ahead since she was 10 and a bit wiser. I was still naive, still waiting for wisdom. Rose's instincts got the better of her. I, on the other hand, wore a mask of nothing. I remembered not knowing how to feel or what to say, or how to move my feet.

Once Rose and I reached mid-driveway, Dad pushed past a few police and firemen and rushed to us. He went to Rose first, as usual, and held her long. He stroked her hair and whispered things into her ear that made her whimper and then crumble to her knees to scream and cry. Dad knelt before her on the ground and rubbed her back while he wiped her tears.

I stood off to the side, alone, with my sunshine-yellow lunch pail and my red rain boots on, and stared at the house and all the flashing lights. A large crowd was in the side yard and a small crowd in front. Not only were there officials, but neighbors and spectators too. I craned my neck to find Mom and couldn't see her. Nobody seemed to notice me but I noticed all of them.

A couple of men in the crowd in the side yard moved away which left a gap. I could see a foot on the ground, twisted in an inhumane way. It piqued my interest and I slowly began to work my way up the driveway and closer to my house. Just then, a police officer approached. I looked up at him and him down at me, his eyes large and round. I didn't speak. The man asked if I lived there and I nodded. He then told me to go find my father.

When I went to my father he was still busy with Rose. I gazed down at my big sister and began to cry when I saw her tears, and I hadn't yet known what I was crying for. When Dad finally told me the news I didn't believe him. But that foot on the ground that had been bent as it was came to mind. I remembered dropping my yellow lunch pail and I ran into the woods as fast as those red slickers carried me.

Nobody had bothered to come and find me. I crawled into an opening between two boulders and cried the night away before sneaking in the house much later to cry myself to sleep in my bed. All night I had tried to block out the gut-wrenching sounds of Rose's whimpers that came from her bedroom.

Rose never quite recovered. Mom wasn't performing back then. Her temper and abuse ruled again. The things she did to Rose and I when she'd hit us were unspeakable- even now. Other kids, I'm sure, suffered worse, but suffering at the hands of your own mother was the most damning fate. I knew how I loved Rorie and I didn't even birth her. It was common practice in our family for siblings to take the young as their own, especially since the real mother refused to step up.

Then came Clyde. He cheered us up with his bright brown eyes and bushy eyebrows. His bottom lip dipped into a frown even when he smiled, but he was always happy. St. Germaines were happy babies, miserable kids. He wasn't any different.

Eventually, Mom grew tired of a newborn and started going out with her friends again. She drank more but wasn't quite labeled a drunk yet. Rose, like with Henri and with me, cared for Clyde like a mother not a sister. A sister made fun of a little brother and laughed when he threw tantrums. Rose bathed him and read to him at nights and held him on her lap listening to 70's rock.

Little Clyde was four years old when he got a hold of one of Dad's handguns and pulled the trigger. He shot his own face and died instantly, no witnesses. Mom had run upstairs to grab a toy for him and, during that small frame of time, he'd found Dad's gun in a bottom drawer of the large oak cabinet in the living room. He aimed at his face as he most likely peered into the barrel. There were even more police and rescue than with Henri's accident.

I was in my early teens and had been out with Carmen and friends all day. We'd been drinking at Carmens' boyfriend's house. I didn't get the news until I went home the next afternoon to grab a change of clothes for another night out with the clique.

Mom sat on a kitchen chair, her head in her lap. Dad stood over her. Uncle Jeremy paced uncomfortably around the kitchen, pulling nervously at his beard that was long in those days. Dad had been out of the house for a while at that point so I knew something had happened when I saw him there.

Upstairs I could hear Rorie crying in her room and I looked around for Rose. A swarm of personnel flocked in the living room. At least they had enough decency to leave the family in privacy.

Nobody spoke until I demanded to know what happened. Uncle Jeremy was the one to take me outside and away from the others to let me know that I'd lost another brother, and only when my soul had begun to find the pain of losing Henri bearable. I didn't cry as hard over Clyde as I did Henri, mainly because I should have seen it coming.

Even before the deaths started in our household, we'd been cursed in other ways- evictions, family tragedy, car accidents, drunken rages gone awry, abuse, addiction... You name it, someone in the St. Germaine line had dealt with. Few had overcome it.

Rose rented a motel room for two weeks and wallowed in her miseries until Uncle Jeremy and I forced her back home. She didn't come willingly. I hurt tremendously too but I had to repress it for everybody's sake. Rorie was three and could comprehend death. Thankfully, she was still young enough to believe in a heaven.

We vowed never to discuss, or even mention, the names Henri or Clyde again- for her sake. She was the youngest now, and female, so we had to protect her. We all protected Rorie, Dad protected Rose, Uncle Jeremy protected Dad, Mom's friends protected her. Nobody protected me. Bret wasn't home yet to shelter me but I imagined he fared better being distanced from the situation.

I got my pain and anger out by partying every single night with Carmen and the girls, by flirting with every guy that caught my eye or whose eye I happened to catch. The year Clyde died was the year I lost my virginity to Carmen's cousin, Dennis, who was 15 and in high school. My spirit was weak and I desperately sought peace and love in any form. I didn't find it. Then Bret came home in the summer and I found love again. Peace hadn't yet graced me but I never lost hope that it would eventually, someday.

The cemetery in Lil Beth was fairly large and blocked in by two-foot-tall stones lined up to form a small wall. The residents kept it plain with very few flowers and ornaments to decorate head stones. The grass was dry and always brownish. But there was no litter, no headstone tipping, no grave robbing- anymore. Nobody buried relatives in valuables nowadays and everyone else knew that.

No other cars were around. I pulled to the side of the narrow drive that ran through the center. The two small rocks that bore the names of my siblings could be seen from where I parked. I turned off the engine and hesitated before getting out. No other mourners were around which gave me strength. I hated being in a cemetery with someone else because I knew that other person had lost someone important to them and that always made me sad. Being sad for them and being sad for myself was too much to handle.

First 'Henri Thomas St. Germaine' and then 'Clyde Antoine St. Germaine' jumped out at me from identical gray

SPILLED MILK

stones. They died so close to the same age. If I ever got pregnant, I hoped it would be a girl because I felt all little boys in our lineage would meet the same end. I couldn't bear to lose another. Losing another would literally destroy me.

Dad's grave was to the right of Henri. Dad's tomb was dark gray with tiny white and black rocks blended in, and covered with a shiny glaze. It was another reason on my list of why I resented Mom. Her sons got plain tombs and the husband she'd ostracized got a grand one.

Maybe I wasn't mature enough yet to factor in things like economy or tomb design availability or who directly was responsible for selecting the stone. I felt Henri and Clyde had been jilted and Dad rewarded for his sins even in the so-called afterlife. Ones headstone should reflect the kind of person they were- a shitty one for a person of the same likeness and an elaborate one for a person of fine character. Henri and Clyde were too young to be tainted. Theirs should've been extraordinary.

I sat in the exact spot between their gravestones. Sitting even an inch closer to ones would've been an insult to the other. Henri's plain gray stone had a small heart etched into the top right corner. Clyde had a butterfly. I wondered for the first time who had selected those symbols and who decided which symbol belonged on which stone.

I lifted my hand and ran my fingers over the etchings of the heart. Then I looked at the epitaph on Henri's stone. 'Gone too soon' it read. I had to look away immediately. The words were so true that it hurt to see them. I thought of the bones which lay in his coffin beneath the ground. I thought of the suit he'd been buried in that shielded those bones.

75

Poor Henri and his broken bones. The landing of the fall killed him. I wondered if he felt every bone crack and died of blood loss or if he smashed his head on the ground and went instantly. I never knew all the details and I didn't ask either. I didn't want to know.

The butterfly on Clyde's stone was small. Smaller than Henri's heart and that pissed me off. 'Beloved son' Clyde's headstone said. Beloved he was. He was a charmer. Rose adored his every feature, his every movement. They spent a lot of time together.

Mom was back to drinking and hanging out with friends at all hours, so Rose picked up her slack. Rose loved the role of caretaker so much so that she dropped out of school to take care of Rorie, but I also think she did it because she hated high school. I, on the other hand, only found relief at school and away from Mom and our lives.

After almost an hour at the graveyard, exhausted from my own thoughts, I had passed out right there on the grass. When I woke back up, I remembered dreams of baby pudge and innocent giggles.

When I got back home and entered the house, Mom was bitching at Rorie about something in the family living room. The television flickered scenes of a yellow sponge and a pink starfish who were best friends. They'd do silly things inside of a pineapple house. Rorie was sprawled out on the sofa, her head propped against an arm rest, remote control in hand. Mom sat on an end table next to the TV by the basement door.

SPILLED MILK

"What now?" I moaned and tossed my purse onto the coffee table in the center of the small room. The runner crinkled as my purse slid a few inches before it rested.

Both my sister and mother looked up at me, then Rorie quickly turned her focus back on the sponge named Bob.

I plunked down on the loveseat which sat against the opposite wall of Rorie's couch. I watched the two of them and studied their dynamics. The slit in Nicole's eyes as she glared down at Rorie was cold.

"Then why the fuck did you do it?" Mom persisted. Apparently Rorie had logged onto one of the social networking sites Mom frequented and had used Mom's profile. Some guy our mother had been chatting with started to message Rorie thinking she was Mom. Rorie played along. It bent Mother out of shape.

Rorie channel-surfed during a commercial break and answered, "I told him I wasn't you and he kept sending messages."

Mom stood and hovered at the end of the sofa where Rorie's feet lay wrapped in purple cotton blankie. Rorie sat up and pushed against the arm rest. We both knew Mom was pissed. It was in the air.

"I read through the conversation string, you lying bitch!." Mom spat. "You never fucking told him you were you and you flirted with him, you little slut!"

"Mom-" Rorie started, at full attention now.

"Who the fuck do you think you are?" Mom intercepted. She moved closer to Rorie and stood tall above her. Rorie moved her face away as if expecting to be slapped at any given moment. "You're a little slut already. I can't believe it.

Look at you," Mom mocked, "with your scraggly hair," and she lifted a strand and let it go in disgust, "and your bucked teeth," she protruded her top teeth and curled back her lip to tease Rorie. "You really think you're pretty enough to be talking the way you do?"

Rorie looked up at her mother, her eyes wide, her small lips slightly agape, her hands together, the fingertips rubbing each other in an act of self comfort. But mother didn't see her innocence like I did. She continued with her insults and I'd heard enough. I wasn't in any mood to hold back. She spoke to Rorie as if she were much, much older.

I stood up and tugged at Mom's arm to pull her away. She snagged her arm loose and went back to badgering Rorie.

"Stop!" I pleaded.

"Mom," Rorie started.

Mom's palm met Rorie's cheek as fast as an arrow pierced skin. Rorie's little face turned red and her eyes widened more. "Don't call me your mother!" Mom hollered while I simultaneously shouted, "Cut the shit!"

My little sister's face started to scrunch up as if she were ready to burst into tears. My emotions became a struggle to conceal.

I pushed Mom aside and ordered Rorie to my car. She bounced up and fled out the front door without grabbing her shoes. I could hear her start to cry before the door slammed.

I turned on my mother and screamed into her face, "She's 10 years old! Have some damn respect!"

She twisted her face into ugly hatred which caused me to step back a little. The mixed emotions of the day enabled me to stand my ground.

"Respect?" she spat, "Show that little twit respect?"

"You mean your daughter," I corrected, "I think she deserves some respect, yes. You can't go on calling your fourth grader a slut."

She chuckled. "Who the fuck are you- Mother Teresa? You're a little slut too," she laughed. I mocked her laughter and she stepped closer. I could smell the Jose Cuervo on her breath coupled with stale cigarettes. Her eyes had a yellow tint I hadn't noticed when I first walked in.

I slanted my eyes at her and cursed my lips before I spoke. My hands clenched at my sides as I begged for the willpower to not punch her pretty lights out. "Well, we learned from the best didn't we?" It wasn't a question. It was a statement that ended in a question mark.

She slapped me- hard! I didn't falter though. I only smiled at her. She hit me again and I began to laugh. Did she really think physical punishment could hurt me worse than my soul hurt me each and every day?

Mom stormed off muttering stuff like her daughters were whores and we'd never be able to snag her men away from her, that we were jealous of her. I stood in the living room laughing yet holding back tears with every insult she heckled.

Rorie waited in my car, seated in the backseat. She sat small, her little shoulders slumped. Her seat belt wasn't on. One of my sweatshirts was scrunched in a ball and she held it like it were a teddy bear.

I looked at her from the center mirror. "What are you doing in the backseat?" My face stung from the slaps and I wondered if hers still did too. She was still flushed.

She sniffed. "I wanted to be alone."

Neither of us spoke for a moment. The silence stressed me out.

"You okay?" I decided I should ask.

She didn't answer immediately and, when she finally did, I regretted having asked. "All I said was a blow job sounded fun. And I did say I wasn't Mom- I swear."

I stared at her via the mirror and she pleaded with my eyes for trust. I cracked a smile for her sake and simply nodded. It was good enough for her.

Her eyes lost some diameter and shifted to the house. I looked over too. Our New-Englander needed a fresh coat of paint along with numerous other repairs and upkeep.

It was a fairly warm day but would be more pleasant if the breeze subsided. I decided to surprise Rorie with some ice cream. She strolled the toy aisle at Walmart while I cashed my paycheck at the customer service counter. Then we drove to the nearby Dairy Queen and ordered one chocolate and vanilla swirled cone and one strawberry cheesecake blizzard. We shared both treats.

As Rorie shoveled chunks of cheesecake into her mouth I stared at the pink of the slap that lingered on her face. I should've told Rorie that nothing Mom said was true, that she was pure and pretty and smart. I should've rubbed it in Mom's face that she was stupid to not realize the gifts bestowed upon her- the gift of Henri, the gift of Clyde, the gift of Rorie. Mom had been foolish for never recognizing them as such.

I wanted to let Mother know that Henri and Clyde dying was all her fault- that she should've been watching. Had she done that one simple act of parenthood I wouldn't carry with me the extraordinary ache of not having them, of having to explain to Rorie one day what exactly had happened and why.

I had to swallow the fact that *I* was Rorie's mother figure and the woman who lived in our house who called herself such had no right to ever touch her again- ever.

CHAPTER 5

My visit with Rose was only a week away. Both times I saw Bret during the last few days he tried to coax me not to go. Both times I'd insisted I was going whether he approved or not. I was nervous and excited to see her but dreaded the prison visiting process. For some reason, I was always the one selected at random for a search. I hated to disrobe in front of a total stranger just to see my sister.

Mom never brought up the fact that she knew I would be seeing Rose. I'd checked my nightstand drawer and noticed the letter in the same place I'd rested it. If Mom knew by the letter there were no signs she'd read it. I couldn't picture her with enough attention to detail to put it back exactly as it'd been. I didn't bother bringing up the topic either. I knew it'd just start another fight I wasn't strong enough to handle.

Uncle Jeremy called in the morning after I got Rorie ready for school. She'd had the last week off for school vacation and spent it with Uncle Jeremy and Sara- not at the same time.

The weather had been unusually warm one day and then teasingly chilly the next. On Monday girls took out their shorts and tank tops then on Tuesday those same girls wore sweatpants and hoodies. It was typical New England weather, and though I'd spent my entire life here, I'd yet to grow accustomed to it.

My immune system felt the same. At the start of winter, when the temperature plummeted, I came down with a bad cold. Every spring my allergies kicked in. I was sure being a smoker didn't help matters much but I refused to quit for my own selfish reasons.

I'd been sneezing all morning, my eyes were bloodshot, my nose stuffy. There must've been pollen in the air. Uncle Jeremy would think I was stoned and lecture me about saving money. I was on my way into town to see him. We were to have lunch and chat it up, just the two of us.

The center of town was so small that finding Uncle Jeremy's truck wasn't hard. The spots next to it were taken so I angle-parked a couple of spots away. He wasn't in his vehicle so I assumed him to be inside the restaurant.

I saw him as soon as I walked in the Wok Inn. The Wok Inn was a cozy Chinese buffet that charged 10 bucks for all-you-can-eat. It was my favorite spot to dine alone. Dropping a 10 plus tip was easier on my wallet than a 20 plus tip. I liked this place because of the name; I found it creative and pledged my patronage.

Uncle Jeremy waved me over. The greeter followed behind, and Uncle Jeremy and I ordered our drinks- two Pepsi's, one with ice and one without.

The food smelled amazing and I loaded my plate with white rice, beef on a stick, teriyaki beef bits, chicken and broccoli, green beans, garlic shrimp, and crab rangoon. My plate was packed. Uncle Jeremys overflowed and everything on it was a different shade of brown.

I gently scolded him for not grabbing any vegetables and plopped a couple of my broccoli pieces and a couple of spoonfuls of stirred mixed veggies on his plate. He frowned at the pile of nutrients. The coloring was still bright so the healthy ingredients hadn't been completely steamed out.

He chewed mouthfuls as I watched him. I hoped he ate good on a regular basis.

"How have you been?" I questioned in between chews. I ate my food at a quickened pace and reminded myself to slow it down as to savor my time with my uncle.

"Good," he said, and sipped at his soda.

"Good?" I noticed his plate was running low on meat and that the veggies I'd placed there had been pushed to the side. "That's it? Just good?"

Uncle Jeremy snickered. "I'm good. How are you and Rorie?"

I tilted my head and gave him a chastising look. "That wasn't the question. How are *you*?"

"I'm doing the best I know how. Been keeping busy."

"Eat your broccoli," I told him, and he hesitantly pierced it with his fork. "Aren't you lonely?"

He looked at me.

I clarified, "Why don't you find a lady friend? You've got to be dying of boredom alone in that house." It seemed I always pushed a woman on him lately.

"A lady friend," he repeated and shook his head. I smiled at him. "Shoot, what would I do with her? Teach her how to hunt deer and how to hook a worm?"

I giggled at him and the rest of our meal was spent talking of normal everyday things.

My uncle paid the bill and asked if I wanted to take a meal home with me. I felt guilty that I'd eaten so well without Rorie and that was the only reason I accepted. I made a mental note to toss him a 10 next payday.

Once outside, we sat on the bed of his truck and smoked cigarettes. I had the day off and wasn't ready to go home. I enjoyed spending time with him. It was nice to have at least one male figure in my life who wasn't estranged or dead. He was blood; he couldn't leave me even if he wanted to- we were biologically bound.

My argument with Mom from last week, when she had slapped Rorie, came up again. I let him know his youngest niece had chatted with Mom's friend and mentioned that blow jobs sounded fun. His expression was blank and I waited for words of wisdom.

"Rorie all right? She seemed okay when she told me about it a few days ago. Did something else happen?"

I shook my head. "She's a trooper. Mom hit her pretty hard though. I wanted to hit her back but you know Mom." I didn't mention the two smacks that Mom had dealt me. It wasn't of any importance.

He blew out a whistle and looked ahead. "She's too young to know what a blow job even is," he rationed to himself and I was sure he was probably right. "I'm not sure what to tell you on that one, Am. That's woman stuff."

"I'm not sure if she knows what it is. What I do know is that Mom read through the online conversation and Rorie told the guy it sounded fun. FUN!," I repeated louder. "She's 10. TEN. She should be dressing up her Barbie doll!"

He rubbed his beard and laughed. "Were you playing with Barbies at 10?"

"No," I answered, although I could've lied to prove my own case. At that age I was busily getting my ass beat by Mom. I was too depressed to play with dolls.

My uncle mentioned that he didn't even recall being that age. He hadn't been 10 in over 30 years. I wondered if I'd remember Mom's ass-whoopings in 30 years or if I'd find forgiveness by then.

Uncle Jeremy had to use the bathroom and pardoned himself to go back into the buffet. While he was gone, I made up some excuse in my head about Mom having left me a message on my cell phone, that I had to go see her right away. Upon his return, I thanked him for the food and the takeout for Rorie and apologized for having to jet so soon.

"Her majesty beckons," I said. "You know how that goes."

He shifted his eyes away then swung them back to me. "Talk to Rorie."

"Yeah yeah," I swore. "Got to head out. Thanks again."

I sat in my car and pretended to search for something in my glove box as I waited for Uncle Jeremy to pull away in his truck. He finally did and gave his horn a couple of toots as he drove off. Once he was out of view, I dialed home to see what Rorie was up to. No one answered.

Rorie was making a peanut butter and fluff sandwich when I entered the kitchen. I heard Mom in her bedroom upstairs, giggling with a friend. The bass in his murmurs revealed his gender. His words were indistinguishable but I knew what they were doing in front of a lens.

SPILLED MILK

Rorie was in good spirits. She took special care on how she spread the fluff. It was white fluff, her favorite kind. Dad preferred the pink strawberry kind.

"What are you going to do today?," I made small-talk with her as I popped open a can of soda and sat at the table. She finished preparing her lunch and plunked down her plate then sat across from me.

She tore off a chunk of sandwich and offered it to me. I declined and told her to run out to my car to grab her Chinese food that I'd forgotten to bring in. Her eyes grew into two big orbs and she rushed out.

When she came back into the house, styrofoam takeout dish in hand, she put her sandwich into a plastic sandwich bag and stored it in the refrigerator. She pigged out on the Lo Mein noodles and pork fried rice that she loved best. Smelling her dish made me hungry again. Chinese food was counterproductive- you could eat two to three plates then be hungry again an hour later. It was the overload of MSG.

"How was school?" I asked.

She rolled her eyes and talked with her mouth full. "Mrs. Anderson gave us a crap load of homework. You should see the math she's making us do. It's college-level work, Amber!" she exclaimed. I smirked at college-level work in the fourth grade.

"You should march right up to her," Rorie carried on, fork suspended in the air before her mouth, "and tell her we're suing her. That'll make her back off."

I chuckled at my little sister and helped myself to one of the fried chicken wings. "We can't sue her, Rorie. I'll help with your math. It's not a big deal. Besides, you just had vacation-why are you complaining?"

"Sara said you could sue for anything. She said a lady spilled coffee on her lap and burned herself then she sued the fast food restaurant! She ended up scoring 100 million thousand dollars!" She nodded and added, while masticated rice and pork threatened to fall out of her busy mouth, "We should totally sue Mrs. Anderson."

I whistled. "Wow. 100 million thousand dollars is a lot of dough. That lady scored."

Rorie gave me a chastising look and spoke, "Am, I said she sued for money. Pay attention."

I looked at her quizzically. She murmured to herself, "Why would anyone sue for dough? That's stupid."

She cracked me up sometimes. "Unless she was a serial baker," I joked. Rorie didn't get it so I laughed alone.

"You're nuts," she let me know.

I polished off the chicken wing. "Tell me something I don't know."

Mom came in then- hair disheveled, lit cigarette perched between two fingers.

"Girls," she greeted. I didn't reply.

Rorie's response was, "Howdy partner." They'd done line-dancing at her school before February vacation commenced. She really got into it and taught me how to do-se-do my partner and how to promenade.

It was fun dancing with her in the basement listening to country music on the radio. We made fun of the country singers who tended to sing about their dogs dying, losing a soul mate, or finding love in all the wrong places.

Mom grabbed a spoon from a drawer and let us know she was going to be home late.

"Glitter's offering overtime?" I asked with sarcasm.

"Smart ass," Mom said to me and began eating from Rorie's dish.

"Why are you going to be late?" I asked my mother.

"Hey!" Rorie suddenly shrieked to Mom, "That's my last shrimp!"

Mom giggled and put the shrimp into her mouth, going "mmm" and chewing slowly to tease Rorie.

Rorie put her fork down and pushed the dish away. She started to pout. "That was the last shrimp."

Mom laughed again and I had to chuckle at Rorie's rage over the littlest things.

"Lighten up," Mom told her youngest, then moved the dish closer to herself.

I smirked away at young temperamental Rorie.

The night before my visit with Rose, I was on edge. I found myself in Bret's driveway. The outside lights came on and I waited for him to show up in his doorway. He didn't. I didn't want to go inside to talk with him.

I honked my car horn a few times and waited. His van was in the driveway so I knew he was home. His front door opened and I waved him over. He raised a finger to gesture to hold on and he went back inside.

I couldn't talk with him about Rose indoors. In his cabin he controlled what happened and if he didn't want to talk about something he wouldn't, and that was the end of it.

During a ride, and in my vehicle, he didn't have a say. He had to listen to me or else jump out of a moving car.

He hopped in my car, baseball cap suddenly on. "What's up?"

"Want to go for a drive?"

"Sure," he could tell I wanted to talk but if he knew I wanted to talk about Rose I knew he wouldn't come.

I put the car in reverse and drove off. "We should drive to the top of the Kanc and hang out by Lower Falls," which was a swimming hole we frequented on hot days.

Once I pulled into the lot of the Falls Bret turned to me. "What's on your mind?"

"What's *not* on my mind?" I countered before I finally said, "I'm seeing Rose tomorrow."

My mind traveled until my thoughts went to a particular time with Rose. Mom beat me with Dad's leather belt- not the belt itself but with the thick metal buckle. I'd lost a free badge given to me at school in the third grade by the D.A.R.E troop.

I used it as a wallet and it was free which meant Mom didn't have to buy me one. Well, I lost the badge-turned-wallet and Mom lost her mind. I never knew why. But she ordered me to get Dad's belt from the hook. I hesitated and she got it herself.

I stripped naked so she could punish my bare nine-year-old flesh. She never gave me a choice. If I didn't strip she forcibly removed my clothes and underwear. Even in front of Dad and Bret she'd do it. It didn't matter who was around during those years.

I cried so hard during that particular punishment because she tied my hands to the doorknob of the bathroom with a handkerchief. On that hard linoleum floor I knelt while she hit me over and over again with that damn belt buckle. Rose heard me crying even through the handkerchief and rushed in to my aide.

She shoved Mom off of me which averted her attention. Mom chased Rose with that belt throughout the house. It was a long chase as Rose would go up the front steps and down the back. It was a round robin until Mom got tired and promised that she'd get her later. And she did- when Rose least expected it too.

While Mom had been chasing Rose around the house, Dad snuck in and untied me. Then he held me long and hard and stroked my hair as I cried into his lap. He told me I was his good girl as he helped me to get dressed.

Once he heard Mom coming to check up on me, or possibly punish me more for somehow being the cause to her charade with Rose, he moved far away from me. Mother barged in and started hollering at how I was useless and lost everything as if we were rich or something. Dad didn't stick up for me. He just stood there when a moment prior he'd comforted me.

The memory bothered me. Remembering it made me more anxious to see Rose. I loved her for sure. I adored her for rescuing me from Mom or taking the majority of the blows when we were punished. We were usually punished together- as if Rose and I were one bratty daughter instead of two separate beings.

"I miss her, Bret. Sometimes I miss her so much that I don't know how much longer I can take it. I miss how things used to be. When's it going to get better, Bret? When is it not going to suck so much?"

He thought a moment. "Good question." He propped his feet up on the passenger seat console to get comfortable. "I'm honestly not sure if it will get any better," he said. "I mean, look at *me*. Mom sent me to that fucking Home when I was nine.

"I had problems socializing in school and Mom jumped to the conclusion I was nuts, stupid, or something equally insulting, and the bitch sent me off. Now look at me- I live in a fucking cabin I had to make with my own hands, and I'm all alone. So, when will it get better you ask?" He shook his head, hoping for the right answer. "I guess it's up to you to make it better."

"How?" I asked. "Let me guess," I answered for him, "It's up to me to figure out how."

"I wasn't going to say that," Bret said.

"Then what were you going to say, wise brother?"

"Shit," he muttered, "I don't fucking know, Amber. Cut the shit, would ya? I don't want to talk about this shit." I made him uncomfortable.

"Fine," I said, the disappointment evident in my voice. "Forget I brought it up."

He looked over at me in the dark car. I could feel his eyes on me from my peripheral vision. He studied my expression to see if he had hurt my feelings. I felt bad- not bad for myself, but for him. I forced a smile and whispered, "I'm just having a moment, that's all. Sorry I said anything."

I felt it necessary to turn the conversation to lighter things so I caught him up with my work life at Movie Magic and how I wanted to look for a full-time job or a second part-time one. He inquired about Frank and his meanderings and I filled him in on the odd and random tales of Frank's odd and random life. Bret had met him a couple of times last year when he stopped in the theater.

Bret liked Frank. Frank said Bret was a nice-looking fellow but he should smile more often and make better eye contact. I chuckled at that. Bret only did those things with people he loved. If he liked you he acknowledged what you said even if what you said didn't make sense or he didn't agree with it. If he hated you, you didn't exist. But if you were somewhere in the middle, you were okay and he'd treat you like a human being.

We chatted about Carmen and my other friends from school. Once I mentioned Hillary, he perked up. He'd always found my friend, Hillary, pretty. She was attractive and knew it. She was one of those girls who talked about how hot she was and how everyone wanted her, then, in male company, wondered if her hair was okay or if her thighs were getting fat.

When she fished for compliments, they rained. It used to annoy me but then I learned to cut her slack by convincing myself she had a terrible home life and her mother insulted her on a daily basis too. That way it felt better being her friend.

I pretended to not hear him when he suggested the three of us catch a movie or go bowling sometime. The thought of Bret and Hillary bowling or flirting during Scary Movie the Thousandth made me sick, so I quickly told him Rorie couldn't stand her even though she never said that. I then changed the subject to the road work on the Kancamagus and how I felt like writing a letter to the state highway department.

We clam-baked my car and jammed out to the oldies station. By the end of the night, thoughts of Rose and of my shitty life turned into thoughts of everyone in my life who had done a good deed for me. The list of names was short but the people on that list were a hundred feet tall.

I thought of Uncle Jeremy and how he stopped by every once in a while. It wasn't because he had to because he didn't. He came by and helped us out with food and a few bucks for bills because he wanted to. I appreciated that. It was a hard thing for me to let him know that and I didn't know why. It was something I'd have to work on.

Then Frank came to mind. When I broke down at work one day, a week after Rose shot Dad and went to prison, he comforted me. He called in some girl, Mary, who worked there part-time to cover his shift and Elvis came in to cover mine, so that he could follow me home and be on-call had I needed someone to talk to. I never did call him or appropriately thank him but I never forgot that gesture of kindness and how he always asked about my family even after all that he knew about us.

Mrs. Huntington was next in my thoughts. She was the only person who came to me after Dad's funeral to see if I was okay. Of course I wasn't okay and she knew it. She stayed with me long after everyone else had left, even Uncle Jeremy who probably would've stayed if he hadn't been smart enough to see I needed the time alone. I made a mental note to send Mrs. Huntington a card one day when I was ready and I'd let her know what she meant to me, to Rorie. Not many stuck around yet she did.

Finally I thought of Rose, who was, by a landslide, number one on the list. Not because she was my sister or that she killed Dad and a part of my guilty soul felt relief, but because she was a mother to my little ones. She'd done enough in her short life, and seen enough hardship, to have someone beside her in spirit.

"What are you thinking about?" I suddenly asked Bret who, too, was off daydreaming. "Or are you passing out on me?"

He started to rock back and forth then busted out laughing, "I'm so stoned!" I laughed with him and his rocking that shook the car made me laugh harder.

"Me too," I turned the car off to save battery juice. He didn't seem to notice or care that the music vanished; he still rocked to the beat. "I can't drive, Bro." That made us laugh harder, so hard that a tear slid down his cheek.

I watched my older brother- grin large, teeth visible- and the moment caused me to lean forward and kiss him on the cheek. It'd been a while since he even smiled. The kiss came too close to his lip that he stopped and backed away in the same fashion I backed away from those who touched me. He noticed he had reacted and carried on with a few more giggles.

Afterwards, I dropped Bret off at his cabin and waited for an invitation inside that didn't come. It was difficult to put the car in reverse and back away as he slowly, still very inebriated from the clam-bake, wandered into his front door.

I crept in the house and checked up on Rorie before I entered my bedroom. Mom was at the club. I crawled into my bed and threw the covers over me, my clothes and shoes still on. I flipped onto my back, kicked off my shoes, and yanked off my clothes.

Lying naked in my room, I tossed the sheets off and let the chill of the room tickle my naked skin. I began to touch myself. I couldn't get to the point of an orgasm so I let my fantasies wander- to myself wrapped around a pole and a red g-string jammed between my tanned butt cheeks, to Carmen's bare-naked breasts and stiff pink nipples as she sat at my kitchen table, to my ex-boyfriend's face wagging side to side between my thighs, his tongue shoved far inside of me. My toes scrunched as I slid a finger inside my flesh and felt the juices leak.

Once the fuzzy feeling passed, I threw on a pair of pink Hello Kitty pajamas and tried to fall asleep. Thoughts of Bret's facial stubble just as I had reached orgasm messed with my head. It was definitely not a topic that would come up during my visit with Rose tomorrow.

CHAPTER 6

I woke up with butterflies. The excuses I could give Rose for not showing up to see her ran through my mind- Rorie got sick and no one was available to stay home with her, we lost electricity and my alarm clock didn't go off and I was so late arriving the guards turned me away, Mom overdosed again and I had to rush her to the ER for the ritual stomach pump, Uncle Jeremy got Rorie a new dog a few months back and it suddenly died and we had to give it a proper burial.

I could rub it in her face how she'd left me stranded over the past year or so just because she needed time away from the world. What about my world? Just because I wasn't sleeping on a dingy cot loaded with back-aching springs every night, shower with 20 other naked women, or swapped stories with other cellmates about kids, boyfriends, families that had been left behind, it didn't make me any less for wear. I suffered too and sometimes the outside world was a scarier place to suffer. She was a coward for deserting us.

I heard Mom as I started down the back stairs.

"Morning," I greeted and helped myself to a cup of orange juice from the jug I'd brought home the other day. It was Rorie's favorite drink and I got pulp-free just for her. Rorie could be heard channel surfing in the living room. "Did Rorie have breakfast?"

Mom was seated at the kitchen table, a mug of coffee before her. She wiggled her fingers inside of a small jar of nail polish remover. The kitchen reeked of acetone.

"She had two bowls of cereal," Mom replied. "What color do you think?" she asked and lifted up a hand. I studied the three nail polish bottles set up in front of her- neon blue, hot pink, and red.

I picked up the red bottle, shook it, and handed it to her. She took it and smiled up at me. She was in a normal mood. "Or maybe hot pink," I suggested. She weighed between the red or hot pink and stuck with the red.

I grabbed a package of Pop Tarts from the cupboard and told Mom I was heading out and that the Huntingtons would be by for Rorie in an hour. She rolled her eyes and started to paint a nail, "Sara's mom is such a snob, don't you think?"

I didn't reply. At the doorway, Mom spoke again, "Have a safe drive. Peru's quite a hike." I stopped in my tracks and turned to look at her. She was unperturbed, as if she had just casually commented on the weather.

"Thanks," I didn't know what else to say. I waited for a series of questions as to why I was going, how I could betray her by visiting her husband's killer, how I tarnished the family name. "You should come with me sometime."

She scoffed, "As if I'd be caught dead at Peru." Peru Prison was in the top part of southern Maine. It was a womens-only prison that housed killers and those with habitual felonies. Most of the women I'd seen there looked as if they belonged. Not Rose though who looked like a librarian in that setting.

SPILLED MILK

Had she not been draped in that standard orange jumpsuit you would think she worked on the administration staff. When she was first sentenced, I worried for her because I knew women like her- shy, withdrawn, sweet and kind, and pudgy- would be an easy target.

I turned to leave. "Amber," Mother called after me, "you're a traitor for going. That fat, miserable bitch should rot in prison and you know it like I know it." She had more to say but I tried to drown it out.

I rushed out and slammed the door behind me as I called over my shoulder to Rorie that I'd see her soon. My wedge-heeled shoes crunched over the dirt driveway and I jumped into my car before backing out in a rush.

Peru Prison was quite a haul from Lil Beth and a very boring commute on a long, straight stretch of bland road. The population from Lil Beth to Sampson was pathetically sad and only a few small cities were in between. The majority of the people lived in the southern sections of the states or on the coastlines.

It was April and Mother Nature blossomed slowly. Trees readied themselves to grow back their leaves of all different colors- gold, green, red- and flowers would soon bloom everywhere. Insects would buzz and the snakes and other reptiles would come out to hunt. Bears, surely out of hibernation by now, roamed the valleys again and the moose majestically displayed themselves.

A family of raccoon had already gotten cozy in the rocks behind my house and the deer pranced by in the open fields a couple of times. I snapped a picture of a mother and her two babies with my cell phone camera and used the picture as the wallpaper so I could see it when I wanted to be inspired. I felt blessed to have witnessed and captured the scene and I respected that mother deer for doing what she was supposed to do, what nature had intended her to do.

The yellow road signs along the way warned of moose crossings and brown signs bragged of tourist attractions like scenic stops and swimming holes. A couple of green signs pointed to cities and towns by the coast where the zoo and beaches were and others further north where hiking trails, tramways, and breathtaking mountaintop views reigned.

I could see tramways going up and down steep green hillsides carrying tourists looking for rare views of the nature and the wildlife that claimed these mountains as their own. I should take Rorie on one next weekend. She'd appreciate the beauty and would probably use the entire roll in her disposable camera before we reached the top. I'd have to see how much extra funds I had.

I started to daydream of some miracle full-time job that I absolutely loved and had fun at every minute of the day that paid a ton of money. So much money that I could buy a nice house in another state, maybe down south where it didn't snow and the weather was more consistent, and I could be close to warm ocean water and creamy tan beach sand.

Enough so that I could buy Rorie her first car in six years and buy Bret his dream motorcycle, house with attached garage, and the huge backyard he always talked about. Enough so that I could send Rose more canteen money than the measly 50 I sent every month.

I'd be satisfied with just enough to go into a store and walk out with what we needed and an item or two of what we wanted without the anxiety at having spent a few bucks too much over budget. I sighed at myself... still naïve enough to dream.

Visions of Bret on his black motorcycle came to mind. His black sunglasses complimented the olive tone of his face and the dark brown carpet that made him so handsome. He usually cruised around with shades, a T-shirt, baggy jeans, and his tan work shoes on. He took my breath away on that bike, especially in motion. I missed riding around the Kanc with him, clutching him from behind and feeling every ripple of every muscle.

We drove around for hours and stopped frequently to sight-see or explore new paths, streams, and caves. If ever Bret and I got lost in the White Mountains, he found a way to get us out and home safely. He was skilled and in tune with nature and spent countless hours outdoors.

The memories of last night and my fantasies troubled me. I hadn't intentionally thought of Bret at that very moment when I peaked. It was innocent. Somehow the thought prior had segwayed into thoughts of him. His strong jawline as he smiled stayed too long on my mind- even now. He was my brother, I argued with my conscience, it was natural to think of him so highly. There was no wrong in praise.

A desperation within me craved his voice, his presence, the way his eyes looked into mine. I wanted to cuddle with him like we used to when we were kids- after Mom would beat me, after Dad had done something he shouldn't have, when he'd visit from the Boys Home. But I was nearly 21 now and he was heading towards 26. I was too old to cuddle with my brother. I was too old to cry into his lap to wait for his rugged hands to stroke my soft, fine hair. Those moments were gone like so much else in my life.

I'd visit with Bret after I left the prison. I wasn't any good at avoiding a topic I wanted to discuss even if it made the other person uncomfortable or sad. I blamed it on being a repressed child and never being allowed to speak my mind. And though I loved my sister Rose deeply I still felt resentful. Resentful not that she'd killed Jack but that she never stopped to think of me before doing so. I needed to let her know how that act had affected our lives.

I've asked myself a million times why exactly I didn't hate Rose for the murder. Dad had always been in my life and he worked hard to keep a roof for his children, food on the table, clothes on our backs. He did what he was supposed to do as the head of household. After Mom would hit me or Rose or both of us together, Dad would visit with me in my bedroom and tell me how pretty I was, how I was his good little girl.

But why didn't he ever make Mom stop? Not allowing her to hit me in the first place would have meant more to me than consolations later on. I figured the main reason I couldn't abandon Rose was that he'd fucked up so often during his life that he himself didn't give a shit about it either. Rose was Dad's Jack Kevorkian- she took his life because somehow he was unable to do so himself. It was the way I could condone it and find some sort of sleep at nights.

My apprehension grew when the road sign read 'Sampson 24 miles'. I'd already crossed the Maine state line miles back and must have missed seeing it. Sampson was closer than I wanted. My gut reaction was to turn my Hyundai around and head back to Lil Beth where I belonged. The frugal side of me argued that I'd already dumped money into the tank of gas and shit be damned if I was to waste that money to get this far and turn around. The human side of me wanted to see Rose's face again. My selfish side wanted answers.

Passing through Sampson was a familiar experience. The town hadn't changed much. Same playground with the rusty old slide, climbing dome, and swings. Same average houses needing paint jobs and a good lawn mow. Same porches and street benches lined with people smoking cigarettes and drinking soda who had eagerly awaited the sunshine that none of us thought would come.

Same Main Street businesses, probably the same employees, undoubtedly the same customers. Sampson was a regular town, like any town anywhere in America. Not a city, not rural, somewhere pathetically in-between.

The jail was smack in the center of town, as if the town was celebrating its main source of employment or the only thing that made Sampson known alongside champion well-knowns like Portland, Bangor, or Augusta. If you asked someone where Sampson, Maine was, they looked at you as if you spoke a strange combination between Swedish, Japanese, and Alien.

But if you asked that same person where Peru Prison was, they gave you detailed directions- jump on Route 44, also known as Straight Shot Road because it was a straight shot to the Canadian border, cut through town, then follow Jumper Lane off of Main Street direct to Peru.

The parking lot of the jail was packed as it typically was on Visitor's Day. I had to cruise around the lot a few times until a beat-up yellow minivan with a fake wood panel backed out of a narrow spot. I had to reverse a few feet to give the minivan room to get out. He tipped his hat at me and drove off, a big smile on his face. He must've been visiting with his girlfriend or wife. I wondered what his lady friend had done to land herself here and what he'd been doing without her, and if her and Rose were friends.

My hatchback Hyundai Accent, whom I called 'Cherry', fit into the spot nicely. I hesitated once I placed the shift into Park and turned off the engine. I reminded myself that Rose needed me. Everyone else in the family had abandoned her and I didn't want to do the same. If I didn't show up for today's visit I cringed to think it would hurt her and I knew it wouldn't rest well on my conscience.

I found the bravery to exit my car and as I head toward the door I straightened my long black skirt and my leopard print top. I wanted to look my best and my car mirror had reminded me my mission had been accomplished. So did the guard at the entrance who held open the glass door for me.

"Thank you," I said and smiled large.

"No, ma'am," he said, "thank *you*." I still felt his eyes on me as I passed him.

The line at Registration was long and crowded with homely-looking women who still tried to look pretty by layering on cheap makeup and by shoving their raggedy feet into flea market low-heeled pumps, bratty kids with food and snacks smeared on their faces who were dressed up in creased khakis and button-down shirts or frilly dresses with pinned-on bows to cover the stains, and with men and women who appeared at ease to be here- unlike me.

SPILLED MILK

Almost every pair of eyes seemed to notice me in my four-inch black sandals, form-fitting black skirt that rested a couple of inches below my knees, and my tight, scoop-necked, animal-print top with sleeves that rested above the Gemini symbol tattoo on my left forearm.

Maybe I was a bit over-dressed for a prison visit but little did these people know that this was my regular wear- more specifically, my normal costume when I wasn't in a deep depression or hating on life. The real Amber looked like this daily but the other Amber- my evil, sad, depressed twin- wore jeans and tight-fitting T-shirts and only 2-inch heels or flats. My shoes always reflected my mood if my face couldn't be read.

The attention made me more nervous and I knew I couldn't flee from it. I looked around for a nearby bench or table to lean against. I felt woozy, hungry, starved. The eyes of homely women, shabby men, and curious children filled me with all kinds of feelings- annoyance, rage, the feeling of being incredibly alone and singled out.

As people were checked in, the line shrunk. I looked over my shoulder to the crowd that stood behind. I was glad I had forced my way in here when I did. I wished I had brought in my purse so I'd have something to do to look busy. I could go through it a couple of dozen times in search for an object I needed to find but couldn't and I wondered what such object would be- my compact, a pen, one of those tiny tubes of sample perfume...

But all I had was the ring on my right pointer finger to distract myself with, so I pulled it off and slid it back on, pulled it off, slid it on... It was a claddagh ring that Mom had given me for my fifteenth birthday. The heart meant love, the hands represented friendship, the crown symbolized loyalty. I wore it always. I'd never let Mom know what it meant to me.

The line eventually dwindled and a few people were pulled out for the random search. I wondered if I'd be the next one pulled. I half-expected it. When I reached the folding table that sat three guards and several clipboards with paper and pens hanging from discolored thread, I gave the guard my name and his eyes scanned a lengthy list of welcomed visitors. He checked my name off and in I went to familiar yet foreign territory.

I surveyed the room for my sister. The room was huge, all linoleum, all white, but for the black outline around the windows. The black would've matched the color of the bars in the windows had they been first painted. Now they were authentic-looking, rusty, and the dark paint was flaked.

Tables lined the entire room- some were full of orange-suited jailbirds and their guests, others only had orange-suited women who awaited the family and friends they prayed would show up. I looked even harder for my sister, my heart racing at the idea that she was one of those waiting women.

I hesitated to walk around to search for her as I couldn't stand all the eyes on me. Men, in particular, snuck glances and the women prisoners who sat alongside them shot glares my way or looks of self-pity. I didn't notice people looking at anyone else with as much interest as they were me. With careful effort, I made sure not to cower by the wall and display my discomfort.

"Hey," a girl called over to me from a table closest to where the guard table was and by the wall where I stood. It was hard to tell if I knew her. They all seemed to look the same with plain faces, hair in ponytails that hung low, and disturbingly bright jumpsuits. She called out something else that I only caught bits and pieces of.

The noise level in the room was deafening if you really concentrated on it. I had learned to drown out noises growing up because I always drowned out the sound of my mother's voice and her screams or hollers.

I pointed a finger at myself and mouthed "Me?" to her. She nodded and waved me over with a smile. Her guests were a male who looked about her own age- mid-30s or so- and a young boy who was pale with freckles and blonde hair that leaned towards red. He was the total opposite of my brothers. They were tan-colored with large bright eyes, long dark lashes, big pink smiles. This boy made me nauseous and I had to look away and focus on the woman.

I approached quickly and had to dash between crowds of people. I ran into an old woman's purse and quickly apologized. The old lady smiled at me while the younger and slimmer woman beside her tilted her lips at me. The younger woman's mouth was a red slash mark across her face; I didn't like her.

"Hi," I said when I reached the table, "Were you calling out to me?"

She smiled again and her green eyes seemed bright against her pale complexion and sandy blonde hair. "You're Rose's sister," She said matter-of-factly, "Amber." I liked her.

"I'm sorry, do I know you from somewhere? Lil Beth or something?" The ugly little boy stared at me and I made great efforts to ignore him.

"I was Rose's cellmate a couple years back when she first came in. Well," she chuckled at a joke or situation only she and Rose knew about, "until she got put in the hole and I got stuck with Nancy." I snickered with her and wondered why Rose got put into solitary. I assumed this woman to be Kara. I remembered Rose used to write about her.

"She's back there," the woman said and looked over her shoulder towards the center of the room. I looked in that direction.

I threw my hands up to gesture 'where?' and she answered, "Over there," and pointed, "by that guy standing with the Nascar T-shirt holding a Pepsi," she could tell I still didn't see, and carried on, "kinda by the far end of the room, by the Nascar dude and that lady with the pink streaks in her hair.."

I spotted pink streaks and then a Nascar shirt. My eyes landed on my sister. She was smaller and she looked younger for some reason. Our eyes met across an enormous hollow room filled with people and united abandonment. I thanked the woman for pointing her out, telling her hopefully we'd catch up again sometime.

Once I reached my big sister's table, she stood up and we looked at each other. Guards stood post around the room and the ones by us watched closely. Rose was sentenced to life for homicide- hugs were not permitted. Although she didn't have a history of drugs or violence she couldn't be the exception. Bodily contact often meant an exchange of illegal substances.

I sat first. Rose just stood there, her arms crossed over her chest, and looked down at me. It wasn't a look of disgust or disappointment to see me even though she didn't smile. I knew she was okay and the look she wore was of contentment. I fidgeted in my seat and twiddled a long strand of my hair until she finally sat down across from me.

"How are you?" my sister asked. She smiled slightly. She was different.

"Good," I lied. "Same old shit, different day."

She nodded and sat back, arms again over her chest. I scanned her from mid-section to head, searing every part of her into my brain, how she was now. She'd lost considerable weight. Always, Rose had been a chubby kid although she'd been born less than five pounds. Mom insisted that she hadn't been premature. Rose, being a fat, shy kid became an even fatter, shyer adult. She was picked on in school. People made fun of her while the rest were noticeably unaware of her existence.

Her arms that used to be flabby slimmed down a good couple of inches and her hands and fingers seemed to belong to someone else. My eyes rose up and noticed breasts that were still ample but had lost some of their largeness. I then wondered if she was eating enough and how often she was exercising on her hour out.

The face I used to know was a wide oval and boy did Rose have cheeks before! Her chin pointed slightly and I'd never noticed that before. Her features were spread out across her face when prior it was face, then eyes, a nose, and tiny lips in the center. Her eyes seemed wider and less slanted. Her eyebrows never changed- still two untweezed, brown, horizontal lines over her eyes. The black St. Germaine eyelashes stayed and so did the long, frizzy, dark brown, almost-black hair.

Brown eyes with dark rings around the cornea stared into mine of the same. I wanted to cry but I couldn't. I wanted to hope that because she looked different meant she *was* different- that she could be free here. I looked around the room and drowned out chatter and laughter, sneezes and sounds of food, chairs moving, and so on, and wondered what her perspective of 'free' was.

It couldn't have been here. It couldn't have been at home. It took some effort to hold back tears and calm the tightening of my throat as I asked myself if Rose *could* ever be free and *where*....and the thought tore at my insides.

What I thought were positive traits about her the world generally took advantage of, causing people like Rose to be the underdogs. I always rooted for the underdog and I'd always root for Rose. She was quiet, kind, sweet, generous, your everyday girl. She had her off-days and yelled and cursed and got into small fights with other girls but those times were rare. Mostly, Rose suffered internally while she pasted on a phony smile and covered herself with goodness because she had to- for us.

"You lost a ton of weight," I complimented.

She placed her arms on the table and lost her smile but not because she'd lost her happiness. "Prison will do that to you. Most people think just because you only get so much time outside or in the gym that you stay fat and lazy. But I get to work out in my cell too and the meals they serve us here... well, let's just say they're not too filling."

"You looked better before," I subconsciously said aloud.

Rose scrunched her face and laughed. "Are you okay, Am?" She gestured to her new self and I smiled.

"Seriously," I said. "You look good now, you do! But you looked better before. You were *you* before. Who is this new person?" This time, the thought of 'you were *with* us before and, therefore, you were beautiful before' stayed unspoken.

"I'm still the same me, jackass," she said and we giggled.

"Yeah," I joked, "minus about four tires," referencing the fat she'd had around her waist and hips when they flapped out of her pants, "and a portable oxygen machine."

She laughed louder. It was one of our many private jokes. I used to make fun of her when we were younger after she'd simply walk half a mile and be out of breath or climb stairs and need to rest.

She was heavy when she was a teen- I guessed probably 250 pounds. I told her by the time she was 25, she'd need an oxygen tank to wheel along beside her. It wasn't funny when I teased her about that before but now it was because now she wasn't obese.

"Tiffany's a good cellmate," Rose went on, "she keeps me motivated. We challenge each other with crunches."

"Good," I urged. "Keep it up. Seriously, don't lose motivation later on and quit."

"You're a trip, Amber," she said. "You really are. I'm not who I used to be. I don't start things and not finish them like I used to. I'm serious about this whole exercise thing and I'm going to keep with it."

"But," I defended, "you used to live in the Procrastination Station and I'm just making sure you're no longer idling there."

"I'm not," she stated.

I looked around the room and caught several people looking our way. Rose noticed too and added to her last sentence, "Well, not until I look like you, Little Sis."

"Shut up," I said teasingly, never knowing what to say to compliments, "you don't want to look like me. Finding a size five in the mall sucks. And try finding a size seven shoe in some of those stores." I immediately wished I had never mentioned the mall or the outside world but she didn't flinch and we drifted onto the next topic which was her cellmate.

Tiffany Bridgeport had five kids and was 47 years old. She'd been in and out of jail since she was 19. She'd been married four times and divorced thrice and had changed her last name so many times that she eventually reverted back to her maiden name. I couldn't imagine a woman wanting to ever marry again after losing so many loves. Rose explained the difficulties of this particular divorce she was going through now. Tiffany was the one who had gotten Rose through her days when she felt she would fall apart.

"Meet any girlfriends?" I asked and peered at her, half-serious. "Drop any soap?"

She laughed at me and said how Bubba always dropped the soap and there were no Bubbas here; well, at least no Bubbas with dicks.

"Seriously, Amber?...," she said and looked around at all the basic and dumpy Plain Janes to prove her point. Her eyes swung to a guard standing near the entryway. "He's cute."

"The skinny tall one?" I asked.

"No," she said, "the one next to him."

The one next to him looked like Dad. I froze for a brief moment and studied him. The guard and our father shared many similarities- the dark hair, their height, the mustache and short beard. It filled me with the creeps.

"What's his name?" I asked and hoped it wasn't 'Jack'.

"Bartholomew," she said. "They call him 'Bart' for short."

I laughed and pointed, "Like Rorie's fish."

"How is my baby sis?" Rose asked and perked up. "How's her schoolwork?"

I wanted to say that Rorie was at the top of her class but I didn't want to lie. I wasn't in the mood to cover up for Rorie's lack of effort nor was I in the mood to admit I was mostly to blame for it. I wanted to rub it in her face that we were all neglectful of our duties since she left. The thread that held us all together was serving a life sentence.

Instead, I told her that Rorie was doing just fine.

"Booga?" she asked about Bret. "He okay up there in that cabin?" The idea of him alone in the cabin tantalized me.

"Sure," I offered.

She looked at me blankly. "And Mom?"

"Mom's Mom." That said enough.

She nodded. She knew what I meant. "What's she doing for work nowadays?"

I rolled my eyes. "She joined the PTA and works full-time at the post office."

Rose pursed her lips and tilted her head. "You know what I mean, retard."

I cracked a smile at being called 'retard' again by my big sister. "Are you seriously asking me this question?" I studied her for the truth. I didn't want to discuss Mom and what she did. Neither should Rose.

"Did she quit that shit?" my sister asked. A child at the table next to us wailed and an agitated father tried his best to control the situation. "She got a real job, right?" Rose didn't seem to notice the commotion.

"Please," I scoffed and straightened my skirt. Mom would never leave Glitter or stop doing porn. She had many times defended her profession saying it *was* a real job. The word 'real' depended on perspective. "Mom's always going to twirl around the pole or spread her business on the internet." Rose looked disturbed.

I made the household work. I fed us. I clothed Rorie. I went to her parent-teacher meetings. I took her to her best friend's house to play. I worried every single night about how my being her caretaker would shape her life and what I could do more to prepare her for a vicious, spiteful world.

That was how I condoned wanting to apply at The Express. Money made the world go 'round and, there, I could get money and make our lives a little bit easier. I wasn't a hypocrite for thinking less of Mom. I wasn't one either for thinking less of myself.

"She promised," Rose said very austerely. "For Rorie's sake, she promised. For *my* sake, she promised she'd quit and be a good mother."

"She'll probably do it forever, you know," I reminded.

Rose chewed at her lower lip and picked at the skin around a fingernail. She was heavily in thought.

"Uncle Jeremy said he found her a job at the lumber yard doing clerical work but she turned it down," I said.

"When was that?"

SPILLED MILK

I shrugged. "I don't know. Last year about this time." I looked her squarely in the eye. It was the perfect time for the golden question, the one I'd been longing to ask her. I wasn't always the best at timing and contemplated if I should wait but I was never any good at thinking before speaking.

"You know, *last year*," I continued, pointedly, "around this time, when you weren't around. When you had that guard come and tell me you didn't want any visitors. When I was all alone and so depressed I couldn't work and Uncle Jeremy had to come over to take care of Rorie's basic needs because our own mother wouldn't. When people were spray-painting insults on our front door about you and Dad still. Remember?"

She squinted at me and flinched. I'd hurt her but she wasn't going to admit it. She always concealed her pain well. "I couldn't see you that day," she explained, ignoring the other topics I'd brought up. "I wasn't in any condition to see you, Amber."

A sudden anger came over me and I mistakenly said, "You always took the easy way out."

She looked cold for a moment but then contained herself and resumed, "You're being awfully bitchy today. I'm trying to explain why I sent you away that day, why I couldn't see you for a while, and all you're handing out is guilt trips. You didn't miss me at all?"

"First of all, I'm always awfully bitchy. Secondly, 'not being in any condition'," I made quotation marks in the air with my fingers, "isn't an explanation and, third, of course I missed you. I miss the help and female company my own age."

She pondered. "What about Carmen? Aren't you girls still friends?"

"I'm not sure," I answered. I wasn't sure where I stood with Carmen. Maybe I never knew where I stood with Carmen. "She's too preoccupied with her geriatric beau," I made fun, "and too preoccupied sitting at our kitchen table topless as one of Mom's friends gropes her boobs."

Rose didn't seem surprised. Carmen wasn't shy. She used her perfect body as weapons to get attention from men and to intimidate women. I hadn't realized it until now- wounded and wiser.

"Seriously?"

I scoffed and nodded, "Totally seriously. She whipped off her shirt and went upstairs to Mom's room."

"*The* room?"

I nodded again. "And then left the next morning."

"Eww," Rose said. I was glad our mood had lightened. "Carmen was messing around with some stripper in our mother's bed? Our Carmen?"

"Our Carmen," I stated. I squirmed again. "Oh my God, Rose, I can't talk about that. It grosses me out. Tell me about what you've been up to."

Without hesitation, she rattled on. She started with why she'd decided on no visitors in more detail. She let me know that ever since she got sentenced she'd accepted it. Then came a bout of denial, anger, aggression, resentment, sadness for things she said she couldn't explain. She needed time alone, simple as that; time away from the things that bothered her most- me, the family, reminders of her life.

SPILLED MILK

In her solitude, she found a different sort of acceptance. She learned to accept that she'd abandoned her family and her responsibilities to us but she never did utter a syllable of what led to her pulling the trigger. I couldn't bear to ask either. All I could do was listen to her voice and soak it in.

Although it killed her to know we needed her and she couldn't be there, she understood what was done and that it could not be altered. A judge had sentenced her to 40 years and she had to make the most of those 40 years without us. Our absence was the hole in her heart.

"I miss my girls and my Booga," she said, "but what am I going to do, Amber?" she threw two slimmer arms up. "I can write to you and hopefully you'll write back. We can talk on the phone- they have those prepaid calling cards here. And hopefully you'll come back to see me more. You can mail me pictures of Rorie and Bret too. I want to see how much they've grown."

Seeing her sitting before me as a prisoner, eyes glazed and layered with wisdom she should never know, made me want to reach for her and hold her close.

I watched her hand on the table, fingers still caressing one another in comfort, and I ached to touch it, to feel her skin on mine, so that somehow we could be whole again in some cosmic way.

"Earlier," Rose suddenly said and glanced down, allowing me an opportunity to wipe away an edge of a tear that threatened to fall, "you had said you missed me."

I was confused and questioned her with my eyes.

"You used the past tense," she pointed out.

I stupidly froze. I didn't know what to say. I hadn't meant that I didn't currently...

"Rose-"

She put a hand up to stop me and spoke again, "Does she remember me?"

I knew who she referred to. "Of course she does. She's a kid not an imbecile," I said. Rorie in pigtails and jumping rope with Sara flashed through my mind.

"Will you tell her I never meant to leave her?"

My throat constricted and I swallowed hard. I had to force myself to speak. "Of course. She already knows it wasn't your intention. But how do I explain you left nonetheless?"

She sucked in a deep breath and sat back. Her expression was troubled. She searched for words.

"I love that little girl," she said, an octave above her previous tone. She pulled her body forward and propped her arms up on the table and looked at me deep. I almost couldn't blink. "That girl is why I'm okay with things. She is why I can finally breathe."

It made sense but not fully. I had so many questions still that I wanted answered but the clock on the wall warned that our time was short.

"She's a good girl," I agreed. "She needs a good role model around."

Rose smiled. "You are, Amber," she said softly, "you just don't realize things like that. All you see is the negative side."

"The real side," I countered.

"You're gorgeous, you're smart, you're funny. Do something. Just because you have a little sister to look after doesn't mean you can't put yourself out there like you used to and enjoy things. We're not little kids anymore- there's nothing to run from."

There was always something to run from.

"I do miss you," I switched topic, "I mean, I miss*ed* you and I miss you. You were always a good sister."

Neither of us spoke for a moment. I occupied the awkwardness by grooming my cuticles and inspecting my nail polish. She twiddled with a strand of coarse, dark hair. When she was around Rorie's age, she sucked on her hair like a piece of licorice and her hair would be drenched. As an adult, she never quite lost the compulsive urge to play with her locks even if she did lose the urge to suck on them. Her consistency fascinated me.

If Rose had to choose only one person that she loved best it didn't have to be mentioned that it was Dad. She had killed the one person she loved most in the entire world and she *still* did- tremendously. Even after all the healing she'd tried to do over the last year or so, she still couldn't accept that the reason Dad was no longer around was because of her.

No one else but her. That had to be hard to recover from.

CHAPTER 7

When I pulled into the driveway after the long ride home from Maine, Dennis Huntington's white Mercedes was parked in front of my house. Sara and Rorie were on the trampoline. It was so refreshing to see her on it again. It'd been a while since I'd last seen a bouncing, tumbling Rorie. Heidi sat on the grass, Indian-styled, and watched them in contentment. She must've swapped cars with her husband for the day.

"Hey," I said behind her.

She rose immediately. "I didn't hear you pull up," she looked at my ratched Hyundai at the far end of the driveway. "I was busy watching the girls." She looked to Rorie and Sara and her smile said it all. You could tell she loved being a mother.

"Amber!" cried Sara, her yellow hair being tossed around with every jump.

Rorie waved at me and begged me to get on with them. I declined and said maybe next time.

"Thanks for letting me take Rorie today," Mrs. Huntington said.

"Any time," I said and meant it.

"Rorie's getting real good with that mini-golf club. Her and Sara were having a friendly competition as to who could sink the most holes." I was sure, when Heidi didn't mention who came out the winner, that it wasn't my baby sis. I didn't ask because I didn't want to hear that little Sara beat best friend Rorie at yet another friendly competition.

My eyes followed Rorie's body- up and down, up and down. Her pink leggings and pink-and-white horizontally-striped shirt went up and down, up, down, until finally the stripes blurred together.

Heidi broke my trance, "You never returned my call."

"What call? I never got any messages." I hadn't.

"Last week. Your mother answered."

"Oh," I said disgustedly. "That's why."

"I asked her to let you know I called and to give me a ring back."

"Why did you call?" I looked at her, into her crystal blue eyes.

"Let's sit," she said softly and positioned her bum onto the ground. I followed suit. It made me nervous any time anyone told me to sit. It usually meant bad news.

"Yes?" I asked gently, hoping she'd get to the point if, in fact, there was a point to be made.

"Nothing specific," she explained. She smiled at me and when she smiled so did her eyes. They squinted in a way that made her appear genuine.

"How's the home front?" Always the same questions. There was one- there'd be about 99 more.

I shrugged. "Same old, same old. You?"

She softly chuckled. "Dennis is a riot," she said and explained no further.

I nodded even if I couldn't confirm how much of a riot Dennis Huntington was. "That's great you two still get along."

"Yeah," she said and smiled to herself. "You'll find your Mr. Right soon."

Never once had I ever talked romance with her or ever hinted that I was in search of a Mr. Right.

"Rorie tells us you're seeing a young fellow."

I shook my head. "Don't believe everything Rorie tells you."

"Well, you'll find your guy. You're so pretty it's hard for me to imagine you'd be single forever. I'm sure you get asked out a lot, am I wrong?"

"Totally wrong," I said and managed a small laugh. She had no clue how wrong she was. Men either wanted to have sex with me or they wanted nothing to do with me when and if I didn't give in. None of them could be depended on.

"They're intimidated by you. Quite often you see people that are attractive but it's uniform attractiveness. Every once in a rare while, you come across someone who is noticeably uniquely beautiful and your eyes can't help but linger a second longer. You're one of those people, Amber."

I didn't know what to say or if I should say anything at all. Compliments embarrassed me and left me speechless, and being left speechless embarrassed me even more.

"Thanks," I managed and still didn't know if I should call her Heidi or Mrs. Huntington. I felt I should call her 'Mrs.' because she took care of Rorie and treated her with respect and 'Heidi' was too impersonal. It was important Rorie be shown that women in this world could respect each other and get along.

Should I just call her 'ma'am'? How about 'H'? One of these days I should just throw my arms around her neck and say, "How goes it, chicky?" It'd be cool if her response was "Not much, homey!" but I doubted it would be.

We were quiet a moment and I glanced at her profile. I should have told her she was pretty too but there was a five-second rule when it came to things like comebacks or returning praise. Five seconds was long gone.

"Rorie's a good girl you know," Mrs. Huntington said but didn't turn to look at me. I was grateful for that. I was more comfortable in conversation with her when we both looked ahead and not into each other's eyes. I feared my eyes always said too much that I couldn't take back later. "She misses her sister."

My breath caught and I shrunk when I realized Mrs. Huntington had noticed my reaction. Rorie must have mentioned where I'd gone. She must have overhead Mom this morning.

"She knows where I went today?" I asked softly.

She nodded. "She heard you and your mother arguing."

"Is she okay with it?" I asked and listened closely for sounds of Rorie's voice or laughter.

"She's pretending to be okay with it, let's start there," she looked concerned and I had to look away. I felt guilty that our lives caused her worry. "Have you talked to her about your sister?"

I plucked a blade of grass from the earth and played with it slowly, delicately, painstakingly compulsively. I needed to focus some attention elsewhere or else crumble inside. "Not since it happened," I admitted and wondered if she'd pull a Dr. Phil on me and counsel me to death about what I *should* be doing and what I *should* be saying.

"Hmm," Heidi Huntington pondered to herself, probably conjuring up a plan on how to save the day, "Well maybe tonight if she doesn't bring it up *you* can. Kind of explain to her why your sister is in prison and what she's doing to make her life better. I think that would help Rorie with all of this."

"Is she okay with this?" I asked again with more persistence. "Is she mad at me for seeing her?"

Mrs. Huntington thought a moment and tried to find the right words to not set me off. She'd witnessed my mood swings and negativity many times in the past and was learning how to get around those things. It was another thing I felt bad about- the idea that possibly my being who I was caused her to walk around on egg shells. Maybe I was being paranoid. Maybe Mrs. Huntington did like me after all. Maybe a St. Germaine, besides Clyde and Rorie, tickled her affections.

"Your sister did something terrible to somebody Rorie loved. It's been a couple of years since it happened and Rorie's older now. She was old enough to understand back then. Maybe she's interpreted the situation now and developed her own conclusions."

"In English," becoming annoyed with her psychological babble.

She looked me square in the eyes and I couldn't look away. "She's torn, Amber. She's pulled in two directions. Your sister did something terrible to your father and I think that if Rorie talks to your sister or sees her she feels she is wronging your father. And I believe that she thinks that if she admits love for your father she thinks she is betraying your sister. Either way, that poor little girl feels she can't win. She feels she can't love them both and that's got to be tough for a kid her age. At that age, kids want to love."

It was true. Rorie loved her fish, Bart, even though it did nothing but float and eat. She loved purple although purple couldn't love her back. She loved Frosted Flakes and we all knew Frosted Flakes only loved milk and spoons.

I let what she said sink in. She was full of wisdom tonight. I weighed my words in my mind and decided on what I'd say before I actually said it. It was a conscious effort and one I reminded myself to make more often.

"Rorie hasn't spoken of Rose or our father since just after the funeral. She kept asking where Daddy was and when Rose was coming home. After a while, and after many emotional breakdowns and arguments, Mom intimidated Rorie into never bringing it up again. Mom used to go psycho with either rage or crying fits whenever someone or the media brought up Dad's case and Rose's sentence.

"She thought it reflected poorly on her. I couldn't disagree. After a while, Rorie seemed okay. It seemed everyone had forgotten. So I made sure not to remind her of those times or of them. So far its seemed to work. Maybe I was wrong. But what do I say- 'Hey, Rorie, I saw Rose today. You know, Rose- your older sister who abandoned you because she felt she had to kill our father? Yeah, that sister'."

Mrs. Huntington smiled at me and moved her hand to cover mine, but she thought against it and stopped. She knew by now that I didn't like being touched and she was probably sick of the humiliation every time she'd tried and I'd retreated.

Her words were careful and spoken sincerely, "That's a tough one, Amber. What does anyone say to someone they love when there is great loss to deal with? Maybe you can ask Rorie if she has any questions about it and go from there. Be open, be honest, but be sensitive as she's very young and not yet soured by life. She's not yet jaded like the rest of us- not completely. I'm sure she'll be open to discussion. She seemed to have no problem talking about it with me. Just know that little girl loves you, Amber.

"That little girl has one goal in life and that is to be a good girl. When I asked why that was her goal, she said 'because it's my job to make it easier on Amber'. Understand that and realize that since your mother refuses to speak of your sister or your father that it is your job to do it."

I could only stare at her and picture white-sand beaches and exotic, colorful birds to take my mind away from her comment and stop me from bursting into tears. I already knew it was my job and couldn't deny that I wanted so badly to just be Rorie's sister.

I wasn't a terrible person for just wanting to play with her and teach her about boys instead of molding her life and worrying that *my* actions could derail *her* future.

"I'll talk to her," was all I said about it. "I'll talk to her tonight."

"Good," Mrs. Huntington said and looked impressed. "Are you going to be okay talking about it though?"

"I was fine enough to see her today," I said, referring to Rose, "so it'd be bitchy of me to not be fine enough to talk to Rorie about it, right?"

"Not necessarily," she answered though it was a rhetorical question and not one in which I'd expected a response to.

"Why can't you say their names?" I suddenly asked as the thought just approached. I looked into her eyes and saw a trickle of sadness. Mrs. Huntington was an open book and her emotions easily read.

She breathed deep and said, "Because I respected your sister. She was a good woman. And I have to respect your father for creating the kids he did..," her voice trailed off and she focused on the mountains in the back yard.

"Rose," I said to Mrs. Huntington, "Jack. Those are their names."

In one sentence, I'd bombarded her with bad memories. I secretly wanted someone else to hurt with me just as I secretly wanted someone to hold me. It was an internal battle-wanting those things and not wanting those things at the same time.

"Rose was a great girl," Mrs. Huntington finally said. "Your father created a fine woman in her and I am sorry she is gone."

"Gone?" I asked. "She's in Maine. That's not gone."

I plucked out more grass and fiddled again.

"Yes," she said. "You're right, Amber." She didn't know what else to say about it and I damned myself for making her feel awkward.

"Jack," I said again. "Why can't you say his name? Jack. Jack." I watched her expression turn blank and I swear I saw a spark of anger cross her face. Did I piss her off? Was she going to finally let me have it?

She swung her eyes at me and her voice was stern when she spoke, "I will never say his name. Hearing his name fills me with feelings I'd rather not feel in this short lifetime. I give the man credit for who you and Rorie are as people and for Rose's kindness and determination to raise the St. Germaine children but I can never give him credit for much else."

Her eyes were so sincere I couldn't bear to look away. I needed the kind of empathy someone like Mrs. Huntington was capable of. I needed her sympathy too.

"I know what your father did," she said. "It's okay if you want to talk about it. I fully comprehend what that must have done to you and I commend you for being as strong and independent as you are. You've been through so much in your short life. Both you *and* Rorie have. If you want to know why I can't speak his name, it's because of you and because of Rorie."

I tried to restrain myself and not show emotion. It was hard but I achieved. She studied me for a reaction; I didn't give her one. If I showed anything at all, I feared I'd lose it completely.

"Why the heck do you care anyway?" I asked in a whisper and finally pulled my eyes away. I heard Rorie shouting in the distance to Sara. Giggles echoed. How could I ever be sad when Rorie had been through so much and still could frolic and laugh and play? I had no right to dwell. "It's well-known that the St. Germaines are pieces of shit."

"Never speak of yourselves that way," she scolded and it surprised me. "You are far from shit. You have so much potential and so much ahead of you. Just do me a favor, would you?"

I raised my eyebrows at her. "Sure."

"Promise me you'll reach for your dreams and keep reaching until you get them."

"I'll try," was all I could secure myself to.

Mrs. Huntington and I started to casually converse about simpler things in life, cup-half-full topics. Our conversation about Rose and Dad and reaching for my dreams turned into Rorie and Sara adventures and then talk of summer plans.

We made unsecured plans to take the girls to York Beach in Maine or one of the beaches along the southern coast of our state. We also made tentative plans to enjoy the local water park and nearby theme parks like Santa's Village or Story Land where Rorie loved riding on the swan boats and riding fairy tale-themed roller coasters.

Both Mrs. Huntington and I knew that these plans would probably happen but most likely without me. I had a tendency to make plans and not follow through. It wasn't anything personal; it was that the presence of people discouraged me and my tolerance level depended on my mood.

Mrs. Huntington checked her watch and whistled to herself, "Oh golly!" she stood and brushed the grass and dirt from her bottom, "I didn't realize the time. My husband is probably starving and eating away at his own limbs." I chuckled.

She hollered for Sara who ran into her mother's arms and circled her waist with two frail arms. "Time to get home for supper."

"Can Rorie come?" she asked and Rorie skipped up from behind, her brunette pigtails swaying side to side in unison.

"I'm taking her out for pizza tonight," I intervened before Mrs. Huntington could answer.

Heidi smiled at me through her blue eyes and kissed Sara on her forehead, "Well, there's your answer, my silly girl."

I walked Mrs. Huntington to her car. Rorie and Sara trailed behind holding hands and whispering secrets back and forth.

"Thanks," I said to Heidi Huntington at her car door.

"You're welcome," she said, "although I don't know why you're thanking me."

"For everything," I smiled at her.

Rorie and Sara hugged goodbye and we waved as they pulled out of our driveway.

I put my arms around Rorie's little shoulders and looked down at her as I swatted one of her pigtails, "So, where do you want to go for pizza tonight?"

"Chuck-E-Cheese!" she shouted and raced into the house to grab her purse.

I wasn't really hungry. I was exhausted from the day's events. I'd lost some weight in the past year or so. Stress and depression were never good for an appetite. My lifestyle and worries only allowed for one meal a day and maybe a snack here and there.

I didn't make enough money at Movie Magic to buy an adequate amount of food to see us all through for the recommendations on the food pyramid. I made sure Rorie got her three meals and that was all that mattered to me.

Once we reached the Chuck-E-Cheese in Temple and ordered our pizza, Rorie saw one of the girls from her school and they went off to play in the tunnels that hung from the ceiling. I told her to stay close so that I could beckon for her once the pizza arrived.

Alone at our table, I had nothing to occupy my time so I was forced to look around the room and notice all the families and smiles and loving touches given. Maybe it was superficial but it was all real to me, a slap in the face as to what I didn't have and wouldn't ever.

I thought of Bret and was sure I'd lose sleep tonight. I felt insecure at the visions that maybe he hadn't been home when I stopped in because he was out with someone else, possibly a girl. I didn't like him having anybody when I had no one.

I waved to Rorie who peered out the clear box that she'd crawled into. It looked like she had four eyes through the plastic. Her friend from school found other girls to play with and was off playing in the ball pit.

I gave Rorie's friend the evil eye and hoped she looked in my direction. I puckered up my lips and blew Rorie a kiss. She giggled and pressed her face against the cube so that her nose scrunched. It made me laugh but I still wanted to kick her friend's ass for ditching her.

Soon, our large pepperoni pizza with extra cheese, onions, and green peppers arrived and I waved Rorie over. She didn't notice my first couple attempts and when she did finally and saw the pizza on the table she practically ran over. When she got to the table I looked down at her pink socks and asked where her shoes were. She pointed to a plastic cubby.

"Go get 'em," I ordered. Instead of moving, she plopped down on the bench across from me and sipped at the Sprite she favored.

"I'm hungry," she pouted and reached for her first slice. Maternal instinct kicked in so I got up and got her shoes myself.

When I got back to the table she looked up at me, scrunched her eyes, and went "mmm" while she chewed loudly. I chuckled at her and sat down. Rorie had placed two slices on my plate ready for me to eat.

"Why thank you, Rorie," I said and ritualistically scraped the topping from slice number one. I ate the pizza first and then the topping last. So delicious that way.

"You're so weird," she said to me as I piled the toppings together on a corner of the paper plate. She'd seen me do it a hundred times and she'd said how weird it was a hundred times.

"Hey," I countered, "it doesn't matter how it goes in, it all comes out the same."

"Ew," she said, mouth full. A piece of masticated food fell out of her mouth. She laughed.

I did too. "Ew," I said back at her.

Rorie and I had a good time at Chuck-E-Cheese. She beat me in Skee-ball and ended up walking out of there with a ton of little toys and a brand new desk mirror and comb she'd gotten from all the tickets won.

"Want to see what Uncle Jeremy's up to?" I suggested and Rorie eagerly nodded. So, off we went and for a moment I pondered stopping off at Bret's cabin afterwards. It'd be a great excuse to see Bret without feeling weird because I'd have Rorie with me.

The ride to our uncle's house was eventful, full of Rorie's stories jam-packed with the girls at school, her music teacher whose slip always showed under her dress and her nylons always had runs in them, and the funny things her and Sara did.

Uncle Jeremy was working on his motorcycle when we pulled into his dirt driveway. Rorie hollered "Hey, Uncle Silly Pants!" from the car window before leaping out and into his arms. He held her close, grease all over his clothes but Rorie didn't care. He tipped his Red Sox cap at me and smiled large, "What brings my girls this way?"

I shrugged, "Stopping by to see our favorite uncle."

"Your *only* uncle," he corrected and Rorie giggled.

"What can I do?" Rorie said excitedly, grabbing at random wrenches, nuts, and bolts. She was always eager to help the men in her life. She very visibly held a preference toward men, just like me, Mom, and Rose did. Women had so often done us wrong.

Uncle Jeremy handed her a scrap piece of metal that was lying around his yard and a couple of screws for her to tinker with. She was quickly at the project at hand and used a green screwdriver to twist that screw into place even if she didn't know what the heck it went to. My uncle bent down and started tinkering with his bike again while we small-talked. I offered to help but he declined and assured he was almost done and couldn't wait to get his hog back on the road.

During spring and summer, he cruised the mountains. Sometimes all the way to the Canadian border past Pittsburg, our states northernmost town that was more populated with moose than people. There was a long strip of road in Pittsburg called Moose Alley where sightings were guaranteed.

Dad liked taking us girls up there when he was alive. Rorie loved when she saw the babies and would try running up to them to pet them and get a closer look. Of course, Rose- motherly and concerned- would chase her, scoop her up, and chastise her. Then she'd say, "What would I do if a moose ate my sweet little Rorie?"

We hung out with Uncle Jeremy until he finished his bike project. His smile was huge when he sat on that motorcycle and revved it. Rorie squealed and climbed on the seat behind him and wrapped her skinny arms around his waist.

"Ready!" she squealed. Uncle Jeremy laughed and promised her a ride when he got her a helmet.

"Make it purple with glitter," Rorie said.

"Deal," he said and they pinky-swore on it. I had to laugh although I knew I wouldn't allow her on the back of a motorcycle for a few more years.

Uncle Jeremy let us know he was going to go for a cruise before it got dark. He invited us back over for dinner around nine but I let him know it was a school night and we'd have him over for supper mid-week. Rorie splattered big kisses on his scruffy cheeks. He laughed heartily and claimed it tickled. It made her do it more and I smiled on the sidelines, savoring every moment, etching their grins in my mind.

As he sped off with an arm in the air as he waved, Rorie cooed and insisted, "When I'm 16, I'm definitely getting one with pink streamers."

"Of course you are," I chuckled. I pictured her wearing a purple helmet as she sat on a bright purple motorcycle with hot pink streamers off the handlebars, laced with silver glitter, flapping in the wind. It reminded me of her bicycle when she was six. The bike had a banana seat that had a picture of a purple unicorn on it. The unicorn's spiraled horn ended with a pink star at the tip. She loved that bike until someone had stolen it from our front yard.

She cried for three days straight until Dad rushed to the nearest Walmart with Uncle Jeremy to scoop up another bike, this time one with Barbie on it. It was originally pink so Dad splurged on purple spray paint before they presented her with it.

Mom had bitched at Dad that night about spending money they didn't have. I remembered Dad telling her to shut up, that she was six and it made her happy. My love for him was huge that night. Even now, as I thought about how he made Rorie happy that day, I cringed at the guilt of still possibly loving him despite all he'd done.

We sat in my Hyundai in our uncle's driveway listening to music until I gathered up the nerve to bring up Bret. Rorie hadn't seen Bret in quite some time, a number of months, and I wasn't completely sure she'd want to see him. She rarely spoke his name anymore and he rarely spoke hers although I fully knew she was in his thoughts.

Instead of asking Rorie if she wanted to go, I took the ride up the Kanc towards his cabin. She hadn't been to his cabin in over a year and I wondered if she knew where we were headed.

My sister busily bobbed her head to the radio and watched the passing trees. She commented that she hoped she'd see a moose and it brought me back to the time Dad crashed into one. Did she remember?

As we climbed higher up Mt. Jolly I kept looking in Rorie's direction awaiting a reaction from her; she had to know where we were going. Once Bret's road neared, she sat up straighter and her face looked more alert. She didn't appear uncomfortable nor comforted.

I looked to her again and spoke, "Do you want to see Bret for a little bit? See what he's up to?"

"I don't know," she replied.

"You want to wait in the car while I run in?" I turned the radio down.

When she didn't answer, I said, "Rore?"

"Fine," she spat.

"Fine?" I pulled over into a lot with a scenic view of Mt. Washington, Mt. Cranmore, and other small neighboring mountains. "Fine, as in okay? Or fine, as in whatever?"

"Fine as in fine," she repeated and sat back, blank.

"What's wrong, baby sis?" I asked softly and so badly wanted to reach out and stroke her cheek and tell that her I loved her to the point that it left me breathless.

She fidgeted with her finger and began to scrape off purple nail polish from a thumbnail. "Nothing" she said but her words didn't convince me.

"You can tell me anything," I encouraged and I tried to muster up the strength to touch her. But I felt if I touched her I'd love her more than I already did and I couldn't imagine that I'd survive the weight of that love.

I watched my baby and smiled at how beautiful she was. Her dark eyebrows and long lashes, the full rosy lips I saw on our mother, and her soft olive skin. She reminded me of a

Precious Moments figurine. She was maturing at an alarming rate and no longer my little girl.

Before I knew it she'd be grown and I knew she'd need me even more. I hoped I was strong enough to withstand the problems she may encounter. I knew how I was and if she was anything like me I'd be in for it. My teen years weren't too far in my past but I felt old, aged, broken. I couldn't conceptualize living to be an old lady. I wasn't sure my will was robust enough.

I tugged at one of her pigtails and forced a chuckle. "Share what's on your mind, kiddo."

"Well," she considered what to say, "what if he doesn't want to see me?"

It bothered me to think that she'd ever wonder of Bret's feelings for her. He loved this little girl more than words.

"Why do you think he wouldn't want to see you? He loves you. Of course he wants to see you. How could you ever think otherwise?"

"He's good at forgetting love," she said. Five simple words. Five. Four. Three. Two. One. One simple word. Simple yet so complex. I just couldn't figure out whether the most important word was 'love' or 'forgetting'.

"What do you mean?" I sat back in the shadows.

She scrunched her lips. She shrugged and twirled a long strand of silky soft hair. Rorie and Rose and their hair obsessions- their comfort zones. "He's good at pretending he cares when he really doesn't. One minute he's cool, the next he sucks. When he visited us, he only visited you. He didn't give a shit about the rest of us."

"Watch your mouth," I cautioned her then immediately focused on the topic at hand, "What do you mean 'forgetting love'?"

She looked at me dully and I scooched back into the shadows. "He loves you one day and the next day he's over you."

"Yeah?" my voice came out a scratchy whisper.

"He's a moody asshole and Mom says he's a pig perv."

"A pig perv?" I repeated then cleared my throat. I feared specifics. I didn't want to know what exactly made him a pervert but I needed to at the same time. My soul always ached to hurt because it knew no better; it always asked direct questions and demanded direct answers. It was self-sabotage.

"Mom says he used to sneak off all the time with girls in town and do stuff."

"Stuff," It wasn't a question.

"Yeah," Rorie nodded, "Stuff. Like sex and shit."

"Watch your mouth. Describe 'shit'."

I leaned back deeper into the shadows until the door frame blocked further movement. I was trapped and Rorie's truths came at me. My ears throbbed, my throat constricted, my mouth dried. The car was hot.

"Mom said he's a male slut. He gave some girl some harp disease."

"'Harp disease'?" I pictured a large, shiny, golden harp and a contaminated blonde woman with flowing hair, wearing a white dress, busily plucking at strings.

"Mom called 'em 'love bumps'," Rorie giggled and I cringed. "Plus Mom says he's a liar and a thief and she's glad he doesn't come over anymore. She said he's no longer her problem. She said he's the reason Dad left to live with Uncle Jeremy instead of living with us."

"That isn't true," I defended. "He'd never make Dad leave. Dad left because Dad left." No one else had anything to do with Dad's decision to leave his kids in a house with his crazy wife while he drank beers and partied with his brother across town.

I rolled a window down and breathed in the fresh mountain air. I fumbled for my pack of cigarettes.

"Amber?" Rorie asked.

"Yeah?" I puffed in a drag and watched the smoke float away into the black sky. The wind tousled my hair and caused my forehead to itch. I used my shirt sleeve to relieve it and eyed the cover-up that smudged on the material.

"You okay?"

I looked at her. Why wouldn't I be okay? Did she sense my mood change or read it on my face? Hiding in the darkness hadn't worked. "I'm good," I answered.

"But if you want to go see Bret, I will. I'll do it for you. He can't suck entirely if you still like him."

"You don't?"

She shrugged and thought. A smile spread on her pretty little face and she looked over at me. "He's still my brother. Of course I like him. All I'm saying is I wish he liked me more. All he cares about is you, you, you. If he liked *me* more maybe I'd like *him* more."

"He loves you," I said in all seriousness.

"Not as much as he loved you in those movies," she said.

"What?"

"Mom said he really, *really* loved you in the movies and that Uncle Jeremy's a dick for loving you too."

"What movies?"

She squinted in her little girl way and couldn't come up with an answer. She shrugged and looked at me again. "I have no idea. Mom didn't tell me the name of it."

I looked ahead and noticed there were no more stars out.

"Let's go," she said.

"Where?"

"Bret's," she answered.

"No."

"No?"

"No."

SPILLED MILK

CHAPTER 8

I couldn't sleep that night. My thoughts were jumbled yet some parts were so clear it was surreal and frightening. I wasn't frightened like a kid who was afraid of the dark. I wasn't convinced the bogeyman lurked in every corner and his mission in life was to kill me.

Around my eleventh birthday, when Rorie was just a baby and Dad had just moved out, I remembered Mom and Uncle Jeremy talking together in her bedroom about something that had to do with me. I was on my way out to ride my bicycle down the road when I heard my name mentioned several times and Dad's name. Of course, I lurked outside her bedroom door and listened, as still as could be, and soaked in every word I could make out.

I'd eavesdropped well into their conversation. All I caught was something about me, Bret, and Dad, and how Uncle Jeremy knew. Uncle Jeremy, each and every time she brought it up, swore he couldn't have known, that if he'd known he would've killed "him" with his bare hands.

He cursed out Mom, calling her a "dumb bitch" for even thinking he'd keep "the shit" in his house. I had no clue back then what they talked about and I still hadn't a clue. I didn't care. The word "videos" had been mentioned.

Remembering Mom's voice saying "videos" and Rorie mentioning "movies" seemed somehow correlated.

The thing that bothered me the most was the comment of forgetting love. I couldn't fathom it. The act of forgetting

141

love had to take a lot of energy and anger. I hadn't seen my little brothers in years yet I still remembered my affections for them.

Sometimes I forgot what they looked like or some of their mannerisms, and that made me feel guilty, but I couldn't forget how deeply I loved them. I loved Rose; she murdered our father and I still loved her. I was mad at her for different reasons than killing Dad and I hated her at times but eventually I got over it and went back to loving her.

I closed my eyes tight and twisted my mouth semi-grotesquely as I readied myself for the sobbing that welled up so strongly inside of me. I felt I'd explode if I didn't let it out sooner rather than later. But it didn't come. All that came was odd and random sexual pleasure. Goosebumps layered my skin, my nipples hardened, and my crotch tingled.

I flung off my blanket and tore off my clothes in a horny rush. I laid down on my bed and fingered and stroked myself to a welcomed, frenzied orgasm that lasted quite a while. No one could screw yourself like yourself.

After my senses returned I felt better. Instead of crying, a small smile spread across my lips and I brought my fingers to them to taste my own come. I'd been with girls before. I used to daydream about Carmen's breasts and what I'd do to her if I had her alone in a bedroom under the right circumstances.

I used to sit on a bright green bean bag while my friend Trinity sat on a red one across from me. We weren't wearing underwear and we'd watch each other masturbate. I remembered how excited I felt when she'd close her eyes to get off. We were 12. I still saw Trinity around town once in a while. I could still picture her pussy.

SPILLED MILK

I figured Rorie was passed out in her bed and contemplated driving out to Bret's house. I wasn't even sure I'd go in. All I knew was I wanted to drive there.

Quickly I got dressed in a pair of jean shorts and a white tank top. I threw on a pair of wedge-heeled, tan sandals and made a mental note to paint my toenails later on. I glanced in the mirror and fixed my hair. After a little eyeliner and mascara touch-up, I head downstairs after I had confirmed Rorie was asleep.

The night was unusually warm which typically meant we'd see a storm of some sort either the next day or the day after. It was far from a clear night; the stars didn't want to show themselves. Spring would hit hard. Soon, there would be tourists all over the place backing up town traffic and swarming the local shops and eateries. Our local businesses depended on the money from tourism. Without it, we'd probably cease to exist.

I looked at the car clock- 2:02am. I wondered if Bret would still be awake.

The clouds that floated around the moon, just a sliver tonight, took my breath away. The trees were black vertical streaks across the skyline and they were beautiful. Bob Marley jammed out in the background and the warm breeze played with my hair through the cracked window.

It was one of those moments in life when everything seemed all right even when it wasn't. The natural environment exuded calm vibrations, as opposed to city life where things like cars and more cars, big boxy apartment buildings with lousy neighbors, and alleyways with big green trash barrels marked with apartment numbers ruined the Feng Shui.

143

When I pulled into Bret's driveway I noticed a lit candle in the window and curtains half-drawn. Was he awake? I quietly got out of my car and tiptoed on the gravel. I held my breath until I reached his doorway.

Just then the door opened and my big brother loomed before me. He had on a baseball hat, his work jacket and boots, and had his keys in hand.

"What the fuck?" Bret asked.

"Sorry," was all I could say.

"What are you doing here, Amber?" He looked confused.

"I couldn't sleep," I said.

He smiled a little and moved aside for me to come in.

"Aren't you leaving?" I asked as I walked past him.

"No," he said and tossed his keys into a dish that sat on a small table by the doorway. I looked at him, questioning with my eyebrows, and sat on the couch. He sat on his chair and kicked off his shoes.

"Seriously," I said and removed my jacket, "where were you going at this time of night?"

Bret's eyes lingered on my chest then to my face and he answered, "I was headed to the house."

I assumed he meant my house. "Why?"

"I figured you'd be awake."

I smiled and struggled to breathe normally. He had been coming to see me as I came to see him. "Well, you figured right."

His eyes flicked to my chest a few more times. Suddenly, he snickered and asked "Where'd you get those?" while pointing to my tits.

SPILLED MILK

"What?" I laughed and glanced down at two hard nipples clearly seen through a thin, white tank. I hadn't bothered with a bra. "I'm a woman."

"That you are," he said quietly, a bit uncomfortably. "My little sister is growing up."

I didn't know what to say. I felt prickles on my inner thighs and on the sides of my vagina. It caused an overwhelming rush throughout my body. I wanted to be penetrated in every hole, gentle then rough.

"I've been grown for a long time, Bret."

"I know that," he shifted in his seat. He looked away and I lit a cigarette.

I enjoyed watching my brother steal glances at my breasts. I waited for the guilt. It didn't come but I knew it would.

"Got a girlfriend yet?" I badgered him.

He laughed, took off his hat, messed with his hair, then replaced it. "Got a boyfriend yet?"

"Several," I joked.

He only looked at me.

"What?" I said. He wasn't laughing anymore. "I was kidding."

"Am," he said, this time in a brotherly way, "don't give yourself away."

"I was kidding," I said again and had to laugh at him.

"I know you were but I'm being serious. You're a pretty girl. Guys like pretty girls. I'm just saying don't just give your pussy away."

"Uh," I sat back, "thanks?"

He got up, went into his refrigerator, and returned to the sitting room with a 30-rack of beer. He offered me a can and opened one himself. Within the hour, we were both drunk.

Logs burned in his fireplace which made me sweat. "Open a window," I begged and, without thinking, I peeled off my shirt forgetting I didn't put on a bra. Bret didn't falter. It was as if girls whipped off their shirts in his living room on a daily basis. The crossing thought made me blush and I felt a brief surge of jealousy.

Bret didn't open a window. A few minutes later, my pants and shoes came off. My white laced thongs stayed on. I sat on his sofa as if I were fully-clothed and worthy of respect. Bret, being a man, had forgotten who he was to me and came to sit beside me.

He leaned closer and put a hand on my knee, "You're a funny girl, Amber. We need to do this more often."

His hand felt warm as it cupped my kneecap. I wanted his hands all over me. I wanted things inside of me. I wanted to be violated. His eyes roamed my body and he licked his lips. The room swirled around us.

"Oh my fucking God, girl," he breathed and licked my ear. I moaned and arched my body forward until both of his hands caught my breasts. He squeezed them together as I positioned myself on his lap and he attacked them with his tongue and lips.

His fingertips furiously tugged and stroked my nipples. The sounds he made while he feasted at my chest drove me crazy. It was as if they were his last meal, his favorite meal-tasty and filling.

SPILLED MILK

I pushed against his crotch and felt his manhood press
against me. He was hard. Oh, yes, he was.

"Fuck me," I ordered. I couldn't be blamed. In the heat
of the moment I'd forgotten who we were to each other, who
I was to him, and especially who he was to me. I was fucked
up- high, drunk, blurry. I had to remind myself to keep
breathing.

"Oh yeah?" he groaned and cupped my ass with his big
hands. "You want me to fuck your little pussy, baby?"

I didn't reply. I only bobbed up and down on his groin
desperately wanting his penis to fall out of his pants. It felt
smothered and wanted to breathe. My tits bounced and he
flicked at them with his tongue while he squeezed them into
his face. I opened my eyes and looked down at him. I enjoyed
watching him fondle me.

"Fuck me," I begged in a small, anticipating voice.

He looked up at me. His hands stopped moving. His eyes
lost some of their gloss and he looked abruptly ashamed.

"I'm sorry," I whispered and dumbly froze on his lap,
waiting for a reaction, any reaction. "Don't be mad at me."

Bret made a noise- a mix between a flabbergasted
grumble, a grunt of pain, and a hiss of disgust. He scolded,
"What the fuck is your problem?"

I looked down at him, my long hair flowing down both
sides of me. The strands softly tickled the sides of my breasts.
I should've covered myself.

"Don't be mad at me," I pleaded in a child-like voice.

He looked up at me and our eyes swallowed each others.
His hands found me again. He held my hips and his rugged

147

hands climbed up the sides of my body then stopped right under my armpits.

I leaned down and dared to kiss his neck, loving every moan he let out. I could tell he was fighting with himself internally. Did he want to be my brother or invade my body in a thousand different ways? I wanted both.

He caressed my breasts as they hung before him then lowered his hands to caress my bottom. I licked his earlobe and grew increasingly excited as he squirmed underneath me. He tried to resist me.

I inched my way towards his mouth. He must've realized what he was about to do and tossed me off of him. I landed against the thick wooden coffee table with a painful thud. I didn't utter a sound. All I could do was watch my brother.

He couldn't find it in himself to move. He couldn't find the will to look at me. Against his chair he reclined, ignoring the sweat dripping down his neck that soaked the top of his shirt.

I shrunk on the floor, afraid to move, feeling dirty as I sat there naked. He wasn't naked. Only I was.

"I'm sorry," I managed to whisper, my arms across my chest. I couldn't pull my eyes away from him.

"You need to go," he barked. He still didn't look at me.

"Okay," I said softly, still unable to budge. I couldn't bear the thought of him angry at me. I crawled to him on my knees and sat before him. "Please don't be mad at me, Bret."

He looked down at the floor behind me but I knew he saw me. I urged him to look at me but he wasn't ready. I sat up high on my knees and reached for his hand. He jerked it away and said again, this time with more urgency, "Go. Amber, just get the fuck out."

I didn't bother covering up as I knelt before him. I was already cloaked in shame. What was another sin added to countless others? It wouldn't make a difference in my destiny.

"I'll go," I continued, "if only you'll tell me you love me."

Finally he looked at me, but not at me, at my chest. His eyes lingered on the nipples. He then looked into my eyes. "How can I tell you that right now?"

"Tell me you love me," I wanted to break down in tears.

"Amber," he pleaded with me and sat as far back against the sofa as he could. It made me want to die.

"Touch me," I tried to control the rasp in my voice. "Tell me."

"Go," he begged again, his eyes shut tight. "I'm serious, get out. Get the fuck out."

"Fine," I spat with venom, hurt and disrespected. "I'll fucking go!" I stood up and looked around for my shirt and pants. I put them on as fast as I could. I found my keys and scooped my shoes up from the floor.

"You're a fucking asshole!" I shouted at his doorway. He was frozen in the same spot and I wondered if he'd spend the night on that couch cushion. Our eyes met before I slammed the door.

Once I got into my car, I leaned against the steering wheel. I couldn't help but wonder what I would've done had he followed my instructions.

I would have been afraid to turn him away.

CHAPTER 9

I woke up in the afternoon and rushed around to get to work on time but ended up clocking in 15 minutes late anyway.

"Nice of you to show up," Frank greeted, soda and Twizzlers in hand.

"Well if it weren't for those big dollars I wouldn't be here," I said which brought a chuckle from him.

"Yeah? What would you be doing?"

"Decorating my mansion," I answered. Another chuckle from Frank.

"Do I get my own wing in your mansion?"

I reached into the plexiglass snack counter and pulled out a cupful of popcorn and helped myself to some lemonade. "We'll see," I promised Frank about his own wing.

I felt bad for him. He was middle-aged, single, and living in north country while working full-time at the local movie theater. He was such a genuinely nice fellow. He deserved better. But deserving better and earning it were two different things.

I hoped I wasn't here at his age. When I got to be his age I'd take Rorie and we'd get our own little house or cabin in some other state. Somewhere where it didn't snow or rain so much. Somewhere warm 12 months out of the year. Somewhere where Rorie could thrive and completely forget her past. That was my only future goal. Maybe Bret would come but I couldn't ever imagine him leaving here. It was all he knew and all he cared to know.

The work night was redundant. It was a weekday and business was slow. I longed for a sudden flood of people dying to see the latest blockbuster or a ceiling leak so I could mop all night. It would've distracted me from thoughts of Bret and of last night.

Frank mentioned how he'd overheard another conversation our boss, Elvis, had with someone on his office telephone. Something about him having to get rid of a couple people as business was doing poorer than this time last year and he didn't foresee it picking up.

We lacked in everything a business relied on to survive-sufficient revenue, strong management, prime location, excellent customer service, advertising. I knew Elvis was running through his small roster of subordinates, deciding which one or two or three to let go. I was sure I was at the top of his shit-list.

I daydreamed that I suggested to Elvis he demolish Movie Magic and build a drive-in. Drive-ins went out of style and most were taken down. But times were changing and reverting back to the old ways- cars, music, everything but morals.

Maybe drive-in venues would be a new thrill since our generation never got to experience them. People could pull in and watch a flick while sitting in their own cars where they could smoke, have a beer, puff on a pipe, or have sex with no interference or embarrassing consequence. My age group would dig it.

I imagined that Elvis thought it such a brilliant idea that he promoted me to upper management. Elvis and I would team up and build other franchises and, by the time I was Frank's age, I'd have some savings and could live comfortably with Rorie. I'd always take her with me.

Frank had run into town to grab a couple of burgers and we chit-chatted while we ate. We agreed that whoever finished last would mop the floors while the other wiped down the snack counters. Frank, being a man, as expected, finished first so I was appointed the mopping duties. I didn't mind. Frank usually did it and I was glad to give him a break.

I could tell by the way he walked lately that his hips were giving him trouble. He'd fallen down the stairs at his house a couple of years ago and every now and again his hips bothered him. He was good at keeping his pain to himself but I could tell he wasn't faring so well.

"How's your sister?" Frank asked as he wiped mustard from his mustache.

I shrugged, "Rorie's fine. She's doing good- her teacher says she's doing extremely well in English and Spelling. Her Math sucks but she's a St. Germaine. All of us suck at Math. She's still super close to that Huntington girl."

"Ah," Frank commented, "the Huntingtons. Heidi and Dennis- good people. Their little girl is Sara, right?"

"Yes," and I had to giggle. "Sara Huntington...what a head trip."

"Cute kid."

"For sure," I said and continued on about how Rorie was using the trampoline again and that was a good sign and how she was excited about her book report because she got a B and expected an F. I blabbed on and on about Rorie's accomplishments, her silly comments, the funny little girl things she did. Despite her attitude sometimes, I was proud of her. If only she could see in herself what I always saw in her.

"How's your pretty mother?" Frank furthered.

"Good," I hated how he had called her pretty. "She's probably busy performing right now," I rolled my eyes in disgust.

"Oh yeah?" he perked up. "She's a good-looking lady all right. Any man would be lucky as heck to be with a little lady like her. What's she perform in?" I couldn't give him the details and make Mom look bad. "Home movies," I answered simply.

He nodded. "Well she's a talent for sure. You let her know your buddy Frank said 'Hi'."

"Will do, Frank, will do."

I excused myself to do the mopping and clean the women's bathroom before I sat back down to dilly-dally and eat until closing. Frank picked up the phone and dialed someone he loved; I could tell by the way he greeted the other person when they picked up his call.

He was a sweet man even if he did like my mother. He was a man though, a flesh-and-bone-and-penis man. I couldn't hold it against him for thinking her attractive.

10pm rolled around quicker than expected and by 10:05 Frank and I had locked up the theater. It was a warm night for late April. I couldn't wait for spring to get rolling and for summer. I loved warmth, detested the cold. I knew I didn't belong in the northeast but I'd been born here and was stuck.

Uncle Jeremy's road was bare- he lived where houses were spaced a quarter mile apart from one another. The lights in his house were off. He was definitely sleeping. I pulled off to the side of the road and killed the lights before shutting down the engine. I didn't pull into his driveway as I didn't want to wake him. I didn't want him to know I was there.

I wasn't even sure what I was doing there. He was sleeping and couldn't talk to me anyway. I didn't even know what I'd ask him. I thought about that all night at work, about what I'd say and how I'd start the conversation. I just figured I'd talk about Dad and Mom and how they met then I'd get to the dirty skeletons.

I crept up my uncle's driveway using baby steps. It was dirt and gravel and my choice of footwear didn't help. I fumbled a couple of times and cursed at my wardrobe for never having benefited me when it sincerely mattered.

His front door was unlocked as expected. The living room was quiet and dark but for the digital clock on the side table. I passed items I recognized in the spots they'd always lain. I passed Dad's recliner before finding the basement door and turning the handle.

The door creaked a little before it opened completely. The wooden stairs leading to the basement were rickety, old, worn, falling apart.

My hands searched the air for the dangling chain that turned on the bulb. It took a while but I found it, gave it a yank, and the dim light switched on. Dust particles danced in the air. The basement looked like it always had- drab, dusty, dirty. It felt unsettled. I felt like a kid in elementary school who had just watched a horror flick and didn't want to admit they were scared. Although I was old enough to know better, I still looked around for monsters.

SPILLED MILK

The basement was a square room with three smaller rooms coming off of it, all three rooms accessible through doorways without doors. Only the bathroom had a door. The three smaller rooms were used for storage and the main area was used for miscellaneous things.

I took a seat on a green chair that smelled stale. The entire basement smelled pungent. It seemed like it hadn't seen a soul since Dad died. I wondered if Uncle Jeremy came down now and again and thought of times he'd spent with his brother.

Tools- allen keys, wrenches, screwdrivers, saws of all sizes, hammers, screws, odds and ends- lined the wooden shelves. Old books, maps, photo albums, and scrapbooks sat upright, covered in aged dust. The entire room reeked of neglect.

I stared at the wall ahead of me and, oddly, the cracks and scuff marks seemed familiar. It was as if I'd studied this wall before but I couldn't imagine when or why. I shivered and my eyes moved to the floor beneath me just as ash fell off my cigarette. The lines in the floorboards caused me to shudder uncontrollably. The planks blended in with each other and the dark lines that streaked them started to swirl.

'Not as much as he loved you in those movies' and *'Mom said he really loved you in the movies and that Uncle Jeremy's a dick for loving you too'* echoed in my head. Rorie's voice seemed to taunt me with things I didn't know, that maybe I didn't need to know. I tried to lift my head but it felt so weighed down by thoughts.

I forced my body to stand. I must have stood too quickly because I wanted to puke suddenly. Instead of rushing to the bathroom I foolishly vomited in the corner. The sounds that came out of me made me sicker and I bent over and held my stomach as I continued to disgorge out thick, whitish mucus. I started to whimper and turned to leave. The boards beneath me creaked oddly and felt loose. It was a really old house. Maybe if I got rich I'd build him a new house.

I made my way through the dreary basement, past Dad's chair, past the shelves that held randomness. I raced up the steps, my shoes clicking on the wood as I climbed. Once I pushed open the door that led to the living room Uncle Jeremy was standing there.

His facial reaction matched mine. "What the fuck?" he grunted in unison to my "Holy shit."

I slipped into the living room and stood before him. He had just woken up; sleep still in his eyes. Maybe he had gotten up for a sip of water or to take a leak. He looked around confused. I could only stare at him, my eyes wide at the thought of him disappointed in me.

Immediately the excuses spewed forth, "I wasn't taking anything, I swear," I put my hands up before me. "I wouldn't-"

"Seriously, Amber? I honestly wouldn't think you were here to steal from me." He rubbed at his eyes. "What the hell are you doing here though?"

I froze.

"I thought I heard something so I woke up," he explained. "And apparently the thing I thought I heard was, well, my niece sneaking around my house in the middle of the night."

I couldn't speak.

He shook his head at me and cleared the tiredness from his throat. "What the hell, Am? What the fuck is the matter with you?"

A mini face-off.

SPILLED MILK

One, two, three...

"Amber?"

Four, five, six....

"Am?!"

Seven, eight, nine...

"What the FUCK are you doing in my house in the middle of the night?"

Ten...

"You better start speaking, girl."

"I dunno," was all I could manage.

"Speak," he ordered again, visibly agitated. "Now. I don't have time for this shit." He shot a glance at his digital clock to check the time.

"I had to go," I began. "I had to go in the basement."

"What?" he looked confused. "Why the hell would you have to go in the basement?" We both looked down the open doorway to the dingy, worn basement floor.

"I don't know. I know it sounds crazy but I had to go there, you know?"

He shook his head again then sat down on his living room chair. "No, Amber, I don't know. Explain it to me."

"I'm sorry to bother you," I said and started to leave.

"Now wait a minute," my uncle blared, "you sneak into my house at the ass crack of dawn-"

I interrupted, "It's not even midnight."

"I'm old," he excused himself. "Midnight is late for a guy like me."

"Midnight is hardly dawn," I said.

"Regardless, you have some explaining to do. What's going on?"

I sat on the sofa across from him, unable to meet his gaze. We sat in anticipating silence for at least a full minute. It was amazing how 60 lousy seconds seemed like an eternity.

"Do you ever miss Dad?" I randomly questioned not knowing why. I hadn't talked about Dad in depth with Uncle Jeremy for over a year. Uncle Jeremy never brought him up either except with a mention here and there.

He ran his fingers through his hair awkwardly. "He's my brother," was how he answered. He was like a deer caught in headlights. I felt guilty at his discomfort.

"And he was your friend," I pointed. Uncle Jeremy nodded. "Do you think about him a lot?"

He shrugged. "He's my brother," as if that was explanation enough.

"Do you ever go to the cemetery?"

"Now and again. Sometimes in passing." I may have detected a hint of sorrow in his brown eyes. He wasn't the type of guy to show he cared. His only weakness was Rorie. Nobody could resist Rorie- her laughter was like a symphony.

He looked at me sincerely, "I was there yesterday. The flowers were a nice touch."

"Spring must be early," I said.

"No, the pink ones. Was it you who left them?"

I shook my head. I never left flowers at Dad's grave, only Henri and Clydes', and I hadn't even done that for a while. I made a mental note to do so. I'd been a bad big sister.

"No." The anxiety started to form inside of me.

"Well, someone had just put them there. They were fresh. Think maybe your mom stopped on by and left them?"

I snickered. "Are we thinking the same person? Nicole St. Germaine?" I didn't expect an answer. "The only person she'd get anything for is herself."

"Well, who do you assume it was then? It sure as heck wasn't me. Pink flowers," he muttered. "Why pink? Why flowers anyway? They just sit there and eventually die; no one gets to really enjoy them."

"It was a woman," I said. "Only a woman would get pink flowers."

The women in Dad's life crossed my mind. Who randomly thought of my father one day and went to visit his spirit as if he had one at all? People like him didn't last long and neither did their souls. There wasn't any room for assholes in the afterlife.

"Well, regardless, your dad ain't dead to someone out there," Uncle Jeremy speculated. I twitched my eyebrows with ingratitude at who my father was and who on earth would see him as respectable. Everybody knew about what he'd done.

"Did my brothers have pink flowers too?" I couldn't help how confrontational I sounded when I wasn't that at all. I tried to contain the quiver in my voice.

I shouldn't have asked. I knew the answer.

My uncle looked sincere. I scolded myself for bringing up his little nephews. "No," he answered softly.

I wanted to go. I stood to leave but I didn't move. The childish part of me had always wanted someone to convince me to stay, someone to remind me that even if I left they still loved me. Uncle Jeremy just sat with his head bowed. I waited another second or two then I bid him farewell before heading out the door.

Veronica Christopher

I drove out of Little Bethlehem and toward Prescott Notch. I wanted to see what hope looked like and remind myself losers still had something to aim for.

As soon as I entered Prescott Notch I could tell the difference in class. I yearned for one of the houses in town with a sprawling lawn and a view to die for. Lil Beth was just as pretty as Prescott Notch and Eastman Valley- it was the people and their neglect that made it ugly.

I couldn't stop thinking during my ride. I turned down every side road I came across, desperate to fill the time. The thought of returning home frightened me. I wasn't in the right state of mind. I felt off, unbalanced. Home, along with my uncle's cellar, was too much to bear. The tears wanted to gush but I wouldn't let them. I'd do whatever it took to keep the liquid contained within the lids.

Without realizing it, I was close to the Huntington's road. Naturally they'd be asleep. Only stragglers like myself were up at this hour. It was 3am- only wildlife roamed. They were the reason I never wandered the woods at night. I never went further than the backyard. There were too many trees, hills, and strange noises behind my house.

Unable to control my emotions, my eyes watered up and I struggled to see the dark road through the blur. I blinked hard and caught the sight of a mailbox just in time to swerve. My car went far left and I swerved again to miss a ditch off the side of the road. I turned the wheel too hard and ended up in a grassy dip. I braked harshly and jerked forward as my car came to a stop.

I clutched my steering wheel and let loose. 'Sweet Home Alabama' blasted from the stereo. Salty sadness rushed down my cheeks, outlandish noises escaped my body, mucus poured out of my nose and dangled off my top lip. I felt weak; I couldn't repress my despondencies any longer. It'd been a long time since I broke down like this.

I wanted Bret. Despite all the immorality of what had been done, I yearned for him. I needed to feel his skin, the muscles on his arms, the prickle of his manly chin. I needed to hear his deep voice let me know that he'd always protect me and save me, not only because I was his little sister but because he loved me completely. But Bret wasn't that kind of guy. He'd never let me know that if he even felt it. I couldn't bear the thought of seeing him again yet it scared me to ever be away from him.

The car was hot or maybe I had just overheated so I stepped outside. I bent over and coughed so hard I almost puked. The cold breeze increased my nausea. I scurried around the floor of my car to find a half-empty water bottle. I drank it in one sip in a manner of one who'd been lost in the jungle for a week. It helped to stop the coughing but not the tears.

In the background, Lynyrd Skynyrd blended in with 'Behind Blue Eyes' by The Who. It made me cry even harder because I was the sad man, I was the bad man behind brown eyes. My bum hit the ground with an uncomfortable *thud*. My legs couldn't hold my weight any longer; they'd carried enough in their time.

I wasn't even 21 yet and I felt well into my 40s. I just sat there, like a baby, on the side of the road next to my car with only the sounds of wind and The Who around me. It was a miserable moment. I hated that I endured it alone.

My car idle and smoke exited the exhaust in hesitated spurts. I didn't give a shit if it ran out of gas or the battery died. I'd just sleep here and get a ride from Sara Huntington's mother in the later hours of the morning.

My car stuttered then struggled to stay alive. I quickly switched the ignition back so that just the battery was on. Still, Cherry barely managed. I should have gotten up and turned her off completely but I couldn't- I needed the music.

I finally stopped crying after a couple of songs and wondered what time it was. The sky was a light blue decorated with gray smudges of clouds. I could tell dawn was near. Roosters would be hollering soon.

Sleep threatened to come several times but each time I narrowly fought it off, eager to see the sun rise, eager to see something beautiful. I rolled on my side and tucked my hands between my legs. My eyes rolled in the back of my head and my lids slowly lowered. I mumbled silently "sun rise, sun rise...."

Beauty never came, darkness did instead. I never got to see the sun rise majestically into the heavens, only dreams I hadn't dreamed in a long time. Dreams never made sense and neither did this one. I was in it, the old me. How I was, how I'd never be again. It was a good thing *and* a bad thing- either way, it haunted me.

CHAPTER 10

I'd waken up to Rorie crying. She was less than a year old, little and pink. We'd lost Henri a few months prior and the family was still coping. I heard Mom in her bedroom yelling for Rorie to shut up. Dad was in the kitchen, pots and pans clanking around, as he cooked breakfast.

I got out of my bed quickly and slipped two small, cold feet into fuzzy pink slippers. I went through Rose's room to get to Moms. Rose was still asleep, not caring her alarm had already gone off a couple of times.

Rorie squirmed in her crib, blanket wrapped around a tiny chubby leg. She was 'Sephora' when she was a baby. We didn't call her 'Rorie' until preschool when other kids somehow found 'Sephora' hard to spell. 'Rorie' proved less complicated.

Mom looked agitated propped up against her headboard, a stack of pillows behind her. Her hair was a mess and the previous days makeup smudged underneath her eyes. Clyde was still asleep in the bed beside her, spooned against her side.

It was a normal morning in the house. Dad was his normal self. Rose, as usual, slept in late and made us tardy for school. I'd left Rorie in the playpen in the living room like I always did before I head off to run after the bus with Rose. Of course, we didn't catch the bus and had to turn around to beg Dad for a lift.

School was normal. The ride home was normal too. The bus driver, Ed, who jokingly referred to himself as 'Right Said Ed', cracked his usual jokes and told his usual stories. Kristy yapped on and on about her brother and his friends and how they always talked about girls. Kristy and I weren't old enough to sweat over boys yet minus the usual kid-crush here and there.

It was when the bus pulled up to the house that the normalcy stopped. Mom and Dad were in the front yard yelling and throwing things at each other. I could hear their voices inside the bus. The other kids seemed interested in what was going on in my front yard. My yard held a lot of excitement recently. Henri had fallen from the window only months ago and our house had been surrounded by law enforcement, spectators, and news crews for days straight.

"Fuck," I grunted when my feet stepped off the bus step and onto concrete.

Rose stepped onto the ground beside me, "I'm so sick of this shit."

I nodded in agreement and the bus pulled off. That day Ed didn't honk his horn with two quick 'toots' as he drove away. He knew the vibes weren't right.

Rose walked forward with a steady pace and, as her head hung low, she went straight past the commotion and into the house.

Dad wanted to leave. His stuff was already packed. Some of his bags were already in his truck and some hadn't yet made it that far. They were under hostage with an infuriated Nicole.

He'd even moved his broken-down ATV into the bed of his truck underneath a healthy pile of trash bags filled with other possessions. That thing hadn't worked in years and he kept it around saying it was his next project. I couldn't imagine he'd take it with him if he didn't intend on staying away.

It confused me how Mom screamed for him to go and, when he tried, she hollered for him to stay. I didn't understand how you'd ever beg someone to stay when they didn't want to. I couldn't understand how two people who fought so much and seemed to resent each other would stay together. Sometimes love wasn't strong enough.

Sometimes someone had to be the bigger person and walk away. Neither Mom nor Dad ever walked away for long. Yet this time Dad had packed more than just one bag. I somehow knew he would never go back to that house, to Mom.

She was beautiful, sexual, sensual, exotic, everything a man desired, but she wasn't enough on the inside to keep people around her for too long. She didn't have enough substance. Eventually, everyone left Mom and I would too someday. Misery loved company and she was miserable.

"Get your ass inside!" Mom ordered when she noticed me standing at the end of the driveway, exactly where Ed had dropped me off. My feet quickly moved and I fled straight to Rorie. Rose sat at the kitchen table with a whimpering Clyde on her lap. The tension in the house was heavy. I'd known anxiety from a young age.

I crept out the kitchen door into the back yard. Mom was crying and begging Dad not to go, to stay here with her, with the family, with the children who loved him so much. He wasn't yelling anymore. Quite possibly he'd succumb to the sight of her overcome with agony and tears.

A beautiful woman on her knees whimpering could soften any man, or any man that was worthy enough to be called such. His voice was a masculine stream of mumbles. I tiptoed closer to the scene. I'd found a rock to sit on behind a cluster of trees in direct view of my parents.

She was on the ground, crying as if he'd died, wrapped around his legs. It was hard for me, even as I sat there with a fresh welt on my left inner-thigh from when she beat me with Dad's belt two nights before, to sit there and watch her cry. I wanted to rush to her, wrap my arms around her, and cure her of every ache, pain, and hurt unlike she'd ever done for me.

I watched Father explain to his wife why he had to go. I experienced sensations inside myself I hadn't yet felt before and they were confusing to me at 11. They were hard to describe, hard to comprehend, too adult for the likes of myself.

I knew at that time that life had more downs than ups. I shouldn't have cried so much. I shouldn't have lost so much sleep at nights so entangled in my own thoughts and dreams of a happy tomorrow. I shouldn't have had to wear so much cover-up I'd stolen from Walmart to conceal the bruises and scrapes I'd borne at the hands of my own mother.

She usually hit us in ways that couldn't be seen though. She'd smack us against our heads over and over again with her hands but mostly with objects to knock some sense into us. It never did though. It just left knots hidden underneath a carpet of dark brown.

SPILLED MILK

Usually she punished us with Dad's leather belt. Only she didn't use the belt part as much as she used the buckle. She'd smacked me only a few times on my behind as usually I lost my breath and collapsed against the cold bathroom floor after a good three or four strikes. She wanted to hurt us but not in a way that would get her into trouble or get us taken away from her.

No one could know. I wanted to tell people so many times that Mom hurt me but I couldn't. I could only tell Kristy; she was the only one who understood.

I didn't want Dad to go. I knew Mom would go mad and hit us more if he wasn't there to eventually say we'd had enough. He was my father; wasn't he supposed to stay in the house with us for simply that fact, if for no other reason?

Mom finally stood with his guidance. She reached around his neck and pulled him to her. I couldn't tear my eyes away as Dad tried to resist her. Soon, they were naked and rolling around on the ground.

I felt ashamed watching their sex act but I was secretly intrigued. It was crazy how sex affected men and benefited women. Even at that age, I'd made a mental note and would reference that moment frequently in the upcoming years.

I silently urged Mother to stop, to let him go. I wanted him around but I wanted him far. Jack made me feel dirty. He made me feel that way with how he pulled my friends into his bedroom when they were over and closed the door. I never knew what went on in his room, only that I wasn't allowed in and neither was Rose. He said he was just talking and playing games with them. One of my friends told me that my father had spanked her butt once and asked her to spank his. I never asked her if she did. Rose knew about it too. She just never brought it up. She and I had that in common.

Eventually Mom and Dad got dressed and he drove away to live his new life in his brother's house on the edge of town. Mom stood in the yard for a long time and stared off into the distance, her arms firmly around her chest. I wasn't sure what she felt. I wasn't sure if she felt abandoned or if she felt a huge weight float off her petite shoulders. I supposed even if I asked her I'd never know.

I snuck back into the house as I saw Mother head toward the front door. I didn't want her to know I'd been outside and that I had seen and heard too much. Rose was in the living room tending to Rorie and Clyde. The lights from the television screen flickered off of Rose's face. She looked stoic, lost. Clyde was in a playpen at her feet and nibbled on colored plastic blocks. Rorie squirmed around in her bassinet by the basement doorway. She wasn't happy and started to squeal.

The days dragged after Dad left. Once the two-week mark hit I knew he had moved out for good. Rose let me know he'd called one day and checked up on us. He wanted to make sure Mom was taking care of us and that we had food in the fridge. Dad was happy, he said, staying with Uncle Jeremy. I worried that our uncle wouldn't have a reason to visit us anymore.

Mom was more irritable and slept most of the days away. Rose had to learn to get up early to take care of baby Rorie who Mom started to ignore and little Clyde who was too active for Mom to have patience with. Rose never complained at first but, after a couple weeks, she was grouchy all the time.

She griped about how she was a human being and needed
sleep. She moaned that she was 13 and wasn't the mother. But
no matter how much she deplored her new situation she
always followed through with us. She played her role in not
only womanhood but parenthood.

Rose made sure I made it on time for the bus because she
couldn't drive and Mom wouldn't leave her bedroom to do so.
She made sure we all ate enough and she saw Dad often who
made sure we had food, including baby formula for his
youngest daughter. Dad also gave Rose spending money so
that we could get the little extras like new notebooks for
school or shoelaces for aging sneakers.

He sent Clyde candy bars and little toys he'd found at
stores in town. All he sent to me were his kisses and I didn't
want his kisses. They caused me discomfort. I would have
rather had a couple dollars so I could get a snap bracelet I'd
been eyeing at the market at the end of Sandman Road; it was
bright orange with black polka dots all over it.

I didn't like school so much anymore either. I felt like
everyone was looking at me as if they knew I wasn't even
good enough for my own father. I was embarrassed when I
had no reason to be. Fathers left their children all the time,
even around here. Besides, what did I care for? There were
enough rumors about my family to circulate for a lifetime.

One night when I dreamed and remembered it I dreamed
of him, of Jack. I smelled his cigars even in my sleep. I was in
my uncle's basement. It wasn't dusty and drabby while it was
still in use. I was a part of how it was still put to use.

Rose sat in a chair in the corner, a black box in her hands.
Dad stood tall; his silhouette blocked out the light from the

narrow window. He looked like a bloodcurdling beast- the kind that lurked in basements, territorial, that hunted scared little kids and befriended those that weren't in order to recruit them to the dark side.

Dad called me to come closer, *"Am, hey Am..."* The echo started off quiet and the tone increased with each second until it finally exploded and hushed. He just stood there as I continued to sit. His mouth moved and I could see his lips spread, close, pucker, then open in an 'O' as he spoke my full first name. I shook my head at him. He beckoned me again with more intensity. I grew more and more nervous with each second.

He looked away from me. His profile showed a large nose with a bump on the bridge from all the fights he'd gotten into and from all the accidents been in. His dark lips moved differently. This time the echo started high-pitched and loud then faded to a chilling whisper. He spoke a name but I didn't know what it was. I froze in panic, unable to comprehend what was happening and what Father was saying.

A door opened, then footfalls sounded. My toes scrunched up so that the knuckles turned white and a charley horse started to form. I jumped up to escape but I was frozen. Some unseen force held me in place. I tried to cry out for help but no sound came out of my throat no matter how much effort I put forth. The more I tried to scream, the more it hurt to do so.

I was suddenly so woozy but the footfalls grew closer. I felt the urge to scream again and tear the hair from my head. Tears streaked my face. I blinked numerous times in order to see through the blur. A shadow stood right before me. It wasn't my father. Jack stood where he'd always stood and Rose sat where she'd always sat.

Cold, clammy hands cupped my chin and forced me to look up. All I could make out was a male outline. I opened my mouth to scream again. I tried mightily but nothing came out; it drove me wild. I couldn't hear myself. All I could hear was the sound of father's laughter blend in with Roses'. They mocked me until I could take no more and I finally gave in to what they asked of me.

I didn't want them to cast me away. I wanted to be welcomed into the arms of their love.

CHAPTER 11

I clocked in at work exactly seven minutes early. Frank was proud of me. He double, triple, and quadruple-checked the clock to make sure he wasn't hallucinating. The day seemed to slip right on by. We actually had customers; four of them- two girls in their tweens who caught the latest high school dancing movie and an elderly couple who checked out the new love story that came out a couple weeks prior. The love story made serious bank during its opening weekend.

At the end of the shift, Frank offered to follow me home to make sure I made it all right. I had almost nodded off a couple of times at work. I assured him I'd be okay, that Lil Beth was right around the corner. He hesitated at my denial and got into his car. I wouldn't be surprised if he followed me anyway.

I was eager to get home that night. I made it home just in time to catch Rorie at the fridge chugging Barq's root beer from the bottle.

"Hey, babygirl," I greeted and pinched her cheek. She hated when I did that and said it made her feel like a little kid, to which I retorted that she *was* a little kid.

"I was just up to get a drink," she explained when I reminded her it was almost 10:30.

"Soda?" I shook my head at her. "Caffeine isn't exactly a nutritious refreshment before bedtime."

She screwed the cap back on and placed the two-liter on a shelf in the refrigerator.

"You have milk," I scolded and then later realized I had forgotten to pick up a gallon the other day when she had told me we ran out. Leave it to Rorie to remind me that I had forgotten. I told her that she should have reminded me to get it and she replied, "I'm 10. It's not my job to tell you more than once to get milk. You know I need it for my cereal."

I laughed and promised I'd grab some in the morning. "Now get to bed, K?"

"K," and she scurried up the back stairs to her bedroom to rest her pretty little head.

I followed right behind her and crawled right into my bed. It wasn't long before I passed out. The last thing I remembered before the darkness came was silently blessing Rorie after she sneezed four consecutive times. Her sneezes always came in fours.

When I finally woke up, I only had 20 minutes to get ready before I had to leave for the prison. I congratulated myself on my timing as I hadn't even set an alarm. I was jittery with excitement and nervousness.

I dashed around my room and threw on my best clean outfit. Laundry hadn't been done in a while. I was thankful I had enough outfits to last a few weeks. I was a clothes hoarder. My weight fluctuated so much that I never tossed my old clothes if I grew out of them because I never knew when I'd grow back into them.

Once I left my bedroom, I inspected Rorie's and learned she'd already left for school. I didn't even get to kiss her goodbye and it bummed me out. I found a page of notebook with scribbles all over it and tore off a corner to jot down a quick note to her in case she beat me home: *Hey R, I missed you this morning. Hope you had a good day. Let's play Trouble tonight. Love you, A.* I left a kiss mark with my fuchsia lipstick on the bottom where I wrote a small 'xoxo'.

The traffic introduced itself the closer I got to Sanford. It was a sunny day and warm sunny days attracted more people. I hated traffic; I was guilty of road rage. The parking lot to Peru Prison was even more congested. It wasn't a small lot but there weren't enough spots for everyone.

One of the officers eyed me longer than usual. I eyed him back and swayed my hips side to side as I walked away, knowing he was checking out my back side. I practically felt his eyeballs burning holes through my butt cheeks. When I glanced back at him and found out I was right, he finally looked away after I smiled.

I found a spot on the back of the line and waited for my turn through metal detection. I made friends with a little girl around Rorie's age whose mother looked like an anorexic crackhead with her scraggly hair and cheap outfit. The mother wore pink and gray vertical-striped drawstring pants that hung low on frail, bony hips and a pink top with sheep on it. I told the little girl I liked her moms' pajamas. The mom overheard and sneered at me thinking I was making fun of her, which I was.

The little girl's name was Olivia and I complimented her on her name. "Mommy wanted to name me Bernadette after my grammy but Daddy said that name was stupid, that my nickname would be Bernie and that made him want to puke all over the place." I giggled and glanced at her mother's hair grease again. It didn't bother me too much that she looked like white trash but it did bother me that wanted to name her daughter Bernadette.

I leaned in and whispered to Olivia, "I'm glad you're an Olivia and not a Bernie. Bernie's the name of my old houseplant," and she snickered along with me.

Once her Mom passed through the metal detector my turn was next. I said goodbye to my little friend and told her I hoped to see her around. She called to me, "You should give Mommy your phone number so we can play sometime." I waved at her without giving her mother my number. Olivia made me think of Rorie and I missed her even though she was just at school and I'd see her soon.

I hesitated by the entrance of the large visiting room once I saw Rose at a table waiting for me. She didn't spot me and I noticed her glance at the clock on the wall over and over again. I suddenly felt the urge to leave, to just turn around and jump in my car. It almost became a reality but then she had seen me. Her face lit up and she waved hysterically. I lit up too.

She was better off where she was than with us. Maybe it was being with us that drove her crazy in the first place. The judge had determined that Rose was of sound mind and body when she pulled the trigger. Pleading insanity would never go over well. I had hid in my room during her entire trial, so Rose had no character witnesses to speak on her behalf, to convince his honour otherwise.

I felt self-conscious as I walked over to her table, as if she was studying me. I'd never felt judged by Rose but I did then.

175

As soon as I was a good five feet from her my skin broke out in goosebumps.

"Baby," she greeted and stood as if to hug me. I wanted so badly to be in her embrace. We both knew at the slightest touch, I'd get booted out and she'd get searched as soon as I left.

When she first got to prison she had to be in protective custody; no one was an aficionado of patricide. Parents brought us into this world and it was never expected that they'd be taken out by the hands of their own children. She was in P.C. with other women- women who'd killed their children, women who had raped or molested young children, and those who killed close relatives.

One woman in prison that Rose had told me about was Mary Claire. Mary Claire was highly respected in Peru. If Mary Claire didn't like someone, no else could either. Don't let her name fool you- she was a savage.

Another reason everyone respected Mary Claire was that she killed her handicapped grandfather who deserved it. Her grandfather had molested her son since he was two years old. It went on for six years. The boy cried every time someone tried to change his diaper as a baby and when he got older, to the toddler stage, he acted up a lot and threw violent fits.

His sphincter was frequently red, raw, and would sometimes bleed. That should have been a dead giveaway as to what was happening. Mary Claire found out her grandfather had sodomized her son with different objects throughout the years- his penis, a broom stick, a 20 oz. of Mountain Dew, his wife's purple dildo, the dog.

SPILLED MILK

Mary Claire held the grandfather hostage for three days and starved him. She ordered Chinese food and pizza and ate it right in front of him. She dripped pizza grease on his lips and mocked him as he licked it in an insatiable frenzy. She fed him urine to drink- her urine, not his own. She played pornography all day long- most often kiddie porn she'd dug up just for that occasion, and tortured him every time he looked or grew aroused.

She thrilled in that torture and loved it every time she plucked out a pubic hair, every time she crammed sewing needles underneath his cracked yellow toenails, every time she cut him with a razor blade and spat or pissed on the cuts afterwards.

It turned out the UPS guy had heard him crying out in pain one afternoon while delivering a package in the neighborhood. It wasn't until the cops showed up in the front yard that Mary Claire had enough. She took out a hammer and smashed him all over his body, from his feet up to his crown. She hit him over the head a good 50 times before the police finally busted in.

His face apparently looked like ground beef. He had been dead a while before- probably with the first hit to the temple. The Russian Dnepropetrovsk Maniacs would've recruited her in a heartbeat.

Her son had been in the other room the entire time, quiet as can be, hiding under his bed. The cops found him eyes wide open, lips shaking with fear, tears and snot all over his face. He was in bad shape. She probably fucked him up even more but, in her eyes and many others, justice was served. She offed the pedophile who had corrupted her little boy. No more red, bloody, raw ass hole for him.

Rose was different. Rose was still pure regardless of what she had done. Something had to have taken place that was so bad she felt she had to save herself, or save us. I wondered if Kristy's family had felt they got their justice once my father's death was publicized.

I wondered if my friends in elementary school found solace in their older years when they found out. I wondered if the bullet hit Dad out of the blue and he passed right away, or if he saw Rose with the gun in her hand and wondered what he had done that was so wrong. I wondered if he forgave her once he realized what had happened, and who was to blame.

"Hey Rosie" I greeted my older sister and smiled. We sat down in unison. "How goes the battle?"

She shrugged her shoulders, "The usual humdrum. Trying to occupy my boredom. I can only read so many Harlequin romance novels without them all seeming the same. The dudes they put on the covers make me want to barf." Apparently she wasn't a fan of Fabio look-alikes.

I laughed. "So how's your cellmate?" and we small-talked about her celly for a bit before trailing off onto other random topics. As the moments ticked by and the clock let me know our visit was only so long, I grew more and more anxious. I didn't have much faith in myself that I'd talk about what I wanted to. It was easy to dream up a scenario but it was another thing to actually go through with it once you were faced with it.

"Do you ever think about him?" I questioned. I wasn't sure how I found the strength to ask.

SPILLED MILK

She paused briefly before answering, "How could you ask me that? I'm reminded of him every day," and she glared distastefully at the walls of the visiting room. Naturally she'd think of him each and every single day for the rest of her life. He was the reason she was here. Or was she the reason?

"So am I," I said. "I'm reminded of him every time I look at Rorie's face. She looks so much like him. She looks more like Mom like she always has but, as she's growing older, I can see Dad more and more. I think by the time she's a teenager, she'll look more like Dad than Mom." Rose smiled softly in remembrance of her youngest sister. "She has Dad's mouth. She has his feet."

She laughed, "Wonder if she'll inherit his hairy big toe." I laughed with her. We used to make fun of Dad every time he took his socks off. He grew an unusual amount of hair on only his big toes and they were long black hairs, and his feet reeked. We called him Sasquatch Feet. He didn't mind; he went along with it and would make Bigfoot howls at Rorie who'd giggle like there was no tomorrow.

"Do you think of our mother?" I asked.

She didn't know how to reply. She sat back against her chair and crossed her arms.

"Does she think of me?" Rose retorted. I wasn't sure what I detected in her tone. I wasn't sure I'd heard it before. "Does she even talk about me?"

She assumed her own conclusion. She threw her right hand in the air in an exaggerated gesture and smacked it on the table between us, "Of course she doesn't talk about me or think about me." Rose was agitated at Mom; there was a lot of resentment. "Does she write me? Did she ever answer any

179

of my calls? It's like I don't exist. She forgets about her children so easily."

It saddened me that Rose knew her mother didn't cared, that her own mother didn't support her. Nicole St. Germaine was torn. Who did a wife defend in circumstances such as these- her dead husband or her jailed daughter?

What could I say to soften the blow? What could I say to assure Rose that she was still something in the eyes of the woman who had given her life, without it being a lie?

"Well," I began cautiously, "do you still write to her? And I don't ever hear that you called."

She shook her head. "Why should I? She owes me."

I agreed with bombast. "She owes each and every one of us."

"No," my sister looked dead serious, "she *owes* me. She is indebted to me." Then she stopped. It drove me mad.

"How?" I asked; Rose had taken away her husband. "I bet Mom feels the same. We both know she's selfish and doesn't own up to her mistakes but she did lose her partner and a child, a couple of children actually. Even if she is a bitch, I like to tell myself that she felt that loss, that she still feels it today. She can't be that insensitive to not miss you."

"She didn't lose a husband that day," Rose commented in a manner that was addressed to herself, a thought spoken aloud but a thought she wanted me to hear nonetheless. "He left her long before."

She studied her fingers and gnawed on her pinky nail. I could have been mistaken but she looked satisfied. Rose stopped chewing on her nail and leaned in closer to me. She didn't frown. She didn't smile. She simply began to speak nonchalantly, intentionally.

"He loved me best," she said. "Mother thinks he loved her best but he didn't. He told me so. He told me that since I was a little girl. Mom couldn't take care of his children the way I could. I took care of everybody. She hated how Henri and Clyde and Rorie loved me the most, more than they did her. She hated how Daddy loved me above her, how he always defended me above her. She hated it."

I looked to my side and focused on a spot of some man's shirt. I had to remind myself to breathe. I didn't know how to feel or why my heart skipped a few beats.

It was a different kind of love, the way Dad felt about Rose- a paternal love. The love he had for Mother was romantic. I pushed the thought away that maybe Rose confused the two. It'd be normal for a parent to love their kids more than they did their spouse. I loved Rorie more than I loved anybody else, more than I ever would. But the way Rose described it, it made me queasy.

"Dad always loved you best, out of all of us kids," I confirmed. "We all saw it. Even Bret, who should have been the one getting most of Dad's time, saw it. Dad should've been taking his son out to kick a ball or do outdoorsy things but, instead, he was always with you." I resented that; Rose basked in it.

"He loved us all," Rose chimed in, a bit of pleasure in her demeanor.

"Yea," I said condescendingly, "But you were his little favorite. Wonder why," I contemplated.

Rose immediately grew defensive. "What is that supposed to mean?"

"I don't know," I said, surprised at her reaction. I hadn't really meant anything by it. "What *does* it mean, Rose?" My question caught her off guard. "Why do you still defend him?" I had to ask as my heart pounded with each second of the clock. *Three, four, five, six...* "You weren't so defensive of him when you shot his brains out. He had a closed-casket funeral because of you."

She wasn't taking any of my shit. "Is that why you came, Amber? To harass me? To throw questions at me and expect me to come up with answers that'll please you? I know what I did. I was there, remember?" I hated myself at that moment. "You weren't there," she pointed emphatically. "You weren't there, Am. I WAS."

I didn't know how to proceed. I was too uncomfortable. I felt I could have exploded at any moment. One more word about Dad I could crumble.

Our time was almost over. Rose noticed a couple of people departing at a neighboring table. She wanted me gone but she didn't want to see me go.

"I love you girls," my older sister said softly. "Don't ever, for a second, think otherwise. I think of you guys every single day. I love Bret even if he never wants to see me again. What I did, I did for you kids. I would never have done it if I didn't have to."

I couldn't take my eyes off of her. She was so composed. I admired her so much for that composure.

"Will you ever share those reasons with me?" I asked. It would be unfair to rush her. The planning of Pearl Harbor took time. Rose's revelations would too.

"Someday. When you're ready."

I was offended. "I've *been* ready."

"No," Rose shook her head, "you're not. No offense, little sister, but you have a ways before you're ready." She studied me. "You don't remember *any*thing?"

I was confused beyond belief. "What?"

She didn't answer me. She feared she said too much and she hadn't really said enough.

"I remember a lot," I pitched in, in assumption her reference related to our childhood- Mom's beatings, Dad's perversions. "What else is there to remember?"

Her face said much.

"What, Rose?" I persisted. I was on the edge of paranoia.

"Nothing. Just forget it, Amber. I didn't mean anything by it."

"What do you know?" I was near hysterics. My sixth sense detected so much more than she let on, so much more that I needed to know, that I should have known.

An announcement echoed throughout the hollow visiting room on the loud speaker that visiting time was over in five minutes.

"I know I love you," she said. "I know Dad didn't deserve what he got. I know Mom's not fulfilling her part of the bargain. I know I fucked Rorie up by what I did. I know I fucked you up, too, and I know by the way you're looking at me that you'll never admit it. I can tell you're not okay with this yet. I can tell a lot of things about you, little sis."

183

I was sick of her examining me. "Can you tell that I don't give a fuck anymore? I'm going to pack all my shit and find a one-bedroom apartment somewhere far away from here and start a new life. I'm going to change my name and forget everything about this fucking place. Can you tell that?"

"You're not serious," she threatened. It ticked me off. A guard reminded us to wrap it up.

I stood up; she didn't. "I'm fucking serious, Rose. You ran away from your responsibilities. It's not my job anymore. You don't care, I don't care. You can have Daddy's love. I don't fucking want it. I never wanted it, not like you did. You were never your own person," I ridiculed, "you were the shadow in your father's footsteps."

Her eyes narrowed.

I didn't know what to say, how to feel. I couldn't deny the shame I felt in degrading her considering the circumstances. I couldn't pity her or anyone else anymore. If nobody else in my life gave a shit about what happened in the past and what would happen tomorrow then why should I? Why was I so concerned about being Rorie's mother? She had a mother. It was a crappy mother but it wasn't my problem.

"You're just jealous. You always were," Rose said.

I hated her words and how she spoke them. I didn't reply. I only listened before the guard shooed me away. Rose just sat there and mocked me.

"You could never accept it, Amber. *I'm* Daddy's little girl. You were nothing. Why do you think he didn't give a shit about you and did it anyway? Why do you think I helped?" Helped with what?

"You fat bitch," I cursed. The guard wrapped his arms around me. I floated on air. I couldn't hear the guard, only my words and Rose's hideous laughter. "You're a fat, miserable bitch!" Others took notice. I'd caused a scene.

"At least I was somebody's fat miserable bitch!" she called out, finally on her feet. She couldn't let me get the last word. "You were never anybodys! You'll never be anybodys!"

"Fuck you!" was all I could say. I didn't have a comeback to that. She was right and that was hard enough to admit to myself let alone her.

CHAPTER 12

Consumed with guilt, with rage, I drove wherever my instincts led me. I feared they'd lead me to Bret. I wasn't ready to face him yet. I could still feel his saliva on my breasts.

Halfway through the Kanc, I pulled into a viewing spot called Rocky Gorge. There were a few other cars. Tourist season was underway. The weather had cooperated nicely, unselfishly. A couple of cars displayed Massachusetts plates. Our mountains were popular all year round, especially late spring through early autumn.

Tourism slowed a bit around October until the snow began to fall and they came back to ski, tube down mountain trails, and snowboard. If the snow didn't fall on time, although it usually did, ski resorts were busily producing makeshift snow from high-tech snow machines.

I got out of my car and pulled a dingy beach towel from my trunk. It smelled rank. It'd probably been in there since last summer. A dog noticed me walking toward a trail and barked to his owner to let him loose so that he could sniff me out. I nodded to the man at the end of the leash and pat his dog. It tried to jump up and lick me but I wasn't having it.

I hurried past the beach area where a couple and their baby tested the bitter coldness of the water and a couple of other spots where people took picturesque photos. The water rushed down from the mountaintop and looked crisp, refreshing. A woman dared to wade across to a sandbar on the other end. Once she got there she shrieked and shivered in exaggeration toward her boyfriend who laughed at her from the other side. They were happy, in love.

I cut off onto a side trail. I knew a place about a quarter mile down that led to the river's edge, a place that only true locals knew of, a place away from exploratory travelers. The Pemigawasett River was my friend, I knew it well. I'd lived in Lil Beth my entire life and knew these parts. Often, when I was much younger, Dad brought me to a lot of places on and off The Kanc.

He'd been here his entire life and knew it like the back of his hand, better than I ever could. He knew the mountains' secrets, its' tricks. I was still a bit naïve to its beauty and allowed it take advantage of me. I still had a tendency at times to get lost if I strayed from trails even if I thought I knew how to get back.

We were lucky we lived in Lil Beth. It was so close to North Connolly and Temple where there were places to work. Jobs were scant but they existed. We had McDonalds and convenience stores people could find work. If you were lucky, you landed a job at a clinic or the hospital in North Connolly. I wasn't one of those lucky people.

I'd probably work at Movie Magic my entire life as long as I got to work on time and did just enough to not get fired. I'd probably be the female version of Frank. I'd probably be Nancy who worked first shift and lived in her rundown rental in Red Center, barely 50 but face full of wrinkles, self-neglect, and resentment, with four misbehaved children and a disabled husband whose needs took up all of my spare time.

I didn't care where I ended up in my life. I wanted different for Rorie's future. I never wanted her looking back at her life with wishes that she'd done things better. I never wanted Rorie, of all people, to feel second-best. She was my best, my shining golden trophy. Everybody paled in comparison to my baby.

I could picture her when she was older. She'd be the same height as the other girls in the family, about 5'4. She'd keep her dark brown hair long like we all did. Only Rose had wavy hair. The rest of ours was straight and tended to frizz when humid or wet outside. She had big brown eyes with wings for lashes like Mom and I did.

No doubt she was beautiful and would grow even more so as she aged. No doubt boys and men would take notice of her like they did Mother and myself. I worried about that. I had to teach her well and to do the opposite of the females before her.

I had to teach her to save herself for the ones that earned it, to save her love for those who deserved it. I had to make sure she understood that affections were never free. I wanted Rorie to be anything but like me. I wasn't a great role model.

I found the spot I had been looking for and was alone. No one could know this place existed. The mosquitoes had come out and I lit a cigarette to deter them. I placed the stinky blue and white striped towel onto the sand by the rivers' edge and sat down.

It was sunny with only a few puffs of clouds in the sky. The breeze that swept by often was gentle and cool; not cold enough to send me back into the car. The Pemigawasett, what locals called the Pemi, flowed strong where I sat. The foam rushed up against the rocks and boulders that were strewn about in the water. A couple of feet in, past a large rust-brown boulder and a few larger rocks- gray, brown, white- was a pool. It was clear, only a tinted green from its depth, which I estimated to be about five feet or so. A couple of trout swam about.

Despite how pretty my surroundings were, I couldn't shake the feeling of despair. It wasn't the usual despair, like the week before your period when you felt like crying and was depressed all the time. It was a different despair, an indescribable one, one only known via firsthand experience. Everyone had their own story. I surely did and no one else in this entire world had lived mine.

I hated how I hated Rose right now and I hated how she may hate me too. I hated knowing Rorie's fate was up to me. I hated Mom. I hated how Bret was all about himself. I hated how my uncle hid so much. I hated what Dad did to those girls and how I didn't stop him, how I didn't help Kristy.

I hated that she killed herself because of it. I hated how I would never find myself no matter how hard I looked and how I still blamed everyone else for my shortcomings and broken dreams.

After six cigarettes, one joint, and countless minutes spent pondering, I had to go and leave this place. The river and the trees, the gorgeous sky and mountain views made me feel an unbearable sadness, a sadness that wrapped its claws tightly around my stomach and chest. I choked it back as I jumped into my car and fled down the Kancamagus toward Prescott Notch.

Once I reached the familiar road little Sara lived on, I slowed my vehicle in hesitation. I had been a fool to go there. Rorie wasn't even there. What would be my excuse for just showing up?

Their white Mercedes and silver minivan were gone. The house looked lonely. I felt stupid for coming. I felt let down. I pulled at my hair and slammed my wheel several times, screaming my frustrations. I cursed at myself for failing everything, for never amounting to shit, for thinking that people like the Huntingtons would give two craps about a lowlife St. Germaine.

I'd exhausted myself with my antics and lowered my head to the wheel. I clutched it as if I never wanted to part from it. My shoulders shook hard as the dam let loose. I cried and wailed as I may never have before, unlike how I had cried all those times Mom hit, slapped, spat on, strangled, and belittled me or all the times I'd cried at funerals. It was everything in my entire life that had ever hurt me entangled into one ball of sadness.

A loud, frantic knock on the window startled me. I looked up and there stood Heidi Huntington outside of my car. I didn't move. I regretted I'd gone there. I wanted to start the engine and pull away. I wanted to speed home, jump in my bed, and not get up for days and days. But I couldn't leave her. I knew that she wouldn't have left me.

"Amber!" she shouted as I stared at her through the driver-side window. She tried the door but it was locked. "Please, open the door."

I shook my head and cracked the window. "I'm sorry I came. I have to go."

SPILLED MILK

"No!" she shouted louder. "Please don't go. Open the door," she tried to open it again, pulling hard with both of her hands as if it'd magically open. "Please just talk to me, Amber."

I didn't move. I held her in suspense. I felt stupid at having been caught in the state that I was in. I'd never be able to look at her the same afterwards and I feared the reciprocate.

With a small whimper I unlocked the door. Once Mrs. Huntington pulled it open, I fell into her arms. I shook violently and cried uncontrollably as she comforted me. She stroked my hair like Daddy used to after Mom hit me. She stroked my back and whispered "It'll be okay" into my ear. Her knees must've hurt from the gravel on her driveway but she didn't complain nor budge. She just held me and let me get it all out. She knew I needed to find release.

When I couldn't cry anymore and all was silent she stood up and gently pulled me up with her. I looked up at her through the blur. She looked down at me, a small tear coursing down her face, and she smiled as she held my hand in hers. We walked hand-in-hand to the bench-swing and sat down beside each other in serene calmness. There wasn't a single sound, just two human beings engulfed in unspoken understanding.

After a while, her soft voice came, "Whatever you want to talk about, Amber, talk to me about it. I'm here to listen. Say everything you ever held back. Say what you need to. You deserve to be free."

I couldn't look at her. I let her words soak in and they gave me goosebumps. I thought carefully about what I had to

191

say and rearranged the words carefully in my head. I wanted
what I said to have purpose because maybe purpose lead to
closure.

. "Do you mind if I smoke a cigarette?"

"Of course I don't mind. Light it up."

"They're in my car," and off she went to retrieve them. I
watched her walk with the soft sway in her hips and graceful
pace. I hadn't noticed before that she was barefoot. On her
way back, I noticed a couple of small pebbles clinging to her
knees and she had a small trickle of blood on her left shin. I
felt bad about that and wanted to kiss her cuts away.

She sat back down beside me and rocked the swing we sat
on gently. She even lit my cigarette for me and she was the
furthest thing from a smoker. It was small things I
appreciated and I soaked in the goodness of that because it
meant I was human; it meant I was good and I could feel. If
no one else saw that small quality in me at least I did and I
could feel okay about that.

"So, what's up?" she asked after a while. A breeze tousled
her hair.

"I'm sorry I bothered you," I apologized.

"No bother!" she exclaimed. "What's going on,
sweetheart?"

"I saw Rose today," I started. The mention of my sister's
name caused my voice to crack. "It was uncomfortable and
weird. Too much time went by without us seeing each other
and, now that she's ready for visitors again, it's different. It's
like she felt she had to see me again, not because she wanted
to but because she had to. Because she knows I'm lonely and

that I need somebody. She doesn't think I can make it out here alone."

Mrs. Huntington said sincerely, "She sees you because she wants to see you. Maybe she needed that time to herself to think about things. You have to understand her point of view-she made a huge mistake and now she's paying the price, away from you. Honey, that's the part she's got to be most suffering over."

"I don't know what to do with everything that I'm feeling. It's all so bottled up. I have no one to talk to. Everyone I know is just as fucked up as I am. How can they help me? How can anyone help me? I'm so fucked in the head why would anyone want anything to do with me? My own mother wants nothing to do with me. How does that make me worthy? Huh? How am I worthy?"

"You are worthy, darling," she told me, so much promise and meaning in how she spoke it. "We are all worthy, especially you. You may think you're alone in all of this, that everyone's forgotten what you've been through. That's so far from the truth, Amber. Just because years have passed doesn't mean you don't have the right to still grieve. Nobody could survive what you have the way that you have- that's what makes you strong. There is no time limit with suffering."

I didn't know how to reply so I said nothing.

"What else is on that mind of yours?"

"Jesus," I scoffed, "if I spoke whatever was on my mind, we'd be here all day."

"It just so happens I have all day free," she stated in all seriousness and settled back to listen.

193

We rocked forward, backward, for quite a time before I finally spoke again. Heidi didn't rush me or make me feel awkward in any way. She probably had a lot to do inside but she dropped it all for me.

"When I was a kid, I used to dream that I'd get away from this place and do something amazing with my life when I grew up. But what if this is it? What if this is as good as it gets? What if I'm not destined for better?" I had asked it but I hadn't expected an answer.

She replied anyway, "As long as you smile in the thought of being where you are and who you are, wherever you may end up, then it's okay. 'Good' is only as good as you make it."

"But Rorie…," my voice trailed off. "What am I going to do with Rorie?" I looked deep into Mrs. Huntington's welcoming blues. I desperately needed an answer; a logical, honest, hopeful one. "She's special," I practically whimpered, "how am I going to show her a good life if I'm so messed up?"

She loved Rorie well and carefully chose her words. "Rorie is very special. The best you can do for her is to keep on doing what you're doing. Help lead her way in life; help her to do better than those before her. You're a good role model for her, Amber. If only you'd see that. That little girl adores you."

"What about later? When she's my age? When she's 30? Her tomorrows are going to be a result of her todays." That killed me inside. "And *I'm* the one responsible for her todays."

"You take on too much. You put too much responsibility on your shoulders. How does your mother feel about all of this?"

I had to look away to prevent myself from crying again. Mom was always a sore subject.

"Please," I spat, "like my mother gives a shit. If you think she takes care of Rorie, you're wrong. If you think she took care of any of us, you're wrong. She's selfish," was all I could say. "She doesn't care about any of us."

"If you decide to go," Heidi spoke carefully, "you can go and find your way. You shouldn't let your past bind you here unless you want to be here. This isn't such a bad place," she admired the views around us and breathed in the fresh mountain air, "as long as you don't let it take hold of you and who you are."

"I have to take Rorie," I persisted. "I can't leave her with Mom. I can't stay here. I can't go." I wasn't sure if that made sense.

She understood. "If you feel you have to take her, take her. I know wherever you feel you need to go that you're capable of giving her, and yourself, a good life. You deserve so much happiness in this world, you girls. I can't imagine how you fought this battle for all these years all by yourself."

She took my hand in hers and, with her free hand, she held my chin and looked deep into my eyes. Our souls connected, even if for a moment. "You have so much goodness inside of you, Amber. I see it. I've always seen it. If the people in your life who are supposed to show you love don't see it, it's their loss not yours. You have to stop blaming yourself for every little thing that's gone wrong in your family. It was beyond your control. You have to find the one thing that makes you incredibly happy and do it for the rest of your life."

"Like you did?" I pointed. The Huntingtons seemed so settled with their lives and how everything turned out for them. They seemed so satisfied. It was hard to believe they had any demons that lingered in their closets.

"Like I did," she confirmed. She *was* happy with her life. I knew Heidi was decent and good. Her daughter, Sara, wouldn't have turned out so well if she wasn't.

"Did you know my father well?" I asked.

"I did know him," she answered, "but not well. I really only came across him when I was picking Rorie up or dropping her off. I ran into him a few times in town too."

"When I was around Rorie's age… I was in Mrs. Hanscomb's class so that made it fifth grade…I used to have friends over all the time. Henri was two. Clyde was one. Rorie was just a baby. Bret was still at that stupid Boys Home. Dad still lived with us back then. Mom had reverted back to her old ways- drinking all the time and partying with her friends. Rose had already stepped up. Mom was away a lot of nights so Rose and I had the house to ourselves."

I spoke. She just listened. My mind was so clear.

"Dad spent a lot of time in the basement. Rose did too. Our basement's creepy. It's so uncomfortable. I hated being alone upstairs with the babies. Henri had this cry that bothered me. He was such a cute kid but I couldn't stand that cry. Once Henri got going, Clyde would chime in. It used to agitate me. I'd call Mom at her supposed friend's house and she was never where she said she was.

When Rose was in the basement with Dad, I was too selfish back then to want to take care of the babies. That was seen as Rose's job. But in the fifth grade Dad took up a lot of her time.

"So, I'd have my buddies over and we'd play in my room or the dining room. Eventually my friends and I would get bored. Dad would come up and hang with us for a bit while Rose tended to the babies. He used to pat their bums and tell them to pat his. I always just stood there wondering what the heck was happening. I wasn't sure. All I knew was it felt weird. I remembered wanting to vomit every time he did that.

"A couple of my friends giggled at the spanking game but the other ones looked just as uncomfortable as I did. He'd take the girls into his bedroom..." I stopped and watched for a reaction from Mrs. Huntington. None came; she only listened in attentive awareness.

"He'd shut the door and I never understood what was happening. I should have known. I'm a fucking idiot," I cursed at myself, more angry now than sad, "and I fully admit to that." Heidi reached for my hand again but I pulled away this time, wanting to slap myself, hit myself, and yank out my own hair for being so naive.

"He took Kristy in there a lot. Kristy Gregory," I announced and Heidi nodded. The Gregory suicide was well known and frequently talked about. "She was my best friend, you know. One time, and I remember this clear as day, she came out of Dad's bedroom crying. She left without even saying goodbye. Dad didn't come out of the room for the rest of the night. I don't even know how she got home that night. I don't even know what she told her parents when she finally did get home.

"Kristy came over almost every day until that happened. She suddenly made up excuse after excuse why she couldn't come. Sometimes I went over to play at her house but, after a while, Kristy stopped hanging out afterschool and I found other friends to play with. We wrote notes to each other still but it was different. She was so young and she was suffering...because of my father."

Other memories came in bits and pieces. I didn't know if I should talk about them until I analyzed them carefully and made sense of them, or if I should get it all out this one time, so that I wouldn't have to talk about it ever again.

"Amber," Mrs. Huntington said. She squeezed my arm gently. I must've been quiet too long. I must have zoned out with no recollection at all. "Did he ever touch *you*?" she felt she had to ask.

"No," I whispered because he hadn't, not even to hold me for long. All he ever did was stroke my hair after a beating. "Not me." The question made me seriously uneasy. I lit another cigarette and smoked it with purpose. I was sure my lungs would feel it later. I'd already smoked a good quarter-dozen in the short time I'd been on that swing sitting next to the kindest woman in the world.

"Did he ever touch Rose?"

I shrugged again. "All I know is he loved her best. He *always* loved her best. She was Daddy's little girl. I was shit to him. Aren't daughters supposed to be *somebody's* little angel?" I wanted to know.

"You *are* somebody's angel. You're Rorie's angel," she said and I couldn't deny it. I did have her best interest at heart.

I didn't regret going anymore; I saw it as a blessing. When I left the Huntington home that night, I hadn't found freedom or some amazing relief but I found something close enough, something I could live with- I found the truth.

The truth was that I did feel, I did care, that everything I'd been through affected me greatly. I had dwelled on it too long, allowed it to fester. Change was inside of myself- I had to stop letting my past define me. I quite possibly did have a future and maybe the things I'd gone through made me a better person no matter how hard that was to believe.

CHAPTER 13

I slept a solid 11 hours once I got home after my visit with Heidi. I snuck into my house and up to my room without being detected. I hadn't heard Rorie come into my bedroom but I saw her note when I woke up: *Where were you? I missed you! I'm hanging out with Sara today. XO, Sephora.*

No one had called her Sephora in what seemed like forever. She had put a smiley face after her name which I thought was cute. I folded her note and put it into my nightstand drawer alongside Rose's letters. I still read those letters once in a while. They were usually pleasant letters reminiscing about old, fun times.

Bret wrote me a lot while he away at boarding school too. The envelopes were written out to my parents but the letters were always for me. I kept every single one.

When I woke up from my slumber, I was still tired and groggy. I looked at the clock and realized I missed my shift for work. Elvis was surely pissed at me and I left Frank hanging all alone. I felt worse about Frank than I did my boss. I thought of excuses I'd tell Elvis when I finally did show back up for work. I'd make sure he didn't fire me. I'd make him pity me.

The itch for answers propelled me forward towards Uncle Jeremy's house. I scribbled Rorie a quick note just in case she got home before I did. I didn't expect to be out long. Uncle Jeremy probably wouldn't talk about much.

SPILLED MILK

Dad's older brother looked aged; only now did I notice it. He looked worn. The past started to take their toll. He sat on his porch, beer can in hand, and noticed me immediately when I pulled into his drive.

Instead of standing to greet me he raised his beer can high in the air in salute. I tapped my horn and the *beep beep* echoed in the still mountain air.

"Uncle J," I climbed out of my car. "Got something softer for your favorite niece?"

"Softer? Like soda or something? What you want," he joked, obviously drunk, "a lemonade? Milk?"

"Funny," I said and sat down on the porch step by his feet. He sat on a rusty metal chair he'd had for ages. "Like a Smirnoff Ice? Mike's Hard Lemonade? A screwdriver?"

"You know what a screwdriver is?"

I laughed heartily, "I haven't been living under a rock. Of course I know what a screwdriver is."

"Hey, I'm old school," he defended himself. "I'm not hip anymore."

I laughed again. "No one says 'hip', Uncle J."

We snickered away before he got up to go inside and grab me a drink. He came out with a root beer.

"Good enough," and I popped the top.

"You shouldn't know what a screwdriver is, kiddo," he continued. "You're not old enough."

"Please," I said, "I'm going to be 21 in a couple months."

He thought a moment, "It's nuts how much you girls have grown up. It feels like just yesterday you were both running around in pigtails and watching Little Mermaid."

"Aw man, I love The Little Mermaid. Flounder was my dude," I chugged my root beer.

Uncle Jeremy took a man-sized swig from his Coors can. "So, what brings you here? I'm glad you decided to visit like a normal human being this time instead of creeping around my basement at crazy hours."

"Sorry about that," I apologized again. "I still feel weird about it."

"Don't feel weird or anything. You're welcome any time, just at a decent hour and perhaps a knock on the door."

"You got it," I promised. "Anyway, I wanted to talk to you about Rose and Dad," I said, straight to the point. I was sick of beating around bushes.

"What do you want to know?" and I was pulled back by his adherence.

I looked him square in the eyes, "Everything."

"Simplify."

"I saw Rose at Peru. She had a lot to say."

Uncle Jeremy looked slightly uncomfortable. Either that or I was paranoid. "About?" my uncle questioned.

"Something happened as a kid," I blurted. "Sometimes I have dreams about things. It's only snippets but it all feels so real while I'm dreaming it. I wake up in a cold sweat and I can't breathe. I thought maybe I had recurring dreams because I couldn't overcome my childhood but then Rose kept bringing stuff up.

"About how Daddy did something and how she helped him. How Daddy loved her more. I mean, that was obvious; you didn't have to be an idiot to see Dad preferred Rose. But, why? Why couldn't he love all his children the same? Why

202

couldn't we all be equals? But no, it was all about her. Rose, Rose, Rose." I could relate to the plight of Marcia Brady's sister.

He popped open another beer. "Doesn't sound like Rosie to be that way to you." He burped loud. It echoed. "Rosie's usually a nice girl. Wasn't right of her to rub that in your face." He burped again.

"You're so wasted," I commented. His eyes were glossy. He started to slump in his chair.

He rubbed his beard, "Tell me something I don't know."

"Maybe I'll take a beer," I said and he gladly handed one over. I snickered; he was too drunk to notice his slip-up.

"Gracias," I thanked him and sipped on it gingerly, and tried to ignore the awful taste.

I thought long and hard about the pieces of my dreams that I could remember. "Why did Dad spend so much time in that cellar?"

I couldn't look at my uncle. I couldn't see the reaction on his face; I felt it instead. The tension could be sliced with a knife. "Why the basement?" it came out in a whisper. "Why didn't they just hang out in the living room or the kitchen with the rest of us? Why did they have to be alone?"

"What the hell did that girl say to you?" Uncle Jeremy asked. "Why the hell were you suddenly snooping around my house in the wee hours of the morning? You're up to something."

"What *didn't* she say to me? If only you were there," I shrank in the memories of all that she had said. I hoped it tore her apart inside.

"But I wasn't and you're not making any sense-"

203

"Really?" I swung around to him, nastiness in my tone. "By the way your voice is cracking and how you're shifting nervously in your seat I'm making perfect sense."

"What do you want me to tell you?" his voice rose. He put down the beer and lit a fat, damp cigar.

I was quiet in my approach. "I don't remember much about the year my friend hung herself."

"Little curly-haired girl with black hair?" he held his hand up horizontally to represent the height of a small child. "You two used to run around and play 9-1-1 together. One of you would be the operator and the other one would be the victim of some horrible accident. Yea," he nodded. I was a bit shocked he remembered a piece of my childhood so clearly. "I remember little Kristy."

I'd forgotten our little 9-1-1 game. "I was always the operator," I commented. Kristy was good at being the pitiful victim of some horrendous crime. "That was a long year. It was right before Dad moved out." It was a turning point of my chaotic world.

"If you give a shit about me," I held my forefinger and my thumb an inch apart from each other to represent a measurement in which he should have loved me at minimal, "at least *this* much, then please tell me what the hell happened with this family when I was a kid. There is something I blocked out and I need to know what that something is. I have a feeling you can help me."

His silence angered and hurt me at the same time.

The sky was mostly clear with only a few wispy clouds. The moon would rise soon. I had wasted an entire gorgeous day in bed.

"I knew this day would come," he finally spoke.

I sat back down and prepared myself for a journey of discovery.

"I don't know much," he admitted. "Half of what I do know, I really don't know because I wasn't there. I never witnessed it."

"With Rose?" I held my breath.

He shook his head and rubbed his forehead roughly. He looked tired. With every minute, he drooped lower and lower in his chair.

"No, it wasn't like that with Rose. They were just close," he looked at me quickly. "Your sister was very motherly. She was more motherly than your mother was- "

"Is," I cut in. She wasn't just a bad mother before- she still was.

"She took good care of your brothers before they..." he flicked his eyes my way in realization that he'd brought up a sore subject. I didn't react. I could barely even move.

He continued, "Our mother was like that." I didn't know their mother well. Dad married Mom when he was 28 and she was still a teenager, so his mother stopped talking to him. Mom and Dad didn't wed after their first child, Bret, was born.

Instead they tied the knot after their second baby came along, which was Rose. Mom was 13 when she got pregnant with Bret and 15 when she had Rose and finally married Dad.

The story proceeded to unfold, "Rose reminded us of our mother. It wasn't anything sick," he stressed. "Your father was a pervert, a sick bastard I've heard, but he didn't mess with his kid. Nicole used to accuse him of that but she never had any

205

proof. I know my bro," Dad's brother stated with conviction, "he wouldn't do that shit to his own blood."

"To who then?" I asked and nervously passed him a cigarette..

"After your friend hung herself all those years ago, I ran into her brother after the wake. I was never around when, if, your father messed with that little girl. I never directly witnessed a thing but that brother of hers told me she wrote a note that he found when he got home and found her."

I sucked in a lungful of air. Goosebumps rose throughout my entire body. "She wrote a note?" A suicide note was never mentioned. "Why was it kept a secret?"

"He kept it a secret-"

"Eric hid the note?" I asked more to myself.

"Apparently. He didn't want his mother to suffer more. I guess their mother was in pretty rough shape mentally even before it happened. When he got home after seeing his girlfriend, or whoever, he found her and he found the letter. He read it and got rid of it. He never told a soul. It would have been too much."

"He told you all of this?" I asked in disbelief.

Uncle Jeremy nodded. "Yea, I don't know if he threw it away or what the heck he did with it. But he told me after the wake. I swore to that boy, up and down, that I wouldn't tell anyone and I haven't- until today that is. But I trust and believe you're a grown girl, that you'll keep it to yourself. What's done is done. What's buried is buried."

"You went to the wake?"

"Sure," he responded as if he was a relative part of her life, like he belonged. "I never went inside but I heard the ceremony from the doorway." I hadn't even gone at all; me, her best friend. I was too distraught to leave my house when I heard the news on the television- my parents didn't even have the decency to tell me.

"Jack was a pig. He loved all things sex. Women, girls, pure girls, dirty girls, all of it drove him crazy. He had a lot of fetishes. He hid a lot. When he drank or did coke he acted up. It's not like he went around having sex with everything with breasts. He had a tendency towards asses. Sorry," he realized he was talking to his niece, "butts," he corrected. "He used to tell me that Kristy," he took special care in the way he said her name and I respected that, "had the nicest one of all."

"He only said it messed up. Whenever he was sober, he'd say he didn't like them younger than 16. His standards were pretty low. As long as they could legally drive to meet up with him they were fair game. But Kristy was, what, nine or 10?"

"10," I answered. "She was only 10."

Another *pop* sounded in the air as Uncle Jeremy helped himself to another beer. "So that'd mean that your dad liked them younger than 16, wouldn't it? He never admitted it but he did." His words gave me the chills.

"He said he took her into the basement and they'd spank each other. I won't go into details but when he said he liked it, that she was the best at it, I realized that maybe he'd done it before to other friends of yours. I wanted to believe he was talking out of his ass, making shit up, speaking his fantasies out loud. It was the only way I didn't hurt him."

Chunks started to rise up in my throat. "How many do you think there was?"

"How would I know that?" he shrugged and chucked his empty beer can onto his lawn. His yard was trashed with various random objects in ample supply. It was a mini junkyard.

"You know something else I'd like to know," I remarked.

He widened his eyes and raised his eyebrows.

"The note she wrote," I pictured Kristy's handwriting and childlike graffiti, "what did it say?"

Not verbatim, he told me. It was hard to believe what I heard but, knowing my father, I believed every word.

CHAPTER 14

When I pulled into Bret's driveway, his van wasn't there. Instead of sitting in my car to wait for him, I went in. His front door was locked but a window on the back of his house wasn't. I crawled in like a thief in the night.

I stood there in front of that window and watched dust dance in the fading sunlight. The living area was a disorganized mess. Clothes were tossed about his sofa and recliner. Soda cans, water bottles, snack wrappers, cigarette butts, crinkled up pieces of notebook paper and receipts, a stack of mail, a Maxim magazine, and a popsicle stick all littered his coffee table.

I glanced to his kitchen and noticed the same madness. His counters were spotted, his coffee pot held old coffee, dust balls decorated the floor, the sink was full of dishes that smelled so bad it was hard to stomach.

I went into his bedroom and lay down. I smelled his scent on the pillowcase. I dozed off and was awakened by Bret wiggling my big toe. "What are you doing here?" he asked in a way that didn't make it feel like an imposition.

"Hey," I managed to sit upright. "Sorry to barge in on you." I rubbed at my eyes, then followed him into the living room.

He sat down on his chair, "What's up, Am?"

I shrugged. My heart started to race. "Not much. I was bored and wanted to see how you were doing. Where were you?" I asked like a mother or curious girlfriend.

"I went fishing in the river," he said, "down by the bridge." He referred to the small bridge just as you turned off the Kanc and onto the road that led to his place.

"How was the catch?" and he talked about the lone trout he had caught and tossed back in. He offered me food and I declined- my stomach was queasy in his presence.

Looking deeply into my brother's eyes and watching his movements, I wanted the very best for him. I wanted him to forget his past neglect, to know that someone out there genuinely loved him, to find a wife who'd treat him like a king, to find certain happiness, to be all the things he always dreamed of becoming. I had no choice but to address what had happened, to patch it all up and make it better so that we could move on.

"I'm sorry," I blurted. It was now or never. "I was really messed up and lonely." I tried my hardest not to squirm or fidget too much.

He stared at me. "I'm sorry too. All those beers really fucked me up," he explained. "It'll never happen again."

I was embarrassed that he'd seen my naked self. I was embarrassed that I'd felt his, and how I replayed that night in my head as often as I did.

"I feel so weird about it," I offered and knew that it may have changed us forever. "Did you?" He nodded. "Do you want to pretend it never happened?" He nodded again. "Good. It never happened," I assured with a smile.

"Good," he repeated. My body shuddered with chills.

"Alrighty then," I felt the urge to kiss him and have him hold me while I fell asleep. It wouldn't happen. I was paralyzed on his couch and had to force myself back to sleep in order to avoid the awkwardness that stuck no matter how hard we both tried to pretend it wasn't there.

Sunday morning, the sunlight had woken me through my bedroom curtains. On my way to the bathroom for my morning routine I peered into Rorie's bedroom door as she snoozed away and hugged a pillow close to her. A trickle of drool stuck to her chin in a frozen halt. I closed her door completely to allow her uninterrupted rest. She was growing and needed her sleep.

I made myself a bowl of cereal and soaked up some sun in the backyard. An hour later, Rorie ran out in braided pigtails and her pajamas. She still had sleep in her eyes. She looked so cute in the mornings. I pinched her cheeks and told her to plant a wet kiss on mine.

"When did you get back?" she asked and let me know that Mrs. Huntington sent big hugs my way. "She really likes you," Rorie told me. "She said you're special."

"That's nice." I should have told Rorie to pass the message that she was special too.

I told her I'd prepare her a bowl of cereal and would take her swimming at Sawyer's Rock. She was excited. I'd miss my shift at Movie Magic again but I didn't care. Family was more important and I hadn't spent enough time with Rorie in a while. She spent more time with Sara than she did at home.

She scarfed down Lucky Charms and sped upstairs to change into her swimsuit. I did the same. We met back downstairs in the kitchen. I had to laugh at her dressed in her Hello Kitty bathing suit, purple towel draped around her neck, blue swimming goggles strapped to her head.

"You're funny," I commented when I saw the snorkel in her hand and water shoes on her feet. She was fully geared up and ready to go in record time.

"If only you got ready for school that fast," I joked with her.

"Let's go, let's go," she bounced up and down. I could tell I would have a good day with her. We needed this bonding time.

It was still early. The water was sure to be cold still as the Saco hadn't had enough time in the sun to warm up. I packed a book, a notebook and pen, and a couple of folding camping chairs in my trunk. We'd make a day of it. Only locals dared to risk the mountain waters this early on in the year.

Before we head to our spot, I took Rorie to lunch where we had pizza calzones. She got most of it on her bathing suit but she didn't care; she'd be in the water all day and it would wash off. The next stop was the closest convenience store to stock up on a styrofoam disposable cooler, four water bottles, and a couple of sandwiches for later.

Sawyer's Rock was an unmarked spot so only locals, or those who drove by and saw cars parked on the side of the road, knew about it. We got there before noon.

It was an open area with no overhanging trees to block the sun from soaking into the river. It was warmer than other swimming holes. It had a rock people could jump off of into the pool section that was a good five or six feet deep- deep enough for a good swim.

Rorie and I ended up spending the entire afternoon there. We didn't head home until four. During the ride I asked Rorie why she signed her note to me 'Sephora'. She explained that girls in the grade above her wore bras now and makeup.

She said that 'Rorie' sounded childish and 'Sephora' sounded sophisticated. From now on she wanted to be called only 'Sephora' but I refused her; I told her I knew her as 'Rorie' and, therefore, she was 'Rorie'. I became the only exception; no one else could call her 'Rorie' anymore but for me. I had asked if Mom was an exclusion to the rule too and she said no way. I could tell by the way she said it that she and our mother were not getting along again.

When we got home, we snuggled together on the couch and watched a movie. Mom was getting ready for work and was too busy to talk with us. She had a friend with her, a young girl I'd never seen before who kept looking at me whenever she passed the living room. She looked about 18.

My little sister dozed off on my lap during our second movie. I shook her awake and told her it was bedtime. I held her hand and walked with her upstairs to her room. When I tucked her in, she hugged me tight. "Thank you for today, Amber. I had the best time." A simple sentence from a far from simple girl.

"So did I," I said and kissed her softly on her pineal gland.

I sat on her bed and watched her doze off. Her chest rose and set with her breaths. Her toes twitched as deep sleep took her. I stroked her cheek and moved the soft brown hair off her olive-toned face.

She slept with rosy lips in a pout. I gently flicked the bottom lip and smiled down at her. She was so beautiful, still so innocent, so dependent.

Before I could stop it, a tear dropped from my right eye. I laid down next to her and cuddled up close to her allowing her body heat to seep into me. I held her tight with all the love I had for her and prayed to do right by her. Fears overtook me- fears that I may fail her, fears that she deserved so much better and was stuck with me.

CHAPTER 15

Rorie's school year flew by. She only had a month left and would be promoted to the fifth grade. Fifth graders were the oldest in the elementary school and she was excited. The younger kids would look up to her, she'd get seconds at lunch, she would get to go to all of the cool field trips.

I had a scheduled conference with her teacher. I'd bailed on the last couple of meetings I'd planned with this woman and decided since the year was coming to a close I'd better make an appearance.

When I got to the school, it was lunchtime. I signed in as a guest with the main office and followed instructions to Rorie's classroom. The building was small and easy to navigate. Rorie was in the cafeteria enjoying a lunch of a chicken patty sandwich, garden salad, and a whole-wheat roll. The schools had turned to a healthier menu since childhood obesity had skyrocketed in the last few years. The news and doctors called it an epidemic. It took the families of fat kids suing McDonalds for people to finally see that there was a problem.

A homely-looking woman with copper-colored hair and tired, saggy, brown eyes noticed me at her classroom doorway. "Amber St. Germaine?" She only looked pleasant when she smiled.

"Yea," I looked around the room and wondered which desk was my sisters. I looked for any sign of a unicorn, purple, or glitter. All the desks more or less looked the same. I had forgotten the teacher's name. It was Mrs. Something.

"Please," she rose, "take a seat," and gestured to a chair placed in front of her old, chipped wooden desk. I sat and she joined me.

"So," she crossed her hands on the desk before her and smiled at me sweetly which caused the wrinkles to appear prominent around her eyes. She looked about 50. "How have you all been since I seen you last?" I smirked to myself at her use of grammar.

I had not seen this woman since the last week of August when the school year first started and I had walked Rorie to her homeroom. I looked around at her desk for any mention of her name so I didn't feel rude for having forgotten. Her grade book educated me.

"Very well, thank you," I turned the professional side of me on. I represented Rorie and wanted to make her look like she had come from a good home, that the things she'd lived through hadn't scarred her indubitably. "It's so nice to see you again, Mrs. Cypress."

She slid a piece of paper my way. It was Rorie's last progress report. It didn't look familiar yet my signature was on it. At a closer glance, it had been forged.

I read the comments from Mrs. Cypress on the bottom: *Rorie continues to struggle in math and science. Her use of foul language and behavior in the classroom and at recess are troubling. Most of the time she is a nice quiet girl but when she acts up, she concerns me. Please call me to talk about this. I have put her in a special math course to help her improve in that subject and she is working with Mr. Weymouth on her reading comprehension.*

SPILLED MILK

"I never heard from you, Miss St. Germaine," her smile turned into a pout of concern. "I sent a letter home with Rorie last week about the incident on the playground, for you to call me. I understand you're not her guardian but Rorie insists I speak with you instead of your mother. I suppose your mother can't get out of work to make it here?" If that's what Rorie had told her, I couldn't dispute it.

"She never gave me the letter," I explained. If she had, I would have called absolutely. "And I never saw that report card." I glanced at the report that listed mostly C's and D's. Fourth grade used letter grades opposed to the earlier grades who used S for Satisfactory and N for Needs Improvement.

"That concerns me too," stated Mrs. Cypress. The shade of her blouse bothered me- mustard yellow- and how it was buttoned all the way to her neck. She looked stifled. Her black skirt was loose and down to her mid-calf.

I imagined her class was split- half of them probably liked her since she looked like a librarian and the other half probably poked fun at her. When she smiled she had a smear of mocha lipstick on her front teeth that I didn't bother to point out.

I apologized and promised we'd work on her grades. Mrs. Cypress said that it wouldn't matter much since there was only a month of school left and that Rorie had already been promoted to the fifth grade since she didn't get any F's. What should have been an accomplishment, wasn't.

"At home, she's a great kid," I defended because she was. She didn't act up a lot with me. Then again, I was usually off somewhere or working to be with her enough for her to misbehave. Times spent together were getting more and more scarce. It was a wonder the Huntingtons hadn't yet adopted her. Sara would be ecstatic to have her best friend as her sister. Rorie would be better off and I could visit her everyday- Prescott Notch wasn't that far away.

"She's a great kid here too," Mrs. Cypress said, "but she changes at the drop of a hat. With no warning her mood shifts. She goes from Jekyll to Hyde at the blink of an eye."

That surprised me a bit. Apparently, I looked like a fish out of water because Mrs. Cypress stated, "Maybe I should talk to your mother about this."

I was serious when I spoke to her this time. "Speak with *me. I'm* responsible for Rorie."

"Not legally," the teacher disputed.

In defense, "Screw legality. If something is going on with Rorie I need to address it. I'm the one to take care of it," I looked her dead in her plain brown eye. "Help me take care of it."

She weighed the options in her mind and used her words carefully. "Rorie's been using vulgarities on the play yard and she's been drawing pictures and putting them in the bathrooms. I also found this," she reached into the top drawer of her desk and retrieved an Adlib book.

Rorie's teacher flipped open the book made of recycled paper, the pages tinted yellow. I didn't look at it. My brain was stuck on words like 'vulgarities' and 'pictures'. If the pictures were of sunsets, gardens, and rainbows I wouldn't be here. I had to address that before I could move on to this book.

"Vulgarities," I said. That word said a lot but in such little detail. "In layman's terms," I asked for an explanation.

"Swear words, inappropriate topics of conversation, indecent experiments with other pupils, inability to take responsibility of her actions in the classroom in a mature, acceptable manner."

Confusion shifted to flabbergasted.

"You have no clue what I am talking about do you, Miss St. Germaine?" I shook my head. "She's shown no signs at home?"

I shook my head harder, "No."

Rorie's teacher said gently, "Rorie is obviously troubled. She knows too much about certain things, things that she is too young for right now."

"'Certain things'," I repeated. I looked at the doorway and imagined myself running through them as quick as I could. I was positive this woman would not come after me to make sure I was okay.

"Sex," with a drag on the S. 'Sex' as if it were the worst possible thing in this world full of bull shit. "Rorie tells other kids to kiss and touch each other's privates. She flashes the boys. It's all just gone too far."

"Wow," I needed a minute to soak it all in. It didn't matter that she had been taught subliminally and inadvertently; she still knew about it. She was showing boys parts of her body that hadn't had chance to develop yet. I had every right to be concerned.

"When did this all start?" I asked.

"Well, the language, all year. Again, I've sent many notes home with Rorie and I can safely assume you are unaware and did not receive those either." Disappointment with Rorie's lack of trust in me settled in.

219

The woman explained, "She *is* promoted to the fifth grade but I cannot have her in my classroom if she keeps this up. I will have no choice but to move her to the special education wing of the school and finish the year there."

"Give me a break," I spat. "The girl says 'fuck' and 'bitch' a few times and you want to send her to the special ed class? That's how you tell a girl that you're there for her, that you haven't given up on her? Once you get sick of her you can just send her off for someone else to deal with?"

Mrs. Cypress hadn't meant to but she had upset me. Seeing pretty Rorie sitting beside kids in stained clothes, that drooled or shoved pens in their noses, or pissed their pants all day long irritated me. Very much so. My younger sister was such a good cookie once you scratched the surface.

"Well," Mrs. Cypress said, dragging her L's, "it's no wonder that she uses the language that she does. Quite possibly she learned it from home. Quite possibly she's learned *a lot* from home."

I peered at her through two slits. "Tell me more about the pictures she leaves around. What *kind* of pictures?"

The lady before me breathed deep. "Graphic pictures of men and women. Breasts, penises, buttocks, vaginas. She will draw a nude woman and have one of the boys tape it up on the boy's room wall. She'll draw a naked man and pin it up herself in the girl's room.

"She mostly draws penises. She doodles them on her notebook alongside illustrations of butterflies and colorful fish, stars, SpongeBob SquarePants, typical children stuff. It's very odd, as if nudity and sex are natural in her world, as natural as a picture of Patrick Star in a jellyfish field net in hand."

"I'll make sure to talk to her about this when she gets home today."

Rorie's teacher nodded. She rested a hand under her chin to gaze at me. "And the flashing the boys on the playground?"

"Of course," I said. I had fully intended to discuss that.

"What can I do to help?" she asked out of the blue. "If there is anything I or this school can do, let us know."

"I have it under control," I promised. A bell went off and rang throughout the school halls. It was my cue to gladly leave.

When I drove home, all I saw in my mind was drawings of genitals pinned up on the blue walls of elementary school bathrooms. I wondered to myself how an adolescent girl would draw a vagina- an oval with a vertical line down the center or the front view where it looked like a camel toe. I wasn't sure whether to slap her silly or hold her close later. I wasn't sure whether to laugh or hit something.

I knew it was because of Mom. I sped home eager to face my mother and let her know exactly what kind of person she was and how she had managed to taint her little girl. She needed to find a real job, and I'd help her, so that Rorie could have a good role model in her, so that she wouldn't spoil like the rest of us had.

"How the fuck dare you?" the woman wearing bright pink lipstick asked with venom. I backed up. She had already smacked me across the right side of my face, palms wide open, with intended force. "*I'm* her fucking mother!" she slammed her hand on her chest like Godzilla, her face flushed.

"Then act like it," I said calmly. I was ready. I was bigger and stronger now. I could fight her off if I could just stand my ground. "If you acted like it then maybe her teacher would have called *you,* her *mother,* instead."

"You act like you gave birth to her, you little bitch," she hissed. I hated her at that moment, hated her so much I wanted to claw out her eyes. "You act like I owe you or something." If anything, she owed me respect.

I didn't need to give birth to her for me to be her parent. I didn't need to carry her in my stomach for nine months for her to be mine. "I take care of her," I pointed. "I'm the one who will always take care of her. I'm the one who pays the bills in this house. I'm the one who keeps this household running. I'm the one Rorie's teacher calls. I'm the one who goes to the meetings at her school."

She laughed hysterically and looked crazy. "What a fabulous job you did too. Look at her," she spoke of her own youngest this way, "she's a little slut already. I wouldn't be surprised if she's out there fucking the entire town."

A shiver ran down my spine.

"I bet she learned it from you. Look at you," she eyed my outfit, my shoes, my hair, my blue nails with the silver glitter on them, "you look like a skank. She takes after you. She's going to grow up to be a whore too. I'm going to be a grandmother in a few years, just wait and see. You girls are ruining me."

"Ruining you?!" I couldn't help but holler. She smirked, ready for a battle. "YOU?" I mirrored her laughter. I wanted to throw every dirty thing she'd ever done in her face. I wanted to make her feel small, like she'd made me feel small.

She lunged forward. I faltered and wondered if I showed it. I tried with all my might to stay strong against her. She hadn't beat me in years now. Instead of strike me, she came up to me, so close so that I could smell the tequila and feel the breath of her words.

Her eyes were glossed. The left one had a noticeable red vein just like I had. It was the first time I ever noticed it. "You better watch yourself." Her tone was threatening. She'd done all the parenting she felt she had in her.

I cringed at her and wanted to slap her harder than she'd ever slapped me. She could have been so much more had she reached a little further and worked a little harder. She lost her chance but she still had children. She should have worried about *our* chance.

"Rorie's a good kid," I announced. "She deserves a good mother." I regretted having come to her, having told her what I did.

"She's a slut," my mother said and snickered, amused. "You're a slut. Go on," she waved obnoxiously, done with the sight of me, "go play mommy to that little bitch. Go teach her how to suck a cock. Go teach her how to be as worthless as you," she looked me up and down, and sneered the entire time. My shoulders began to droop in defeat.

"When's the slut going to be home?" Mom asked, a hiss in her words.

I didn't say a thing. My bravery shrunk and, like the coward I was, I left as quietly as I could.

223

Mother continued to mutter. I was still within earshot when I heard her say, "That fucking bitch. Stupid, ugly bitch..." I knew she spoke of me. I shouldn't have cared but it hurt. It really fucking hurt.

SPILLED MILK

CHAPTER 16

Rorie got off the school bus in a bad mood after school. Her and Sara fought during recess. Rorie was upset that Sara went off with some of the other girls and wouldn't let her play with them.

"Maybe Sara is just starting her friendship with these girls," I explained, "and wants to get in good with them. She probably didn't mean to be a jerk, Rore. Or, worse case scenario, she *was* being a douche in front of those girls. Just because she acts like that doesn't mean she's blowing you off. Welcome to Girl World," I said and chuckled. Girl World could be brutal. Rorie was still a preteen. Just wait until she was 15 or 20 or 30… It never ended.

Rorie thought over my explanation, "Still. She's *my* best friend. She was mean and I'm still mad at her."

"Fine," I said, "still be mad. But don't be mad forever over such a small thing." I knew what was small in my world could be huge in hers.

I had made amends with Elvis and had to get ready for my work shift. I told him things weren't too great at home and with Rorie, a half-truth, and promised I'd be better. With my background and family past he understood but barked orders to always be on time, do my work efficiently, and to be there every day I was scheduled or he'd be forced to fire me. He reminded me that a no-call no-show was grounds for termination. I strapped on my helmet, took it all on the chin

225

and gave no excuses, just my word that I'd abide by what he asked of me.

Although I was broke and the bills never got paid in full, we had a roof over our heads and food in our bellies. It really helped that Rorie was on the free lunch program at her elementary school so I didn't have to pay out the 15 bucks every week. Her school served her free breakfast too.

Before work I said bye to Rorie, told her to make a ham sandwich for dinner when she got hungry, reminded her to read her book for 20 minutes, and that I loved her so much. She had the number to the movie theater in case she needed me or she needed a distraction from Mom before she left for Glitter.

I drove slowly. When I pulled up to a gas station on North Connolly's Main Street I didn't recognize Carmen's car in front of me. She wasn't in it. I couldn't just drive off. What if she saw me? My car was the only cherry-red Hyundai Accent hatchback with a rear windshield wiper and a bumper sticker of a big band-aid angled on the side of the back bumper.

I counted out seven dollars from my ashtray, mostly quarters I'd put aside for laundry. Laundry would have to wait. Since Mom had sold our washer and dryer, I drove to the Laundromat in North Connolly called Mt. Wash 'n Tan because it was right alongside Mt. Washington and had two tanning booths.

When the Laundromat first went up I found the name creative but now it was just another business inside of a house that rarely anyone frequented.

SPILLED MILK

When cash ran really low I would wash the clothes in the tub and hang them out to dry when it was warm and, when brisk, I'd hang them around the living room on furniture. There would be socks and underthings dangling off of lamps and side tables. Towels would be hung on the shower rod.

Sheets usually hung on the curtain rod in the living room with a plastic garbage bag underneath to catch the drips. Shirts, pants, and other miscellaneous clothing articles laid strewn about on chairs, tables, including the kitchen table, and the sofas. Rorie was too young to care how her clothes got cleaned. Mom did hers at friends' apartments. I didn't hold airs about myself; I wasn't too good for tub-washed clothes.

"Hey," I heard Carmen's voice.

I had my head down as I separated quarters from dimes and nickels. Even if I did pay with all change at least I had the courtesy to sort it all out for the cashier. They usually appreciated it and didn't give me shit about filling up their tills.

"Hey," I smiled as if I had missed her. "You, like, never answer your phone." I would have known that had I actually called.

She glanced at the cell phone she dug out of her pants pocket. It was small, black, and sleek, and the display came on with the swipe of the screen. It was one of those smart phones I was sure her old man bought her. I still relied on my early 2000's phone with the numbers smudged off and the edges battered from being dropped so much. I didn't care. I wasn't picky. I was so far behind in technology I didn't even own an iPad.

"I never got any calls," she said. She came up and put her arms around me. "I missed you, bitch." She smelled like strawberries and her hair smelled like Herbal Essence. I pictured her in the shower completely wet and naked, rubbing her scalp like the girls in the commercials, and going "oh yes, yes, yes!" The thought turned me on.

"I missed you too," the fruity scents lingered in my nose. "How's what's-his-face?" I asked.

"Brian," she sang.

"Brian," I repeated, thinking of his pale, wrinkly and hairy self on top of her tanned, toned, naked body pounding away at her. "Yea, how is he? How are things?"

She shrugged. "The usual," was her answer, and she changed the subject. "So, what, working too much or did you meet someone?" When I didn't answer, she went on, "You haven't been around to hang out. I miss hanging out with you. That party at your house was, like, one time in how long? Like forever, that's how long. What...too good for me now?"

"I've been raking in hours at the theater," I lied, "and hanging with Rorie," I half-truthed. "I did call you a bunch of times," another lie.

"We need to get together soon. I'm hanging with Hillary this weekend," and I cringed at the thought of my brother's attraction toward her. "You should hang with us, you know, like the good old times."

"Yea," I replied excitedly, knowing full well I'd bail, "give me a call. I got to get my ass to work though," I excused myself, "or else bossman will fire my ass."

Carmen laughed. "Always late," she said. "You'll never change."

SPILLED MILK

I took my time at the register in the store, waiting for Carmen to pump her gas and go away. I even counted out the seven dollars in change for the cashier, an older woman who looked lost as if she didn't know how to count. As soon as Carmen pulled away I was free to go back outside. I thanked Dot- per her name badge- and went off to pump my measly two gallons or so.

Frank was happy I was at work 'punctually', as Elvis would say, and punched in five minutes early. He was, of course, in a great mood. He announced the date and time and said that he would jot down my early arrival to work in his personal journal. He said most of the journal listed me as late or calling in sick. I laughed at him and called him a funny, funny guy.

Of course, he asked about my gorgeous mother and went on about how sweet and nice and regal she was. I didn't even know that Frank knew the word 'regal' existed never mind its definition. Every time Frank placed Mom on a pedestal I took it personally.

Unfairly, I did. He didn't know things from *my* perspective but he still slid down a couple of notches in my book.

After the movie theater was spic 'n span I wasn't in the mood to head straight home. The weather had turned to dark skies and scattered showers. All I wanted to do was go somewhere, anywhere, and have some laughs. I wanted to do drugs and get messed up but I didn't want to do it alone. I thought of my current run-in with Carmen and texted her cell phone of my intentions.

As predicted, Carmen texted back that she would get ready and be on her way to my place in an hour. I head home to get prettied up. When I got there, Rorie was still awake and I had to coax her into her bedroom with Twizzlers and a bag of buttered popcorn I'd taken from work. I knew it was a horrible post-supper but it worked and she retreated, snacks and a coloring book in stow.

I went right to my bedroom and tried the door to Moms. It was locked but I could pick it. I'd done it only a couple of times before. It wasn't rocket science- just a simple, plain, early twentieth century lock. No one ever had a key- not even the previous owners before Dad purchased the house over 20 years ago.

Carmen showed up and entered the house without knocking. She came up to my room and stood beside me in front of my mirror to inspect her own makeup. Like old times, she helped herself to my cosmetics collection and touched up her face. She chose my bright baby-pink lipstick and smeared it on. "Hot," she said, "I fucking love this color."

"You look hot, bitch," I said, "I want to kiss you." She puckered up and we laughed. It felt normal, like she hadn't fucked my mother.

"Your tits look huge," she commented and I revealed a black push-up I'd gotten at Target decorated with lace on the top. My breasts pushed together to form a nice, deep valley.

Carmen blinked her pretty peepers at me, the lids blue and shimmery, heavily lined with dark blue liner, lashes curled toward the sky coated in black mascara. Her lips were bright pink and her light brown hair was long and curled at the bottoms. She looked sensational. She had great assets unlike her frumpy, weathered mother.

SPILLED MILK

A fuchsia V-neck halter top clung to her. She didn't wear a bra and her nipples were obvious. Shredded light blue jeans clung to her, decorated with a black belt adorned with mini silver spikes throughout. She topped it all off with silver five-inch heels embellished with rhinestone hearts that dangled from the sides.

I studied myself in the mirror and liked what I saw. Black hair straightened with my salon straightener that went down to my lower back. Face done up with the same pink lip shade Carmen wore, eyes done up in sky blue eye shadow mixed with crystal and mica for some shine, lashes curled and coated with perfection.

My short-sleeved, form-fitting, red T-shirt and stretchy black leggings had been carefully chosen along with my leopard print heels. They were one of my favorite pairs- a sleek, four-inch heel colored a subtle shimmery gold, and the heels had two crystals on them. The straps were my favorite print, the edges made of crystals and rhinestones. I loved them; they were 25 bucks and felt like a million.

"You're a hottie," Carmen said and hugged me. "I miss you, ho."

Why on earth did every girlfriend call each other 'bitches' and 'hoes'? To prove closeness, to prove sisterhood and affection, to show appreciation? Society was fucked up.

We got into her new BMW that Brian had given her. It was his back-up car in case his Benz shit the bed. He also had a Dodge pickup, a pimping ATV, a Sea-Doo, a small four-person boat, a Harley, and was saving for a saltwater boat. Carmen was just one of his many toys. I should have rooted for Carmen to marry into his riches but I was sure he'd get a prenuptial.

Carmen and I promised we'd never go as long as we had without at least talking, that we'd make every effort possible to spend more time with each other. After Rose did what she did and went away people took on a different persona to me-they became less desirable. The more time I spent in crowds and social settings the more I became a people watcher and the more I disliked everyone.

The dog Uncle Jeremy found abandoned and had given to Rose when we were kids had more dignity and morals than society did. Maybe individually, with pure intentions, people were okay. Socially, only in a controlled setting like school or a club, were humans decent to each other.

We acted like we were 16 again in the car, the music loud, Carmen and I singing along with the songs at the top of our lungs, dancing in our seats.

Carmen filled me in on a couple of the one-night stands she'd had since she'd been with Brian and how one of the guys was a work buddy of his. It sounded scandalous and I wanted to hold it against her, only I couldn't. We were all guilty of cheating, all easily swayed by temptation.

Girls like Carmen had more options than most others so the odds were against her to be otherwise, to be unlike how she was. I hated her and maybe I loved her too. I looked out for her and I rooted against her.

We head toward our old friend Kevin's house. Kevin's dad wasn't home. I saw him once every couple of weeks to pick up my weed and customarily just walked in, but I had company this night so I did the civil thing and pounded a small fist on a hard wooden door.

"Entre!" Kevin announced from inside with a french accent. He was with a couple of his buddies. I recognized one of the three. He recognized me too. He should have. I had gone home with him from a club in Temple one night and had given him the blow job of his life. He smiled when he saw me; he remembered. He had probably exchanged blow job stories with Kevin before I got there.

Carmen turned on her charm and went right to Kevin's lap. "How's my baby boy?" she asked him as if she'd called him that our entire lives. I never heard her call him anything but his given name before. He told her he was fine, that he was offended she hadn't come by since school, that she should give him his number so they could catch up.

When Carmen got up to help herself to a beer in the fridge Kevin licked his lips as he gawked at her ass. He nodded to a friend of his who shared his approval.

Kevin came to me. "How's my main girl?" he asked. "You haven't missed me?"

"I always miss you," I lied.

"Yea, yea," he said, "You miss me when I got shit," he joked. That was the problem, I thought to myself, being friends with your dealer. They always expected you to hang out instead of just mosey in, grab the stuff, and dart out with a simple 'bye, see you later'. This was the reason why I preferred meeting him in a parking lot somewhere for a quick exchange.

"Got any blow?" I asked as if I were a pro. I knew nothing about coke. All I knew was that it made me feel happy, satisfied with myself, confident, free. I'd only tried it twice but I knew I liked it. I didn't feel guilty about things I had no control over.

I didn't worry about if tomorrow would suck just as bad as today or yesterday did. I didn't look in the mirror and dislike the girl who stared back. I didn't see sadness in the eyes of every person I passed. I just had to make sure it didn't take hold of me like it did Mother. *My* dignity would stay intact.

Kevin whipped out an 8-ball and one of his friends, Big Daddy he called himself, Idiot is what I called him, turned on the stereo. Lil Wayne cried a line and Big Daddy rapped along- him and his white self, pants hung low, over sized T-shirt, generic Timberland boots- rapping as if he lived it, loved it, breathed it. It was humorous in a way watching the dynamics of who was in the room.

Carmen, geared up in hot heels and eyes full of makeup and anything but mystery, was in the center of the room surrounded by dudes who would screw either one of us if given the chance. The difference was she flirted and soaked up all of their sexist, disrespectful comments and urged them for more. She gave no second thought to the old man who waited for her at home, who paid her bills, who took care of her. She bit the hand that fed her.

"Come sit next to papa," said Kyle, a tall lanky toehead who I estimated to be about 35 or so. I went and sat beside Kyle instead of on his lap as he gestured for me to do. Kyle looked like a car mechanic, grease on his sweatshirt and hands.

SPILLED MILK

His fingernails were dirty, his hands worn. This man had seen hard labor for many years; it was starting to show on his face. The creases in his forehead would be deeper in no time. The way he leered at me and Carmen made me feel dirty, like I had to cover up and quickly.

Then there was Greg who was our age and Kevin's best friend. A lot of the times when I called or texted Kevin, he was with Greg. Greg went to a high school further up north. Somewhere along the way they became buddies.

Greg was all right looking. He was about 5'11 in height and his face was babylike underneath a tough goatee. He was a bit heavier than the other guys and it wasn't muscle. He seemed nice enough if only he would act like a man instead of the little boy he was. It was as if he just discovered sex and boobs, it was all he could talk about. He was drunk, high; a time bomb.

Kevin was Kevin. In short, a guy who loved women, who maybe thought he was better than women, who thought all women should get on their knees and suck his cock. He wanted someone subservient, someone to do what he asked without complaint. I got sick of sleeping with him after a while for free pot. He smacked my ass too hard when he got rough. I enjoyed it but thinking back, the way he man-handled my breasts and slapped them so he could watch them flop around was demeaning.

I'd let men have their way with me since I was 13 and lost my V-card. I wasn't sure how much longer I could bear it. The curse of it all was that I was horny and loved sex. I loved it rough. I loved to be submissive; I wanted to be controlled. I

235

lavished the attention and wanted, like all women, to be worshiped.

I sickened at the thought of whom exactly I wanted to be worshiped by. I tried to always shake *him* from my mind. I wanted to be under his control, to be dominated. I yearned to be spanked and told I was a naughty girl. I wanted my hair pulled as *he* whispered how good, good, good I could be and I would be too. I'd rock his world; I'd make him forget he was my blood.

We both knew, Kevin and I, where this night would lead. Kevin meant nothing to me. He was just a decent-looking guy who had an okay package. All I wanted was his dick, not him. He knew where we stood, his role. Boundaries wouldn't be crossed.

It didn't take long before we were all wired on cocaine and Jack Daniel. The music was loud and spirits were high. I had sniffed a line and a half within an hour. They were skinny lines- I was on a budget. I had tapped into the grocery fund and now I only had 17 dollars to work with at the market tomorrow.

I hated the burn as the blow entered my nostrils and the phlegm that kept coming. After a few minutes it hit me in one refreshing blast. Everything was fine, nothing haunted me. My inhibitions flew out the door and I partook in a lap dance for Kyle who was turning 44 next weekend. I had been wrong; he wasn't 35. I made a note to ask him later why he was friends with Kevin who was only 21 and what the hell he was doing partying with us when he should be at home with a wife and kids.

The longer I sat or danced or talked to the group, the more intoxicated I felt. I wanted to run around the neighborhood and announce how great I was. I wanted the world to see me and to judge me from the exterior. I wanted to jump in my car and drive until I ran out of gas- which wouldn't be that far- and end up somewhere where nobody knew my name.

Carmen had a grand time. She ignored her cell phone on more than a few occasions until finally she turned it off. The way she laughed and told us all how whoever called wouldn't get her time of day I assumed it was Brian. If only he knew she didn't give two shits about him then maybe he'd find a lady his own age and make a family. Maybe he and I could fall in love and he could take me and Rorie away from this place.

Around three in the morning, after Kevin and I had sex a couple of times as his friend Kyle watched, Carmen finally showed up after she'd been gone with Greg for over an hour. She said she was tired and had to get home. Kevin practically ate my face at the door as he said his goodbye. "Mmmm," he moaned, my ass cheek in his grasp, "I'm gonna miss my kinky baby." I didn't like how he called me his baby.

In the car, Carmen advised she was far from tired, she just had to get away from Greg who she called 'tater tot' for his small penis. If she didn't like him, I brought up, then why did she spend an hour with him? Her answer- he gave good oral.

Carmen was adamant she hadn't slept with Greg or returned the favor. She complained that her boyfriend hadn't eaten her out in a week and she needed it.

I assured her she hadn't cheated on Brian, only because he hadn't provided it. In fact, I felt even a kiss was cheating. I was guilty- I'd cheated on every boyfriend I had and never did I exclusively date. There was always someone else on the side. I hadn't yet found the one that everyone squealed about.

Of all the guys I'd met, dated, flirted with, and had sexual relations with, I couldn't imagine that not one of them fared well enough. I hadn't even been close to falling in love. The closest I even came to lust was with Branden Gildamesh when I was in the seventh grade. He was in the eighth. I danced with him to "End of the Road" by Boyz to Men at a school dance. I thought about him a lot, more than a normal crush, but it wasn't love. He was just a nice boy who my friends talked into dancing with me.

"So when you gonna come hang in Eastman Valley?" Carmen asked and lit us both a smoke.

I shrugged. "Tomorrow," I lied. "Next weekend," I corrected. "When I don't have to work," I covered.

The song on the radio sang "I kissed a girl and I liked it… lips taste like cherry chapstick…" It reminded me of something.

"So," I straightened up in the passenger seat at full attention. I had no inhibitions. I felt like I could talk about anything to anybody at the moment. "Tell me," I said, "kissed any girls lately?" I laughed at myself.

She laughed along, a bit of confusion in her tone. "No," she answered, still laughing, "have you?"

She looked ridiculous laughing with me. I wanted to slap her and watch the blood trickle from her succulent pink lips. I wanted to grab her by the hair and smash her face into her Betty Boop steering wheel cover. "How did my mom taste?" I practically shouted and broke into hysterics. I turned the radio up and sang along, "I kissed a girl and I liked it!"

"You're sick!" she went along with the fun. "I wouldn't know, sicko!"

"Oh she just ate you?" I went further. "Jesus, Carmen," I scolded jokingly, "you got to give a little instead of take, take, take. Have you sucked Brian in the last week? Maybe that's why he hasn't licked your clam."

"Amber!" Carmen squealed like she was so good at, "You're so disgusting!"

"Hey," I put my hand up in defense. I kept the mood light. It was all a joke, all in good fun. We'd look back at it later and think it was funny. "Just saying."

I fished for answers, "You fucked my mother, didn't you?" I didn't put it past either of them and I wanted to know. "You fucked her friend too," not a question.

She laughed. "Nicole has a rockin' body, you know," she said. "Her friend had nice tits." She'd had a threesome with them that night and claimed it as her only all-girl threesome. Carmen said she'd do it every weekend if she could, if only Mother called her up and asked her over again.

Carmen wanted to drive around and smoke some pot. I did too but not with her. When Carmen asked if she should drop me off or drive around town, I told her I should be at the house if Rorie woke up which was a lie.

"Tell Nicky I said 'hello'," she called after me when she dropped me off.

I nodded. "Sure thing."

Mom heard me in the kitchen as I rummaged for a soda. I was wired and knew sleep wouldn't welcome me for a while.

"What the fuck were you doing all night?" Mom came up behind me, her eyes yellow, her hair disheveled, her person reeking of pussy and disgrace.

"I was out with Carmen," I answered.

"Got any more?" she asked. I looked up at her.

"Anymore what?" I asked and looked away.

"You know what. I can tell you're fucked up."

"I can roll you a joint," I offered. I wasn't about to spare any of the good stuff.

She rolled her eyes. Her chest was about to pop out of the light pink and black corset she wore. "I know you sniffed something tonight," she persisted. "Don't you have any to share with your momma?"

I had to keep in my laughter. "You can call Carmen," I said. "She has it."

"How is sweet Carmen?," Mother questioned.

I squinted. "You should know better than anyone," I started, "being you two are so close and all." Carmen was a Latin word meaning 'song'. She was far from a melody. She had no self-respect.

My cell phone jingled beside me on the kitchen table. It was a text message from an unknown number that read *Hi Amber I know you don't know me but I'm Carmen's boyfriend. I was hoping you could give me a call when you get this so I could talk to you. I'm concerned about Carmen. Hope to hear from you soon. Thanks.*

Curiosity got the best of me. I went downstairs and dialed Brian's number. It rang five times before he answered. It sounded like I had woken him up.

"Amber," he greeted. "Thanks so much for calling me back."

"Sure," I said. His voice was deep. He sounded sincere, nice. But I reminded myself he wasn't that nice, that they had no right to be together. "What's up?"

"I had a couple of questions about Carmen, about tonight." He stopped. My heart raced.

"Shoot," I encouraged.

He cleared his throat. He didn't know where to begin or maybe he felt he had no right to ask me anything about her.

"Maybe we should talk in person," he suggested. "I don't have a route for the next couple of days," he referred to his trucking. "Can you stop by? Or, since you're up and awake, did you want me to stop by there?"

I didn't immediately reply and he spoke again, "It'll only take a few minutes."

"What's this all about?" there was an edge in my voice.

"Carmen," he simply said. "There's just things I feel I should know about her before I ask her to marry me."

I could have thrown up had there been food in my stomach. What did he want with Carmen as a wife? She wasn't even a good girlfriend. She'd never make him happy in the long run. It was my motivation to meet him, to let him know what he'd be getting himself into if he got down on one knee.

"I'll be right there. Give me 20 minutes," I hung up.

I went back upstairs to my bedroom to change my clothes into something sexier and re-did my makeup. I needed Brian to know there were better girls out there. I would make sure he realized his mistake in getting together with her in the first place.

241

I knew things about pretty Carmen that would turn him away from her in a second. I was eager to share her business with him, eager to push them apart. She didn't deserve to be taken care of.

In record time I made it to Eastman Valley, to the house Brian shared with my best friend. He waited outside for me. He was average height, neither thin nor pudgy. His arms were fairly muscular in a short-sleeved shirt. He was well-dressed-in khakis and a dark brown top. His hair was sandy blonde, almost brunette. His face didn't look innocent nor cruel.

I stepped out of my car slowly so that he could see my high-heeled shoes attached to long slim legs.

"Brian," I said as I stood up and straightened my top.

"Amber," he said, struck by my beauty. He drank me in and I smiled coyly when he looked up from my bosom.

"It's so nice to finally meet you," I twiddled one of my pigtails.

"You too. Carmen says a lot of great things about you." I found that hard to believe.

"We've been good friends a long time."

He nodded. He looked back at his white house. "She's asleep," he advised. "We can go in the den or the garage if you'd like."

"Garage," I suggested and followed him. I didn't want Carmen to wake up and see us. She would be suspicious.

He led me to a small area of the garage where a green shag rug sat beneath three metal folding chairs. He allowed me to sit on the sole chair that had a seat cushion. I sat down and put an extra chair before me so I could prop my feet up. I made sure to not cross my legs; I knew he'd try to steal a glance or two up my skirt.

"So," I said flirtatiously, "what made you call me?"

He wasn't sure how to begin. I began for him, "You called to discuss Carmen and your future. You're unsure if she's the girl you should settle down with. Quite honestly, I see your concerns. Carmen's a different kind of creature. It's best you watch out before she takes full advantage of you. I'd hate to see such a nice guy like yourself be made into a fool."

"Yes," he said. "I need to know what I'm getting into."

"Well, don't you know already? You've been together a while now. I'm sure enough time has passed for her horns to have sprouted by now."

"I'm 45, 46 in a couple of months," he said. "Sooner than later I'll be 50. I've never been married. It's time I settle down and Carmen seems the most logical person to do that with."

I giggled and didn't try to hide it. "Why?" I laughed again then realized I didn't want to come across as vindictive. "Because she's your girlfriend? *That* qualifies her as the *logical* choice?" I pursued. "I'd like to know your reasoning for wanting to marry her."

"What did you two do tonight?" he asked instead of answered.

I shrugged. "What we always do," I said. "Party hard and live with regrets."

"So you two partied tonight? Where? With who?"

I eyed him. He had no clue she mistreated him. He had no idea she could never be faithful to one man. There was still hope; I could still talk some sense into him.

"With my friend Kevin and a couple of his buddies."

243

"Guys?"

I nodded. "Yes, all guys. Carmen doesn't really prefer female company." I hoped that sentence said enough but it didn't and he wanted more. "We sniffed a couple of lines," I detailed our night, "and then I don't really know what happened. She took off with this guy, Greg, for half the night. So," I said, sugar in my tone, "I'm not really sure what she did, let alone what they did together."

He looked down. I couldn't read him very well. I couldn't tell if he was upset or expected it. "Has she had a lot of boyfriends?"

"What has she told you?" I asked so I could purposely contradict it.

"That she's had a couple, that she's only slept with a handful of men, and lost her virginity at 19."

I rolled my eyes. "Well, I'm sorry she's a liar- especially to you. I don't know why you take care of her, get her cars, buy her shit, give her your all. As I said before, I've known Carmen a long time and I probably know her better than anyone else. She's far from saintly, Brian. She's not the girl for you."

I spilled it all- how Carmen lost her virginity when she was 12 to her babysitter's brother, how she slept with a couple of her fathers friends, the threesomes, the women she's had, the night at my house. He needed to know. I didn't sympathize with him. I wanted to hurt him, hurt her.

Brian just sat there. I put a hand on his knee. He stared at my shimmery nail polish.

"I'm so sorry I had to tell you all of that, especially the way I told you," I spoke softly, sincerely. "You're *such* a nice guy. Nice guys don't always have to finish last."

He looked up at me. He hadn't yet digested all I'd said. He hadn't yet seen that beautiful Carmen wasn't all she pretended to be.

"You deserve so much better." I leaned in and scooted my chair closer to him.

He sat back and breathed deep. "Before Carmen, there was Tonya. I thought she was the one. Then Tonya ran off with my brother to live in California. They got divorced a couple of years ago. Just because I missed Tonya didn't mean I wanted her back. I told myself even if she came crawling back to me, I would never take her back."

"Tonya's a fucking idiot," I interjected.

"I look back now and I realize the reason I missed her was because she *didn't* come crawling back." Then suddenly he stopped.

"Never allow another girl to hurt you," I instructed. "You're too good for it."

He studied me. "Carmen didn't give you enough credit," he said. "You're prettier and nicer than she said you were."

That bitch.

"Thank you." I gestured to his radio, "that thing work?"

He got up and turned it on. I told him what station to put it on and he turned the circular dial. A dance song blared and I started to move my body to the beat. He stood before me and watched.

"Got anything to drink?" I asked. I didn't want my buzz to wear off.

"Vodka," he answered. "I'll be right back."

I continued to dance. I fluffed my boobs up in my bra and watched them bounce along to my movements. I reached into my underwear and sniffed my fingertips to make sure I was fresh enough for when he couldn't stand it anymore and had to touch me. My skirt hitched up higher and my legs looked a mile long. The lighting of the garage accentuated my natural tan.

Carmen's beau returned. In one hand, he held a glass bottle. In his other hand he held two beers, one stacked on top of the other. In his mouth, his teeth held a shot glass that said 'New Hampshire living' with a moose and a black bear both wearing hats and holding shot glasses themselves.

I noticed the way he leered at my young body. I danced harder to the beat. "Dance with me," I said and held my hand out.

"Nah," he said. He held my hand anyway and came to me. He didn't dance. "I'm too old for that."

"You're never too old to dance," and moved closer to him. I waited for the perfect opportunity. I rubbed my behind against his crotch and looked up at him. His face was flushed, his groin hard. It could have been my chance but I waited. I'd wait for when his manhood was ready to bust a hole through his jeans. I knew how to play the game.

He drank faster and didn't even flinch. It was as if the beer tasted like water. He couldn't take his eyes from me. I was confident. He thrilled in that. I wasn't a shy little girl who needed coaxing or a man to train me. I moved close to him and slowed my motions.

I sniffed his neck and told him he smelled good. I guessed at his cologne and I was right. I'd dated a couple of guys who wore the same. I knew the scent well- I'd bought Bret a bottle two Christmases ago. Bret wore it for the first couple of weeks until he returned to his natural scent- pine needles, wood, wilderness.

I looked up at Brian's face. He wasn't handsome but I didn't care. He wasn't tall. He wasn't scruffy nor polished. He wasn't anything I wanted in a man. He wasn't even *my* man. I had no right to be there.

"Do you feel better?" I asked, loud enough to be heard over the music. "You better turn the radio down," I said. "What if Carmen wakes up?"

He rushed to the stereo, beer can still clutched in hand, insecurities all about him. He must have forgotten that she was sleeping let alone that she was home. I must have affected him more than I had thought. He was losing inhibition.

"When she's out," he explained about Carmen's sleeping, "she's out."

"I know," I giggled. Waking her up was like winning the war in the Middle East. "She slept through her aunt's house getting robbed a few years ago. They ransacked the living room while she snoozed on her uncle's Lazy Boy." I laughed.

I leaned against the garage wall and started to fan myself with my hand. Dancing had really warmed me up. The sweat released the scent of my body spray.

Brian flicked on the turbo fan in the corner of his garage which I thought was very nice of him. Maybe he was a nice guy after all and it was just his priorities that were fucked up.

"You are so hot," he said, filled with liquid confidence. "You have no clue how sexy you are, do you?"

I put on an innocent look and pouted my lips. "I don't know what you're talking about."

"I bet crowded rooms don't intimidate you at all."

I didn't know what to say. I was flattered. I needed to hear those things and couldn't imagine he used those exact words with Carmen.

"You're so sweet." I went to him and kissed him passionately. It didn't matter that Brian was taken or that he wanted to propose to another girl. He wasn't my boyfriend and he never would be. I used him to stroke my ego; he used me for the same.

All that mattered was that I felt pretty, I felt womanly, worthy, wanted, and I didn't have to think about anything else besides how good it made me feel.

CHAPTER 17

The day after my rendezvous with Brian, Carmen had called and texted my phone at least a dozen times. I ignored her but never expected her to show up at my house two hours later.

I heard her call pull in. It sounded fast- the tires crunched on my rocky driveway. When I rushed down the stairs, there she was. She had just barged in. It was times like this that I wished Rorie would stop losing her keys so I could lock the door.

"Hey," I managed. It was a shock to see her standing there. She looked visibly upset.

"You whore," she spat. She held up a black thong. I'd left it in Brian's garage, under the chair cushion on the metal folding chair I'd sat on most of the night. I'd left it there on purpose; I knew Carmen would find it eventually and would recognize them.

She'd bought them online for me senior year. On the top right corner was my name written in pink glittery cursive. She got herself a pair too, white with her name written in navy blue cursive.

I was busted. I'd wanted her to know but, now that she knew and was in my house and confrontational, I wished it was all kept secret. Brian was in no position to tell her- he'd beckoned me to his house to discuss his future with Carmen and ended up sleeping with her best friend. How could he face her?

"You can't just come huffing and puffing in my house," I said and slit my eyes at her. I had to ready myself for her; she could be mean. She'd come to hurt me. I'd asked for it but, then again, so did she.

Her eyes were threatening and I admit I felt intimidated. Was I ready to officially lose my last and only friend in the outside world? Was I ready to cut off all ties from a past that I didn't completely despise as deeply I despised my home life? I couldn't falter before her and let her win. Girls like Carmen always won and I refused to be loser again, especially on account of a girl who'd never become a woman.

"Like you came into *my* house and fucked *my* boyfriend?" She finished, "I always knew you were a disgusting slut but I really didn't think I had to worry about you with my boyfriends."

I walked down the stairs and past her. I felt the heat coming off of her. I wondered if she'd hit me as I walked by and was glad she didn't because I'd have to hit her back and I really, really didn't want to do that. I didn't want this to become physical between us. She followed me into the living room, through the pantry, and into the kitchen.

I helped myself to a soda from the fridge and contemplated offering her one. It wasn't the right time for small-talk or peace offerings. Olive branches wouldn't be extended.

"How can you just walk away from me? How can you not feel bad about this?" Carmen practically yelled.

"What's done is done. It just happened," I said.

SPILLED MILK

"You fucking my man does not 'just happen'," she shouted an inch from my face. I calmly sipped my soda. It infuriated her. "You're such a bitch, Amber!" I swear I saw her eyes water slightly. "You're supposed to be my best friend!"

"Best friend?!" I shouted back. I eyed her down. I would never back down to Carmen Sherwood. I knew her too well to ever do that. "Please! You're your own best friend. You're too arrogant and self-centered to ever have a true friend. You can stand there all you want and call me a whore but *you're* the whore, Carmen. *You're* the slut who will sleep with anyone just so you can feel special when you count all the dudes who laid up with you.

"That's what makes you feel good," I said, "you feel like you can live life off your looks. You have a personality like shit and, honestly, baby girl, you're a crappy person, crappy friend, and even crappier girlfriend."

She slapped me. I took it and slapped her back. She froze. I couldn't move a muscle either. We just looked at each other neither of us able to apologize nor continue.

Finally Carmen spoke, quietly, a quiver in her voice, "Fuck you, Amber. You were like a sister to me." Her voice found more strength and the shake went away. "How could you do this to me? I was nothing but supportive to you- always! When Henri fell, I was there! When Clyde shot himself, I was there! When your fat sister killed your pig father, I was there! I've always been there for you, Amber! *This* is how you repay me?"

What could I possibly say that would make it better? I was in the wrong; I had betrayed her. She had been there, yes.

After what I'd done and what I'd said to her, how could I apologize now? I was jealous of her but would never admit it.

Cowardly, ashamed, I said nothing in return which infuriated her more.

Her face was flushed, her blue eyes bloodshot and misted over. Her long light brown hair was unkempt. She looked as if she could break down in tears at any moment as she stood there and shifted her weight from foot to foot, and waited for me to speak.

She hissed at me, "Fuck you." She neither whispered nor yelled; it was more of a threat. "Fuck you *and* the broken-down horse you rode in on. You're a *St. Germaine-* poor, disgusting trash. You'll be stuck in Little Bethlehem and amount to shit just like everybody else in your trashy family."

I shook in my shoes and hoped it didn't show. I'd gotten into my fair share of fights in high school with Carmen by my side. She detected fear and insecurities and used it to her advantage.

She wasn't a good fighter physically, but mentally she was capable of defeating her opponent. I was the same. That was part of the reason we got along so well.

Her words stung and caused my temper to rise. "Get the fuck out of my house. Then when you're out of my house, get out of my life. I want nothing to do with a person like you. I'm just glad I was finally able to get that off my chest."

"*What* off your chest?" she asked.

I sneered at her. "The fact that I…fucking…hate…you. I've hated you so long now. I'm sick of pretending I give a shit anymore." I didn't say anymore; I'd said enough.

She smiled at me through her tears and stormed out. That was it- she just left without a word. I stood there, mouth agape, wondering what the repercussions were of our falling out.

I found out three days later. I'd had a bad feeling in my gut ever since our showdown. My anxiety was high. I felt alone, so godawful alone, and I felt selfishly abandoned. I'd backstabbed my only friend. I admittedly did her wrong, so why was it that I was the one who felt walked-out on?

Rorie had gotten off the school bus at her usual time. I was inside cleaning and mopping before my shift at Movie Magic. Since Elvis gave me the chance to prove myself, I'd made special efforts to be productive and punctual. I'd been arriving to work early.

Even Frank commended me on my efforts and said that Elvis did right by letting me stay. Frank always had my back. He always defended the poor girl with the messed-up family who lived down the way in Lil Beth, and he probably always would.

"Amber!" my little sister shrieked as she bolted in the house.

"What?" I asked, mop in hand, look of shock present on my face.

"There's signs in the yard! They weren't there this morning! Come look!" and she ran back out of the house.

In our front yard were six signs, all secured to sticks and posted on our property. They all faced the road so I couldn't read them where I stood in shock at the front door. Rorie was already halfway up the driveway, her purple backpack still stuck to her. It swayed side to side as did her long, shiny ponytail.

Rorie called over her shoulder, "Hurry!"

I did. I ran. The driveway was long and I almost tripped a few times but I had to see what was on those signs. I looked at Rorie and wished she hadn't been old enough to read. The words were written large and thick with black marker. What those words said was bolder than the print.

"Get in the house," I ordered Rorie.

She hesitated. With concern in her little-girl voice, she looked up at me, "Who put those there? Why would they say that about Daddy?"

I raised my voice, "Get in the house, Rorie!"

She started off yet still stared at one particular sign. Her beady eyes said so much. "Who put that there about Daddy?" she asked again.

"Just go!" I hollered. I couldn't pull my eyes from the signage but I heard her footsteps fade away. I looked up in time to see her disappear and the front door slam shut behind her. As soon as she was gone I fell to my knees; my legs couldn't support me anymore.

I knew Carmen would pay me back- it was only a matter of time. Three days was enough. She had to kick me where it hurt most. Three of the signs said awful things about my father being a child molester and a rapist. One sign mentioned Rose, how she deserved to rot in jail for eternity. One said how all the St. Germaines were deadbeats. The other mentioned how Jack was responsible for Kristy Gregory's departure.

SPILLED MILK

Unsure of how I'd explain everything to Rorie, I got in my car and cried my eyes out. Half an hour later, I went back in the house quietly, told Rorie who sat at the kitchen table to do her homework, that I'd explain tomorrow, and got ready for work.

When I pulled into the bare lot of Movie Magic I parked beside Frank's truck. I swore the day I got rich I'd buy Frank a new one. I realized I hadn't left random things underneath his windshield wiper in a while like I used to- napkins with lipstick kisses and messages written on them like *Hi Frank, thanks for the great time last nite! Love, Bunny*, banana peels, miscellaneous wrappers. He never once mentioned it and I never brought it up. It was mysterious fun.

I made my way across the small lot. At the front of the lot sat a black Pontiac with tinted windows. I didn't see the person inside until he stepped out. It wasn't a customer itching to see the new release. The sight of him stopped me in my tracks. Even a decade later, he hadn't changed much. Should I pretend I hadn't recognized him and keep walking?

His hands were deep in his pockets and he looked unsure of himself. He reminded me of Uncle Jeremy. "Hey," he said to me in a deep, rumbling voice. Black hairs on his chin, from two or three days of not shaving, stole my breath before I composed myself.

"Hi. How have you been?"

He shrugged. "I drove by your house this morning." My mouth dropped; I knew why he was here.

Eric Gregory, Kristy's older brother, stood before me. He leaned on his car, shoulders slumped, hands hidden, head bowed down, hurt in his eyes. I couldn't stand what I saw in those eyes- loss, guilt, indescribable pain.

"I'm sorry you saw that." A particular sign flashed through my mind, the one about his sister.

"Me too," he stated. He looked just as he had as an 18-year old boy- only more defined, stronger, inwardly altered. Eric had been a brother figure to me as a kid. He drove us to bowling alleys, Chuck-e-Cheese, the rollerskating rink, the movies, everywhere. Their mother made him but I don't think he minded.

He studied me. It made me self-conscious. "I'm sorry you saw that too," he finally spoke again.

It was because of me he was here. It was because of me Carmen had left those hateful signs. I hated how I couldn't take it all back. It'd been 10 years- I wondered if he'd healed yet.

"I'm sorry, Eric," I said softly. "I don't know who left those in my yard," I lied, "but I'll take care of it. I took them down and I'm going to burn them."

He went on to tell me that I fared out well, that he rarely ever went to the movies, how his mother and father still asked of me during Christmas-time. He lived in his own house now in Connolly and the woman he just began seeing lived a mile from my house.

I gazed at the side of his face, at his jawline, his eyes. The way he stared at the ground saddened me. I knew his hurt well. Losing a sibling was difficult, not something easily overcome.

"I miss her," I broke the silence. "I wonder what she would have been like."

SPILLED MILK

For a long time now, I'd asked myself if Eric blamed me for Kristy's passing. She hung herself because of something my father had done and everyone knew that. Only a few knew the specifics but everyone knew that he had hurt her. I couldn't have blamed Eric if he held it against me but it was something I'd never ask; I'd let it nag me forever.

His jaw tensed. His hands never left his pants. "Your father raped her that morning, you know," he began. Yes, that's what her suicide letter had said. She'd been at my house since the night before for a sleepover. No one was home but for Dad, myself, Kristy, and Rose. Rose was asleep or off somewhere. Kristy was with Dad in the bedroom. After about 20 minutes, she had rushed out of Dad's room frantically and left my house in whimpers. Dad never came out.

I nodded. "I'm sorry," I said and I didn't know why; it was Dad who had hurt her.

Then, he told me just as Uncle Jeremy had that one night. He told me the words written on a small piece of paper in juvenile handwriting that made me cringe with every syllable.

It said: *Dear Mom and Dad, I'm sorry I wasn't a good daughter. He made me suck it like a lollipop then he stuck it inside of me where I pee. He hurt me and I'm bleeding down there now. I think I'm going to die. I think he did something to make me die. I'm sorry Mommy and Daddy and tell Eric I love him. Your daughter, Kristy.*

He watched my reaction to see if I'd cry or whip out a gun like those in my lineage had. When you came from a family that had a killer in it everyone walked on eggshells around you. It was a curse I had to bear.

I looked into his eyes and he into mine. I could see his soul. He was a good man and had been a great big brother. I hoped he forgave himself for leaving that night. I hoped he had washed from his mind what he'd found upon his return. I wanted him to live his life with no regrets. I wanted to want the same for me.

"What time's your shift start?" he asked.

I checked my cell phone for the time. "Eight minutes ago."

He finally stood straight and his hands left his pockets. He had nice hands, clean and soft. I knew he wouldn't visit again. I knew I wouldn't visit him either.

"Thanks for coming," I told him sincerely. I spoke from my heart, "You know when the sun sets and next to the moon there's this one star that's brighter than the rest? Well, that's her. She's watching. She beat us all to Paradise. She's the lucky one. As human beings who are alive and well we don't see it like that but that's the way it is. That's how I'm okay with it now."

He smiled. I went to him and put my arms around him. He held me back and said nothing. I breathed him in, one last piece of Kristy, one last piece of that childhood memory.

CHAPTER 18

After my outburst, Rose was restricted visitors for two weeks. I'd pissed her off. She'd written twice and said that she had called but the phone was disconnected. I hadn't paid the final notice of the telephone bill.

It was time to see her again. I wasn't sure if I was ready or not. I wasn't sure if I was ready to apologize; I wasn't about fake sorrys. Those were two things I kept sacred- apologies and love.

I recognized the guards and we did the usual routine. I should have known that I'd be pulled for the random patdown. I could only imagine the strip search for inmates-having to spread their butt cheeks, bend over, and cough so the guard could see if any contraband fell out.

I spotted Rose right away. "Hi," I softly approached my sister and waited for an invitation to sit down. She didn't beam at the sight of me. I was late.

"Long time no see," Rose greeted.

"Whose fault is that?" and I added a chuckle to keep it light.

She pouted, "Don't start."

I sat down. "No one's starting," I defended.

She didn't speak right away. She was too busy trying to ward off the quiver that came about her lips.

I looked around the room. There were no smiles. The inmates, in their drabber-than-usual orange jumpsuits, looked

259

glum and so did their loved ones. The vibes were all over. I couldn't put it all on my paranoia. Even the guards that paced about looked more gloomy than usual. Rose, especially, looked different with her long scraggly hair that hadn't been combed in a day or two and her teeth that hadn't been brushed yet.

Her demeanor had changed. She seemed defeated again like she had when she first got sentenced. She read my every movement and possibly my thoughts too. "Is Ma good to you? Is she good to Rorie?"

The anxiety was too much. "No," I said softly. I willed myself to keep it together. I couldn't stand what I saw in Rose's face, in her eyes that had already seen too much. I wanted to heal her of everything. I was willing to take on her tribulations and growing pains atop my own. I'd already forgiven her.

Visions of my mother danced before my eyes. I saw glimpses of her in Rose. Rose took after Dad but if you looked hard enough you could see she was Nicole's daughter. Mom had never been proud of Rose with her extra pounds, her squinty eyes, her gentle shyness. "She's never been good to any of us," I answered.

"You need to get the hell out of that house, Amber," she warned. "Get Rorie out. Mother broke a very important promise to me and it's time she paid up."

My sister sat back against the metal chair. My shoulders slumped, my heart raced. There was nobody else in the room to me- no one but myself and Rose. We were back in our house on Sandman Road, lying on her bed together and talking like we used to, about how things would somehow, someday, eventually change for us.

"Do you remember being kids and how Mom would kick the shit out of us for no reason at all?"

I nodded.

"She was frustrated," Rose explained. "She couldn't handle us and we weren't even bad kids. We weren't a handful. Mom had no reason to hurt us the way that she had. She was always selfish, Amber. Dad told me she was that way even before she had kids."

I was sure she saw me flinch. I wasn't sure, though, if she cared.

"Before Dad….before...," she stumbled, but only for a moment, "before he died, I had a conversation with Mom. She gave me her word that she'd be a good mother, better than she thought she was capable of. She promised, on the lives of her dead sons, that she'd change and step up. But she hasn't done that, has she? Since she hasn't fulfilled her part of the bargain I no longer can fulfill mine."

I was afraid to utter a word; Rose had never been like this- so open. I didn't want to steer her away from this conversation that held such gargantuan importance.

"Dad left to live with Uncle Jeremy, what, a decade ago?" I thought back and nodded. Yes, he had moved away when I was 11. "Do you remember anything before he moved away?"

I thought back. Of course I remembered things, lots of things. There was so much that went on back then. "Like what?" managed to escape my lips that twitched sporadically.

"Like the arguments he used to have with Mom when they didn't think we were listening? Our house was so small how could we not hear them?" They had argued so much, every single day practically, and about nothing and about everything. "About those little girls?"

"I remember him taking my friends into his room. I remember being so young I had no clue what he was doing in there. A couple of my friends told me he would spank them and make them spank him." The subject always struck a bad nerve. "Do you remember one specific little girl?" I pointedly asked my sister. Her face softened; she knew who I spoke of.

"Her brother came to my work a few days ago," I said. "I pulled into the parking lot of the theater and there he was."

"What was he doing there?" Rose asked.

"Carmen," I said. "Me and Carmen got into a fight and she decided to post signs in our yard that had to do with Kristy and Dad. Eric's seeing some lady who lives on our road so he saw. He wanted to make sure I was okay."

"That was nice of him."

"Yea," I said softly. Now that I thought back to it, I wasn't sure how he knew I worked at Movie Magic. I don't recall ever seeing him come in. "I'm surprised he remembered me."

"How could he forget?" Rose said and I nodded in agreement. I wasn't sure if she had complimented me or referenced Dad. Nobody up here ever forgot the bad apples. News rarely happened and when it did it people remembered forever.

"He didn't just spank them," Rose said next which caused me to pull back in my chair. "He used to take them into the basement," she said a bit angry. "You knew," she said so seriously, accusatory, "you just played dumb all this time like you forgot or something. They were *your* friends. You knew."

SPILLED MILK

I wanted to slap her as hard as I could, so hard that the drool flew across the room. "I only knew about the spankings." I was hurt, angry, confused, anxious.

She studied me hard, deep. The moment was almost philosophical, slightly metaphysical. I had a hard time focusing through the vertigo.

"What about the videos?" Rose asked and I shook my head. "Dad used to film them you know. When he moved out he took the videos and the camera with him. The cops looked for them everywhere after a couple of those little girls told their mommies and daddies. To this day, nobody knows where those videos are."

"Oh my God," was all I could say. It was all I could think.

"I love you, Amber. If you ever find those videos, please know I love you." She pleaded with me to understand her affections for me.

"Where do I find them?" I begged. "Where did you put them?"

I knew she wouldn't tell me or if she had been the one to hide them. She couldn't implicate our father even after his death.

I left the parking lot of Peru and head south toward Lil Beth, to my uncle's house.

"Mom said he really, really loved you in the movies and that Uncle Jeremy's a dick for loving you too," Rorie's little voice echoed in my head. My baby's voice haunted me in so many ways. She was my blessing and my curse. I didn't want to be here, to be alive. I couldn't handle it anymore but I couldn't leave Rorie with Mom.

Rorie still needed a new sleeping bag for when she slept over Sara's house. She still needed new sneakers- hers were almost to the soles. I thought of poor Rorie in school where all the other kids had new shoes or pants that fit them and she didn't.

Because of me, she had high-water jeans, tight sweaters, and stained pink sneakers that had been glued too many times. I cringed and cursed myself out for it. She needed hugs too and Mom wasn't that kind of person. There was so much I couldn't do for her yet. She deserved so much more than I could provide.

The hour and a half drive back to town was torture. I sped the entire time and kept a close lookout for cops. My uncle's truck was in the driveway. I had secretly hoped he wasn't home so that I could rummage through the basement on my own, with no pressure. I wasn't sure what I hoped to find. I still had to make sense of all that Rose had tried to warn me of. She was so different. Prison had robbed her of so much.

I knocked and Uncle Jeremy swung the door open. He looked confused to see me in the condition I was in. I hadn't looked in a mirror but I knew I looked a wreck. No matter how I had tried to keep it together, I couldn't. I couldn't stop weeping. I hadn't groomed myself in a couple of days. My face had no makeup. I wore the same clothes I did yesterday.

"What the...," he mumbled and moved aside. I rushed past him and practically fell onto the sofa. I lit a cigarette in a frenzy and ordered my uncle to sit down. He did. I was in no mood for disobedience and he could tell.

"What are you doing here?" he asked. He lit one of his cigars. "You're a crazy girl, you know that?" he commented. "Can't you ever show up here normal?"

"I saw Rose today. She told me everything," I countered. "Now I need to hear it from you." I looked deep into his eyes and saw a story- more like a synopsis. He hadn't yet been entirely read. "She told me about the videos."

My uncle looked around the room for answers or excuses. He sat dumbly amidst a billow of smoke. "I'm going to be honest with you," he finally said as he stubbed out his cigar. "This conversation makes me uncomfortable. Your Jack's daughter for crying out loud. You don't need to know these things."

"*Things*," I repeated.

"Yea, *things*," he said harshly. He was annoyed. "I can't talk about this shit."

I began to rock back and forth in my seat. "I was a little girl," I cowardly said. It wasn't good enough- had I spoke up sooner, my best friend would have never scribbled a note instead of come to me. "I didn't know any better."

"As soon as I found out he was making movies," Uncle Jeremy said, "I made him stop. I put him in his place and he never did it again." He squirmed in his recliner.

"Is that why he left? Did my mother kick him out because of it?" I still had a teeny glimmer of hope that my mother had done something good for us.

"He moved out of there for a lot of reasons."

I still couldn't peel my eyes from that basement door and its hideous poop-colored doorknob. The lock was old-fashioned with a keyhole from what I imagined to be a large

265

brass key. I wondered if it'd ever been locked and who had the key. I thought of the floorboards and instinctively rose and went on my way.

My uncle got up quickly as I turned the knob and allowed my lead feet to carry me down the rickety wooden steps. He mumbled as he followed me down. I plopped down on my knees and felt around.

"What are you doing, Amber?" Uncle Jeremy barked. I had barged in his house without a phone call and looked as if I'd gone mad. I couldn't blame him.

I stood and looked around carefully. There had to have been a reason it all seemed so familiar. "Here," I shouted after a while, the floorboards cool beneath my palms. "Here," I said calmer and stood.

There was a slight creak under my feet. The closer I looked I could see the cracks as clear as day. There was a small square and it had been carefully carved out and made to blend in with the floorboards at first glance. My uncle stood beside me and stared at the spot. "What?" he said. "What do you see? It's just a dusty old floor."

I went to the shelves of the basement wall and found a flat head screwdriver and pried the floorboard as my uncle watched.

"Holy fuck," he murmured. We both stared into a small hole. There was a box wrapped inside of a black plastic garbage bag. It was dusty and dingy, obviously untouched for quite some time.

I reached inside and held it in my hand for a moment. My uncle was just as intrigued as I was. I could tell he didn't know about it. We would discover together.

SPILLED MILK

The bag was tied in a tight knot and I used a fingernail to force my way through it. It tore cleanly and inside was a large black shoe box that once held boots. It had been carefully taped shut with silver electric tape.

"You open it," I whispered. I didn't bother to hide how my hands shook.

He didn't want to but it was his duty as a father-figure to withstand the burden. He used the screwdriver to tear through the tape. "Ready?" he asked.

It had to have been important if Dad had gone through all this trouble to conceal it. I nodded. I'd been weak for too long.

The shoe box was stuffed with polaroids. There were graphic notes on the photos. I felt nauseous, the hot flashes hard to handle. Uncle Jeremy was in pretty bad shape too. I couldn't speak when I saw some of the pictures and their content. Underneath them were eight black VHS tapes and about a dozen clear DVD cases. Those too were marked with vulgarities.

I recognized Jack's handwriting. The tapes and DVDs were marked with names and notes like 'Stephanie- cute redhead, purple panties, loud and squirmy' and 'Angie- sexy brat takes it like a champ'.

"That son of a bitch," I heard my uncle grunt.

I couldn't take it anymore. I crouched over and puked in that disgusting hole in the floor with all of my might. I purged out the sin.

My uncle stood. "That mother fucker," he said loudly, angrily. I looked up at him through cloudy eyesight. I was tired, so very tired. He held out a VHS for me to take. I slowly reached up for it. It said 'Amber and Bret'. I couldn't breathe.

"Oh my God," I released. "Oh my God."

I sat dumbly on Bret's couch. He made sure to stay a distance away from me. The tension was immense. I couldn't control the quaking of my lips and burning in my eyes. I had cried so much and I was sleep-deprived. I just wanted to rest and never wake again. Being awake hurt too much.

After Uncle Jeremy's house, I had barged in on Bret. He'd been asleep in his bedroom. It was late. His door had been unlocked. As soon as he opened his eyes, I shoved the tape in his face and demanded to know what I knew he knew. As expected, he didn't act too surprised. He was quiet and it frightened me.

"Dad used to film it," Bret explained. He was nervous. "We were so young when he made us I thought you'd forgotten."

"What do you mean?" I sounded like a little girl again. I trembled and wanted Mommy to hold me. "Why didn't you ever tell me?"

"Tell you what?" my big brother shrank in his seat. "That our father used to tell us to touch each other and if we didn't he'd tell Mom we did something so that she'd beat the shit out of us? Or that he'd threaten to kick us out on our asses and be banished from the family forever? We were little kids, I thought you forgot about it or moved on. I moved on."

Dad had made us touch each others genitals. He used to make us kiss them. According to Bret, I was about Rorie's age which made him a teenager. He was still staying at the Boys

Home but lived with us during the summer when it happened most. It was soon before Dad had moved out to live with his brother.

Sometimes he filmed us, sometimes he took pictures, other times he just watched. Dad never participated- he only watched and masturbated in his chair, then he'd make me clean the come from his stomach with my tongue. Bret reminded me of everything.

"I'm sorry," my voice cracked. I was frozen. "I'm sorry Dad was a disgusting prick."

Bret didn't say anything right away. I wanted to go to him, to put my arms around him. I never wanted to see him hurt. "I'm sorry too," he finally said with fierce emotion. His shoulders shook with heavy sobs, "I'm so ashamed."

"I have to go," I whispered and got up slowly. I felt dizzy.

As soon as I stepped onto his porch and shut the door behind me I ran to my car and threw myself against it. It was damp with dew. The night was silent but for the grotesque sounds that escaped my lips. My legs crumbled beneath me and I landed hard on the gravel. I clenched at the ground and grasped the pebbles and dirt so tight I felt my hands bleed.

"What the fuck!" I cried. "Why!" Only the coyotes in the hills hollered back. The moon was big and close. I wanted to reach out and touch it so that I could be the only person in the world who wasn't an astronaut to have ever touched the moon. But I wasn't that girl. I'd never be that girl. Too much had happened for me to ever live a normal life.

"I hate you!" I screamed to my dead father. "I fucking hate you so much!" I ranted and raved but it didn't relieve me. He had tainted my kinship with Bret. He had ruined so much

269

of our innocence. All those times he let Mom hit me he had ruined my self-esteem, my trust. I hated him for all he'd done to me, to Bret, to all of us.

Then it dawned on me- the dreams I'd had about a man's facial stubble on my body was Bret. It'd always been Bret. I screamed more and shook uncontrollably. I yelled at God, that if He did exist, to prove himself and to take me. I wanted to be one of those young people who died of a heart attack and shocked everybody in the news.

I couldn't go home. I couldn't go back inside the cabin. All I had was my piece of crap car and I was grateful for it. I fell asleep in the driveway as howls echoed in the valleys and memories of a rotten bloodline nestled within me.

CHAPTER 19

"Baby," Rose greeted. "What's up, honey? You're pale."

Where did I begin? "Elvis fired me, Rorie got suspended for messing around with some kid in the boys bathroom, Mrs. Huntington keeps stopping by the house and calling. Oh, and did I mention I found Dad's videos?"

She pulled back. "Where?"

"Uncle Jeremy's basement. I haven't watched them but I have them. Did you know about me and Bret too?" It was the burning question.

Her eyes grew to the size of nickels. "She knew too." I knew 'she' meant Mom. Was that Rose's way of condoning it, that she wasn't the only one who had let me down?

I couldn't believe it. "Did she make him leave because of it?" I wanted to hurt Mom so bad. All this time she knew that Dad had tarnished her children. Instead of telling us we weren't the ones to blame, and making us feel better, she beat us. She could have divorced Dad and done away with him for good but she didn't. He just moved out and they stayed married. So strange. There had to have been good reason.

"That was part of it. It was a bunch of things. Dad wanted to leave a long time but Mom always made him stay. He was her bitch. She always gets her way with guys."

"Did he fall out of love with her?"

"He wasn't smart enough for *that* yet. Like I said, it was a whole bundle of things. Dad loved his sons, you know that.

271

He loved all of his kids. When Henri was born Dad took to him right away. He had the potential of becoming the favorite," Rose carried on. I pictured Henri's cheeks as he slept in my arms. Pudgy baby toes squirmed when I tickled his feet. I heard the distinct sound of his coo's.

"Sometimes it seemed like Mom got jealous. With all the other kids she had to ask for Dads help. With Henri he just did it. Henri was a good baby. As soon as he could walk he cruised around the house like he'd been running around since day one. When my school bus pulled up, I used to have the bus driver honk the horn so that he knew I was home. He loved it. As soon as I got closer to the house, I could see his little face pressed up against the bedroom window. Then when I opened the front door, his little self would climb down the stairs backwards, one chubby thigh at a time and rush to me.

"He never did that with Mom," Rose pointed out and I was not surprised. "It used to piss her off and she would bitch about it. Dad worked a lot back then. He had two jobs- the one at the lumber yard and the other doing construction on the Kanc. Nobody was home when she pushed him," and here I paid close attention.

"Pushed who?" I asked.

"Mom."

"Who pushed Mom?"

"Henri!" Rose was flustered. "Mom pushed Henri out of the second story window."

I gasped and my hand covered my mouth. I looked around and remembered where I was, that I couldn't lose control again. I had to handle my emotions.

"He fell," I insisted. He had to have fallen.

"No," Rose shook her head intently. "She said he did. The police sided with her. No one wants to believe a mother would send her own child to an early grave. It was easier if it were just an accident, easier for everybody. Our family wouldn't have to live with a mother in prison and the cops wouldn't have so much paper to push."

I didn't want to hate my mother more than I did. "How do you know? The reports said that he had fallen. Nobody ever, not once, mentioned that someone had pushed him."

"Open your eyes," Rose ordered, "they've been shut too long. You're a big girl now. Dad made you and Bret do disgusting things together and your mother killed your brothers. It's a lot to take in, trust me I know. I've spent the last couple of years taking it all in. Now it's your turn."

"'Brothers'. Plural. Bret's still alive."

"Yes," she was careless now. She hated Mom and she wasn't about protecting her anymore. I felt betrayed by Rose for knowing all that she knew and for never allowing me that knowledge. Rose was at a healing stage and there I was- phase one. "But Clyde's not, is he?"

"Clyde shot himself with Dad's handgun," I said. Why was Rose doing this? Why was she bringing up old accidents?

She chuckled again. "Have you been living under a rock?"

"What am I supposed to say, Rose? This is all news to me. I just found a fucking video with me on it! My brother was on it! I have to deal with that, not you!"

"Amber," she warned, "please." A guard took notice.

"I don't know if I'm stupid or if my brain just isn't working properly, but I don't remember everything. I don't remember Dad ever with a video camera in his hands. I never knew Mom did that to them either," meaning my two youngest. "I never knew!"

Rose moved her hand closer to mine on the tabletop and I could feel her electricity. "I know," she said purely. I felt her love. "You've had to deal with so much, sweet little sister. We've all put you through so much." Her eyes flooded over but nothing escaped. They were two pools of emotion. "Everything I'm telling you is because I care about you. I want you to know that and believe in that."

I nodded softly. I felt dizzy. I felt like a zombie.

She continued, "Henri couldn't have fallen. The window was too high for him to have fallen. There was nothing by that window for him to climb on. Unless he was Jackie Chan and did some crazy somersault there is no possible way. When Dad called Mom out on it she denied it but something was off about her.

"She never mentioned Henri after that. She didn't cry at his service. Dad said she seemed paranoid, upset that detectives were there. People from town had shown up to pay their respects but she insisted it was because they were insensitive and thought badly of her for not watching her son more closely. It didn't make any sense how she didn't grieve.

"It made Dad mad. I used to hear them argue about it a lot. Eventually, a few short months later, Dad announced he was moving out to live with Uncle Jeremy. She gave him more shit for leaving her than she did for hurting you and Bret or losing her baby son from a freak accident."

"Did she shoot Clyde?" I could picture Clyde, age four, looking into the hole of the gun. He was a curious child. He loved to take things apart and try to put them back together. He loved to explore and being outdoors. He probably would have been much like Bret had he been given the chance.

"Dad never kept his guns loaded." Dad had three guns and one rifle, plenty of ammo. He was a hunter and he went to the outdoor shooting range operated by the White Mountain Gun Club with Uncle Jeremy a lot. I knew that Dad never kept them loaded. At least he was responsible in that way with so many children running around the house at all times.

"Nobody else was home that day except for Mom. We were at school. Daddy was at work and had a 12-hour shift that day. Someone loaded that gun for Clyde.

"Even the coroner reported that the angle in which the bullet penetrated his face didn't match up with the story. But there was nothing he could do. Everything else led up to an accident and nobody could believe our sweet, pretty mother had any motive. It all seemed accidental. Case closed.

"Dad was already away by that time but he came to see us kids whenever he could. He loved Clyde so it distanced him from the house after that. He knew his wife had done it again but he'd never be able to prove it. It was probably then that he started to fall out of love with her."

Voices echoed all around me. It was ghostly- Mom's phony laughter, Dad lecturing me to sit straight or chew quieter or be a good girl, Rose's whispers that it would be okay, Mrs. Huntington's soft hush as she held me close when I cried in her arms, Rorie's sweet childlike giggles.

"There's a term for it," Rose said. "I looked it up." She had told me before how she had read the dictionary from cover to cover and wanted to read the thesaurus next. "It's called 'misandrism'- when a woman hates the opposite sex so much that, in some instances, she kills him. Mom hates men, as simple as that. That's why she toys with them. She knows she has the power, that pussy always prevails. She hated Dad but she needed him. She hated Bret so she sent him away. She felt burdened by those little boys so she killed them."

"She hated us too," I said. "Why are *we* still alive?"

Rose spoke seriously, wise beyond her years, "Just because she let us stay alive doesn't mean she allowed us to live." How profound that truly was.

SPILLED MILK

CHAPTER 20

Rose's letter showed up in the mail only two days later. She must have written it the day I left. Her trademark heart was on the addressee line. Her handwriting was curvier than usual. Her entire letter was neat and error-free. She had obviously spent time on it.

I didn't read it right away. I couldn't. I needed time to sort everything out in my head and then my heart. I knew I had to get away and leave this place. I knew I had to take Rorie with me but I wasn't entirely sure I could. I hadn't left her alone with our mother since I found out what she'd done to Henri and Clyde.

I never confronted Mom; I just stayed away from her.

I went to their grave yesterday- my baby brothers. Nobody had been there in a while, not even the landscaper. I had three family members in the small lot so I supposed if anyone was responsible for overseeing it, it'd be me.

Tucked beneath my mattress, underneath my pink and blue checkered blanket that I'd had since I was a kid, I retrieved Rose's letter. I looked around my room and sat in silence, listening for Mom.

I was scared of her. I locked my door now and told Rorie to lock hers. She never asked why and I wasn't about to tell her that we lived with a lunatic. I had dreams that Mom would come up to my bedroom and stab me to death. That was my worst nightmare- getting stabbed to death, feeling the slices through skin, muscle, and flesh. I couldn't put it past her- she was not to be trusted.

I'd already packed half my bedroom into trash bags and old backpacks. I would take off shortly. I had 14 dollars left to my name. It wouldn't get me far when I decided to go but it was something. I'd gotten my last paycheck from Movie Magic last week and made sure to only spend it on food and the electric bill. I knew I'd need it. I'd dump ten out of my 14 bucks into the gas tank and stock up on Ramen noodles to live off of. I would eat the noodles for food and drink the broth for my liquid. It wouldn't kill me right off.

As soon as I was positive Mom had left for Glitter and Rorie slept in her bedroom behind a locked door, the paper called to me.

Amber,

I hope you're okay after what we talked about today. I'm sorry I had to tell you. I know how much you loved Henri and Clyde. I did too. Those were my little babies. They will always be my little babies. I take them with me each night before I go to sleep and I hold them close to me every morning when I wake up. You are all the reason I keep going.

You're such a good girl, Ammy. I hope you know that. You don't give yourself enough credit. I've always seen what a good girl you are. I put band-aids on your scratches when you were little. I would watch you sleep and make sure you were warm and comfortable after Mom hit you. I would go days without eating so that you and the other kids had something to keep your stomachs from growling. I cared about you all so much more than myself. Believe me when I say that.

I don't know what you will do with what I told you about Mother but I hope that you will get away from her. She will never change and one day, not too long ago, I thought that she would. I thought that she would realize how special her children were and be a mother to you. She hasn't done so. She hasn't lived up to her promises. She promised me that day, you know, that she'd be a good mother, that she'd never be like she was, that she'd never abuse any of you again. She promised she'd make up for all she had done. That day Dad died, she promised.

There was so much I wanted to tell you during our last visit, our final visit. I couldn't find my bravery and I let you leave without my words. You deserved to hear it in person. I wanted you, of all people, to know why Dad died, how he died. I need you to know and to be okay with it. You're ready.

I'm sure you remember when I took off without telling you for all those months just before I shot Daddy. I never talked about it. I never told anybody details. I never even kept a journal about it. I didn't want to leave any trace. Every time I look into your eyes, I see the void. I see your cracks and I want to fill them. I want to help you move on. The truth hurts but sometimes it gives us strength. I hope you find that strength.

I was pregnant, Amber. You probably thought I was a virgin. I got pregnant with him, with this man, and I hated myself for it. It should never have happened. It was sinful. Mother would kill me. It only happened a couple of times. As soon as I found out, I was about two months along. I wasn't sure how long it would be until I showed. Mom had never talked to us about those things. She never even told us about periods. All Mom ever educated us on was that penis size mattered, to play men to get what we wanted out of them, and to try to marry a doctor, a lawyer, or a dentist. She was always so materialistic and judgmental.

I didn't know what else to do so I left. I took as much money I could find around the house and in Dad's secret stash under his bed. I rented a room for a couple of weeks until I got a job at a convenience store just to use my entire paycheck on the next weeks rate for the motel room. I went far north, by the Canadian border. I stayed in a six-room motel where I was the only occupant. I gave birth in that room. I'd done a lot of research on what to do if a situation like that happened. I was scared. I didn't even care if that baby made it or not. I didn't even care that the room wasn't sanitary. Does that make me a bad person?

The baby died the day after. I buried it. At first I tossed it down a ravine behind the motel. As soon as I healed enough I went down to get her. Animals had gotten to her already. I dug a hole. I buried her good. She was bright blue when I did. It didn't bother me too much back then but now I think of it. It doesn't haunt me, however, and that frightens me. It should haunt me, right? Am I horrible that I can live without that burden?

Right after I buried her, I left again. 'Her'- she never even had a name. I hitched a ride back to Lil Beth. By the time I reached town it wasn't even midnight but it was close. It was a Wednesday. I went straight to Uncle Jeremy and Dad's house on the other side of town. By the time I got there it was too late. Uncle Jeremy was gone but Dad wasn't alone. Mom had found out about the videos. I don't know how. Maybe one of the girls had said something to somebody and we all know how gossip spreads.

When I showed up, I found Mom sitting in the backyard, blood all over her. She was shaking and crying uncontrollably. She pointed and I looked over. In the shadows of the night there was Daddy lying on the ground. I went to him. He was lying in a pool of his own blood. It was so much that even the ground beneath him couldn't soak it up fast enough. Blood poured out of his mouth. He was gurgling. He was still alive but barely. I couldn't make out his facial features. The side of his head had been smashed in with something. You could see the dent and the breaks in the skull.

Ma told me she had tossed the shovel in the woods. She had bashed his head but not hard enough to kill him. She was scared that she had done something she now regretted, in the heat of passion, because she truly did love him- or as much as Nicole was capable of loving somebody else. I can't rack my brain over it anymore. I lost all faith that she holds humanity and compassion. I know her better than that. She knows too.

I buried the shovel somewhere. I don't even remember where. Somewhere far in the mountains, a place very rarely traveled upon. Nobody would ever find it; I am certain. I shot him, Amber. I went inside, got his gun, and shot him. I couldn't watch him suffer anymore. If he had lived, he'd be a vegetable or he would have died in the hospital afterwards. He truly had no chance. Mom had done a number on him.

That was when we talked. I told her that Dad had come into my room a couple of times. I told her I ran off. I never told her that the baby girl I buried was his. I could never speak those words. I never wanted her to feel betrayal no matter how much I disliked her. It is strange how, back then, I thought of betrayal when it came to that pregnancy. Now that I've accepted it as a part of me, I see it differently-how Dad should have never laid up with his daughter, how the baby should never have happened. Momma and Daddy betrayed me.

It was Mother's idea. She told the police that she was over visiting her husband and why would they think otherwise? She told them that when she arrived she found me there and saw me attack then shoot Daddy. I promised Mom I would take the blame. I was depressed back then. I hated life. I didn't want to live in the house Dad had lived in. I didn't want to be in Lil Beth but I had nowhere else to go. I wanted to die, to find a way to kill myself. I didn't care about prison. I thought it'd be easy to off myself there. I'd strangle myself with bed sheets and hang myself like on TV. But the movies are always so distorted and unrealistic, aren't they?

So I took the blame. When they asked me why I did it, I never said a thing. To this very day I give them no answer. All I say is 'I don't know'. I used to worry it made me sound cruel. My intentions were always good. Nobody has the right to judge me. I've judged myself enough. Nobody can crucify me like myself.

Mom promised me that she would be good. Right after I shot him out of his misery and we decided on the story we'd tell, right before I turned myself in, we talked. She told me that she loved me and I believed her in that moment. When I look back I realize they were just words. For her to allow me to take the blame said a lot about her. I'd rather dismiss her completely as family, from any memories, than to have my revenge. Revenge means I'd have to see her again. I never want to do that. She has damaged me beyond repair. She has also taught me a lot about the woes of life and I suppose I have to be grateful for those lessons.

I told her I wanted you and Rorie to have a good life. She PROMISED. Now that she has broken her promise, I break mine. I promised her I'd never tell you about the videos, about what Daddy made you and Bret do, that I was the one who had filmed it all because Dad made me. I didn't want him to do to me what he'd done to you so I listened. I was selfish. I will never forgive myself for that. I don't want your forgiveness either. It's something I should have to suffer with until the day I die.

I promised Mom I'd never tell that she killed Henri and Clyde. I never told her I knew for sure but I told her I believed Dad's accusations. She never confirmed it nor did she deny it. We talked about so much that night, Mother and me. So much I could never repeat, so much that was between just us. She made so many empty promises and it hurts.

Tell Bret what has happened has already happened and no one is to blame. You are all so very special. I hope you can be okay with how our little boys passed on. They're being taken care of now. I believe in God now. I never used to but I have to. I have to believe there is something greater out there. If I don't believe in something I would be just like our mother. We can't torture ourselves over the past anymore. There is nothing else to be said.

I can't see you anymore. I am so sorry but it has to be this way. This is the only way you can leave Lil Beth and live your life. You need to start fresh where nobody knows our name. Do everything you've ever wanted to. Take Rorie. I know you'll be good to her. She needs you. Out of anybody in this entire world, it's YOU she needs. Never forget all that has happened, but allow it to make you better so that you'll never turn out like her, like him, like them. Don't let your pain take away your humanity.

Yours, always and forever,

Rose.

CHAPTER 21

Rose's letter never left my mind. I could still see her handwriting as clear as day. Her revelations didn't make me feel stronger or empowered. I felt less whole, incomplete, fully reckoned with. Rose didn't want to see me again, she said so herself. She loved me like no other but she couldn't see me anymore. Love always confused me like that.

She'd already turned me away before and it really messed me up. This time she promised it was for good. I could see her point of view but it was my choice. If she had so much faith in me, why didn't she have enough faith in me to still be in my life, to still have our visits because it was all I had left? I was worth waiting for, wasn't I? I'd waited for her all this time...

I thought of what Rose had written about God and her faith. I could never believe. I had been let down by so much in life that I was scared to believe in anything ever again. I used to believe in love, in second chances, in dreams.

All the symptoms of sadness were present, all the weight and overwhelming sensations. I hadn't showered in the last few days. I could smell myself. My pink nail polish called 'Amazon Flame' was cracked and some had peeled off. My hair was scraggly much like Rose's was in prison.

I wasn't the attractive girl everyone knew anymore. I wasn't the floral-smelling, dolled-up, brunette Barbie I put off that I was. My own mother failed to love me. My own father, whose job it was to keep me sacred, had tainted me in ways I hadn't been ready for.

My car had been on E since last night. It didn't have many miles before it would stall out but I head Cherry toward the Kanc and risked it anyway. If I ran out of gas I would walk the rest of the way and make Bret get me some. I couldn't stay away from him. He was like a magnet. I was drawn to him like a proton to a neutron. I had to go to him, fuel or not, bravery or not.

I felt my hatchback sputter at the first incline. She made it as far as the sign that indicated the turn to Bret's road. I pulled her over and threw her in Park. I walked the rest of the way to my brother's cabin- a good half a mile. I didn't care that darkness approached.

The trees were tall and started to block the sun. It was chilly and I wasn't wearing a jacket. The urgency in the air helped me to walk. My legs felt like jelly lately. My mind was numb. I hadn't smiled in weeks. My feet and hands got tingly for no reason at all. I must have been losing my mind.

When I got to Bret's cabin and saw his van in the driveway I jogged the rest of the way to his door. I knocked quickly, loudly.

"Who is it?" muffled bass came from the house. He'd never done that before- asked who it was.

I turned the knob but it was locked and I grew frantic. What if he turned me away? What if he gave me some excuse? I couldn't stand the thought that his feelings had changed for me, that now I was just some girl he had a past with that he had to get away from.

I knocked again, louder, urgent. He came to the door. He must have known who had come calling from the way he opened it- slow, hesitant. When he saw me, he frowned with concern. "What's going on?"

I didn't say a thing and stood there like an idiot. My lips trembled and threatened my outer shell. I didn't like what I saw in his eyes. Like Rose, he was pulling away from me. I wasn't important anymore. Just when I thought I couldn't anymore I began to sob.

"Jesus, what the fuck happened to you?" he moved aside to allow me in. His cabin reeked of beer.

"Do you love me?" I whimpered.

"Amber," he said. He didn't feel things as strongly as I did.

"What the fuck. You don't." I stumbled off to the bathroom. I didn't want to show emotion in front of him anymore. I hated our relationship and how it was all black and gray now.

A bright orange towel hung from the single hook on the door. I used it as a surface to lie on. With the lights off and the door locked I curled into a ball for a while and sobbed as quietly as I could. It was intense and I shook with shivers. I hated every moment of it. My brother didn't check up on me.

I must have been too exhausted and had cried myself into a deep slumber. I wasn't sure how long I had been out. When I woke back up Bret was sleeping, his feet sprawled out on the ottoman before him. I watched him for a bit. I wondered what he dreamed of and if those dreams made any sense.

The more I stared at Bret, the harder I thought about my childhood, about what had taken place between brother and sister, father and daughter, man and child, and the more I remembered certain things. I remembered Rose would come get me and tell me Daddy wanted to play games in the basement.

The video came to mind. With the grace of a seasoned thief, I managed to retrieve it from my car and put it into the VHS player in Bret's bedroom. It took a lot of guts to slide it into the console and switch the television on. It took a lot of guts to sit down on the bed Bret rest his head on every night and watch the images that played before me.

The footage wasn't steady. I could tell by the voice in the background that it was Rose who filmed it as she had said. Dad sat calmly on his chair and ordered Rose around, telling her to make me sit still while Bret did things to me. I was catatonic as I watched. I had blocked it all out.

Though I was sure the little girl and little boy in the video was me and Bret, I couldn't recall *all* of it. Pieces were familiar. I could remember being touched but I had never remembered by whom. I knew it wasn't Dad. I never thought it had been Bret.

It lasted about 20 minutes. Most of it was Dad telling me I wanted spankings and to ask Bret to give me some. Dad told Rose "Your sister wants spankings. Tell your sister to make the boy give her some. She's been a bad girl. She needs spankings. Be a good little girl and tell her, baby." Every syllable chiseled away at my foundation.

As soon as it was over I allowed the gray snow to dance on the screen and hypnotize me. The doorknob turned slowly and Bret loomed in the shadows. He rubbed at his eyes. He wasn't fully functioning yet.

"What are you doing in here?" he groggily slurred.

I looked up at him. He hadn't shaved today or yesterday either. I wanted to cup his chin in my hands and feel the hairs poke my palms. He looked down at me. My posture was poor and I looked shabby. I wanted him to tell me I was so beautiful that it killed him to see me this way. I didn't touch his face; he didn't tell me sweet nothings.

He eyed the television. The video had ended and the screen was still jumbled. He didn't ask what I watched. I wouldn't have told him.

He didn't soothe me and I despised the distance between us. I leaned back and flicked my hair so that it tossed behind me. I exposed my neck to him and jutted my chest up. I remembered how his lips had felt on my nipples. I was sure he remembered too.

I offered him my hand and told him to come to me. He studied me a moment. "I need you," I said and he came. He dropped on his knees before me and tugged at my pants. As soon as I was naked he told me to turn around and I did. He cupped my ass in both hands and gave it a pat like he used to. His hands journeyed up to the back of my neck where he held my hair firm.

"Turn back around," he ordered. I was a good, submissive girl. Now he could love me. He couldn't say it but he could show it. I yearned for him. He buried his face between my legs and I laid back and allowed one single tear to slide down my cheek. I moaned and told him that I loved him.

CHAPTER 22

I remembered everything now, how Dad used to beckon me. I rarely put up a fuss. I believed his promises that he would kick me out and make my young life hell if I ever told anybody. He had me convinced after a while that it was normal.

I always felt that it wasn't completely normal but it was what I knew and lived. It didn't happen all the time or even every weekend but it happened often enough to leave its damage. Something about Bret and I together turned Jack on.

The way Bret had touched me in his bed lingered on my mind. He held me with such passion. Every ounce of his attention had been on me. That was the part I needed; I didn't need the rest. I had come in his face. I didn't touch him. I didn't even stroke his hair as he gave me oral pleasure. I only leaned back and pretended I was somewhere else. I wasn't me. He wasn't him.

Mom was awake and greeted me when I got back home. She was in a good mood and told me about a party she was having that night. "You can hang with us," she invited me to join.

I flicked my eyes up at her for only a moment. My heart raced in her company.

"So?" she asked.

"Aren't you supposed to be doing something?" I asked her, annoyed, and swung my eyes to her special room.

289

"You should think about doing it," she chimed. I wasn't sure if she was kidding or not. "You need the money since you're not working anymore." How did she know?

"If it pays so good then why was Rorie hungry last night?" I asked.

"You're always so negative," she scoffed. "I'll give you money to order a pizza. Why can't you be a normal girl? Act your age and party with us tonight."

How could I party? How could I enjoy myself? At a time like this? Did she even know everything I'd been told the last few days? Did she even fathom how much I had to comprehend right now? She seemed to know so much about my personal life, how did she not know all of this?

"Sure," I said, drugs on my mind. "I could go for a party," and later that night I was ready.

Mom was in a spectacular mood. She had danced the late afternoon shift at Glitter but still made good tips. When she arrived home, accompanied by a few friends from the club and Carmen who seemed to have forgiven me, she tossed me a small baggy.

"What's this?" I eyed it.

"Enjoy," she said instead. I dipped a fingertip into the bag and tasted the cocaine. Without a thanks, I prepped a few lines.

Everyone gathered in the kitchen when Carmen pulled me aside to hug me and tell me we were still friends. It was as if an offense between besties never took place. I should have apologized to her but I was still in shock over it, still trying to pretend everything was copacetic even if the vibes weren't right.

It wasn't one of those gatherings where people broke off into cliques. Everyone mingled with each other. I took shots of vodka off of Carmen's stomach. We had already made out several times for the viewing pleasure of our male admirers. They guys egged us on and so did Mom.

It turned me on every time I got to kiss Carmen's soft pink lips. No matter how I didn't want to be drawn to her, I didn't care. I'd thought about her sexually so many times that tonight it all became reality. She was mine for the taking. I still couldn't believe she was in my house as if Brian and I never shared that one night.

"Let's go," I whispered into Carmen's ear and led her to the special room where the bed was bigger. I smelled the apricot scent of her hair. It was soft in my hand. She pulled me to her and tucked her hands into the pockets of my jeans. They were inches from my crotch that Bret had explored just days ago. I had wanted him and I wanted her.

Carmen and I kissed again as one of the men turned on Mom's webcam. When I looked over we were on screen and the chat box popped up. Requests and comments flooded in. It thrilled me. I should have known that I wouldn't be able to live with my deeds once I sobered up.

In the haze of it all, I had my way with Carmen and one of the guys. He sat beside us, watched intently, gave some instructions, then masturbated onto our faces. Midway through, Mom appeared. I hadn't heard her come in but I heard her voice. It didn't stop Carmen from doing what she did all over my naked body. She'd been with girls before and you could tell.

Nicole stripped her clothes off with help from the guy who had jacked off on me. They made out. Streamed online, five bare bodies intermingled. It was a room full of free lust and all inhibitions were out the door. We all kissed each other.

The three of us girls gave both hard dicks equal, and undivided attention. Carmen and Mom had their moment on camera solo and were quite popular. One of the guys read aloud the commentary from viewers. Even women watched us live and couldn't contain their hormones.

Afterwards, we all bragged to the others about what we had done. Mom, Carmen, and another girl were by the sink talking. Mother looked at me the entire time. A part of my psyche knew I would regret everything.

I coddled another drink at the kitchen table and sat on the lap of some guy I didn't even know. He kissed my neck and told me how sexy I was, how he wanted to plug every hole on my body. He wanted to be my daddy and show me how good girls should behave.

I was focused on Mom and the girls. Carmen and Mom peered over at me again and giggled. I only heard whispers and faint voices. I heard "bitch" several times.

Carmen approached, all smiles. "Hey," she said and hugged me from behind. "Want to get some fresh air?"

I was eager to get away from the guy I sat on. I was meat but he wasn't my kind of butcher.

Carmen and I went out the back door. Nobody else was outside. It was a cold night but it didn't affect me. The fresh air felt nice. My mother and the girl- they called her Stephy-came out shortly after. I lit a cigarette. I tried to talk and laugh with Carmen but she stood away from me and shared looks with the others.

Stephy burst out laughing and grabbed Mom's arm. "Fucking idiot," she hooted and Mom joined in.

"What?" I asked dumbly. I was so messed up I wanted to sit but the trampoline was wet from an earlier sprinkle. I wasn't sure what was going on. My question made them all laugh harder.

Mom stepped up to me. "Get her, Nic," coached Carmen from the sideline. I stepped back with instant reaction. I didn't like what I saw in my mother's face, the threat I felt in the atmosphere.

"What the fuck's going on?" I said and searched smirking faces for answers. Mom came closer and I turned to walk away. They ganged up on me. All of the sudden I was the enemy.

"Hit the whore," Stephy told Mom. Carmen smiled devilishly. She wasn't my friend. I'd been foolish to forgive her. I should have known better.

Mother grabbed my hair. My beer can fell to the ground. The grass and damp ground soaked up the drops that trickled out of the aluminum. I yelled for Mom to let me go. She yanked my hair harder and I fell to the ground. The party flooded out the side door to witness the commotion.

My mother was on top of me. She never let go of my hair as she slapped me. Some of the people, especially Carmen, egged her on to hit me harder, cause more damage, make me uglier than I was. She hit me and punched me again and again.

I couldn't get away from her hold on my hair. I tried to cover my face. It didn't work and her fists kept coming.

"Disgusting bitch, stupid whore, worthless skank," things of that nature escaped her pursed mouth. I squeezed my eyes closed the whole time. The hits made my mind fuzzy. I must have faded in and out of consciousness.

Mom held my head up and laughed in my face. I felt warm blood cascade from my nose. I tasted it. My lip had been cut open and it started to tingle. The adrenaline prevented pain. I'd been in fights before.

Mom had hit me plenty of times as a kid but never like this. Through every insult and smack and ounce of betrayal I felt, I knew what was happening. I knew tonight had been a set-up. It hurt like hell inside. I had been shaken into reality.

Carmen walked over calmly and looked down at me. "This is for fucking Brian," and she laid a good punch on the left side of my face. I had seen Carmen pull hair and scrap with other girls before but I'd never seen her lay a punch.

It was a pretty good one- I didn't know she had it in her. My left side got the brunt of it. The eye was practically swollen shut. "And this is for being such a cunt," and she kicked me hard in the stomach. Nicole tightened her grip on the chunk of hair she held and threw my face down onto the ground. I passed out.

When I became conscious again, I was alone outside, covered in blood and dirt from the ground I rest upon. All was quiet. It was dawn. The sun hadn't risen yet but very soon would. I lifted my head from the ground. I had been lying down sideways in a fetal position, my face on that wet sandy dirt, in a small pool of my own snot and blood. The morning dew on my wet clothes caused shivers and my muscles ached.

My face hurt. The fingernail cuts on my arms burned and small droplets of blood still squeezed out. They had done a number on me. I spit out blood and mucus. The blood in my mouth caused me to vomit a couple of times.

Chunks of my hair stuck to blades of grass beside me. My scalp ached too. My nose felt broken or fractured. It must have bled a lot- there was a layer of crusted blood I had to scrape off to breathe properly.

Mom's car was gone from the driveway so I entered the empty house and head for the bathroom mirror. My face was a swollen, bruised, bloody pulp. I began to cry from the pain. It hurt so bad. I searched the medicine cabinet for any relief I could find. All I found was Aspirin.

A frantic search throughout the house and Moms downstairs sex palace turned out worthwhile. I found half a line of blow on a CD case and hurriedly inhaled it. A few roaches from joints in the ashtray helped the aches and pains.

I wouldn't call the police or go to the hospital. They would have too many questions. I could tell on my mother and get her arrested. I could tell them what she had done to the little St. Germaine boys all those years ago, to Jack. I wasn't sure if any statute of limitations existed.

As fast as I could run, I fled out of that house to my car. As I drove down Sandman Road I noticed the Huntington's minivan oncoming. My heart quickened knowing that my little Rorie sat inside. Heidi sat behind the wheel and waved as I sped past. I didn't want her to see me cry again. She had already done enough for me. Her minivan honked but I didn't flash my brakes or slow down.

Just keep going, just go. Get the fuck out of Lil Beth. Little Bethlehem- what a name. Who had come up with it and why would anyone in their right mind think that holiness would be here of all places? It was the people who ruined Little Bethlehem. Without the people, she would be crystalline beautiful. My family had ruined it the most.

I passed the cemetery that held my brothers and father. I wanted to kill my mother for allowing him to rest beside the bodies of those innocent boys. How dare she? Wherever I went I would make sure to forget about her.

The ache in my face was unbearable. I didn't know what to do with the physical pain, the emotional one was bad enough. The tears stung the scratches and cuts. It made me cry even harder. I had to sleep I told myself. Whether I wanted to or not I had to. It was the only way to make the pain go away.

I found an empty parking lot behind a closed-down shop and I smoked the rest of what there was in my glass pipe. Despite all that disturbed me, I was able to doze off. Deep sleep found me. It was to the point where I felt I'd never wake up. I didn't care.

If there is a God, I dared myself to utter my usual prayer before blackness enveloped me from all angles, *please take me away. If you are real, if you love me, if I am your child like all others, take me. Hold me in your arms…don't prove me wrong again…*

He never came. If He did I had missed it. When I woke, the night had begun. I had slept the day away and was grateful. My back ached from sleeping in the driver seat. I thought of Rorie and hoped she would never find out about how Mom had beat me in our own backyard. I hoped she didn't find out about a lot of things.

I should have gone back to her. I should have gone back *for* her but I wasn't strong enough to take care of her. I didn't deserve her- she was angelic, too good for the likes of me. She would push me away sooner or later too. Nobody wanted me, how could she?

I turned down familiar roads and passed familiar viewing spots. I knew those views like a schooled mechanic knew the underside of a hood. The White Mountains were all I knew. I would be doomed in city life. I was sure the hustle would wear me down and get the better of me. Wherever I went, I knew I'd come back to Lil Beth. But I had nowhere to go, nobody to run to.

I spotted the sign for the Red Pass and parked on the side of the road. I got out and unlatched the trunk. I grabbed the rope that I used as a tie-down and started on my way.

I followed the pavement path that led to the Pass. On a clear day you could see Lil Beth from there but it started to rain. The clouds were dark. It would be a gloomy night.

I was high on Mt. Cranmore. I had a lot of memories of this place. Carmen and the other girls from school would come up here. We would swim in the swimming holes and sit around in the sun. We didn't care about much back then except for our tans, our hair, our looks, how other people saw us. That was my problem. I was too busy trying to be accepted rather than accepting myself. It was too late now.

The old covered bridge loomed large. The Red Pass was old. It wasn't huge but it had a presence, especially underneath moonlight. Men, with little equipment and technology, had built that bridge with their bare hands. Why they would take the time to build it here was beyond me but I imagined it was because they lived here, loved here, and thought that all those born after them would feel the same.

I was probably the only person left in the entire world who still thought of those men. I was probably the only person left who still came here just because. Not to take a picture of it because it was historic, or to drive across it to pass from one mountaintop to another, simply just because.

My intentions were clear. I knew what I had to do. I knew what I needed. It was my destiny. It had been written for me, my epilogue.

I retrieved the rope from where I had slung it around my shoulders. I shuddered with wild sobs. I had given up, there was no turning back. I couldn't go back to that house. I couldn't go to Bret- he didn't want me. If I never returned everyone would move on with their lives. It would be for the better.

Every monumental moment in my life from childhood to now played vividly through my mind. None of it was consequential but the memories were there. I thought of all the people I had ever loved and how none of them were with me.

The moon, the sky, the treeline, it was all still so magnificent. The weight was heavier because of it. I didn't deserve beauty. I didn't deserve Bret who I couldn't shake from my mind. I would always want him. I couldn't control it. He was my love, the forbidden. I could never have him.

SPILLED MILK

The rope was suddenly around my neck. My throat hurt from screaming, my soul hurt from existing. I knew there could be no more thinking about it. I had to do what had to be done. I had to rid the world of me. I had to rid me of the world.

The constriction around my throat agitated and consumed me with purpose. Nothing else mattered. I'd done all the living there was for me. I'd never known unconditional love but I'd come close enough. I found a small moment of profound bravery. I gulped in deep breaths and muttered my goodbyes.

I was ready.

EPILOGUE

I still heard her. Above the hollers of the wind my baby's voice cried to me. She was sad. I had hurt her. I shut my eyes tight and willed for her to come to me, to stop me, so that I could have just one more moment with her.

Although her voice was urgent, it was harmonious. Her laugh echoed loudly. I could see her smile on the face of the moon. I held my arms out and the beating rain soaked into the open cuts. The cold soothed it as best as it could be soothed. I reached for her and for the dreams I had for us. I used to dream so big for us.

"I love you, my baby," I whispered to her. "So, so much." I clung to the wet rail. I stepped up and started to climb. It was slippery beneath my feet. I started to cry again, this time a calm weeping. I couldn't deny the relief I felt. I was on my way and I could breathe again. At last, I felt free.

In the wide open where I stood, I closed my eyes. The rain flooded my face and blended in with the tears. My sadness became one with Mother Nature. I was a part of her, her child. She had no choice but to love me. The wind slapped against my body. My clothes clung to me. I was covered in goosebumps but I was so warm. I felt like somebody's baby.

Her voice came closer. It beckoned me. She was my angel. She wanted me and I was ready to go to her. "I'm coming!" I screamed and "Amber, no!" screamed back.

SPILLED MILK

For a brief moment, it felt real. I felt her presence just as the sky turned purple. I grew frantic and clung harder. I couldn't let go. She needed me. I was all she had. I would never be good enough but I undeniably loved her.

I hated everything else in the world, everything else about me, but I had her. I had been foolish to not realize it until now. I had lived so stupidly. I loved her too much to leave her with Mother. Mom did not deserve her; she did not deserve that blessing.

Then I looked over and there she was. I wasn't dreaming; she *was* real. She had come for me. My Rorie had come to save me. She ran to me, her small legs carrying her quickly across the planks of the bridge. I didn't know how she had found me or who had taken her to me but she was there, in the physical, and she was mine.

I smiled at her through the rain and tears.

"Amber!" she cried again. She was so close now, her voice so clear.

"Rorie!" I hollered as loud as I could while the rope hugged my throat. "Baby!"

"Amber!"

I put my leg up to climb back over the railing and lost my grasp. The rails were too wet to hold onto.

Just as I had gone back for her, I slipped...

* * *

A note from the author...

Thank you for reading *Spilled Milk*. This book means so much to me in so many ways. The fact that you read it means that much more. I wrote it for you, for me- for the Amber in all of us.

Ever since I was little, being a writer was my one fantasy. I wanted to delve into deep issues and relatable people in a way that made you feel. I hope this book left an impression on you like it did me. Help spread the word and leave a review at the link below. Your feedback is my air.

If you or someone you know is suffering with depression or suicide, please reach out. You are not alone and you're worth it. **I see you.**

Veronica Christopher

Add your review:
Amazon.com/Author/VeronicaChristopher
or, Goodreads.com/VeronicaChristopher

National Suicide Prevention Lifeline **800-273-8255**